DREW

GIULIA LAGOMARSINO

Copyright © 2017 by Giulia Lagomarsino

All rights reserved.

No part of this book may be reproduced in any form or by any electronic or mechanical means, including information storage and retrieval systems, without written permission from the author, except for the use of brief quotations in a book review.

Cover Design courtesy of T.E. Black Designs

www.teblackdesigns.com

Created with Vellum

For all the romantics out there that believe true love does exist.

CHAPTER 1

DREW

Iris. I swear I could feel her on the breeze, standing here in the serenity of the country. She was my life, my dreams, my love, my wife, but above all that, she was my reason for being. I closed my eyes as memories of the smell of her perfume wafted around me, pulling me into a daydream of her walking toward me and teasing me. I could see her beautiful, huge smile that lit up my whole world. Her sharp, blue eyes sparkled as she gazed at me, my chest aching, knowing this was all a dream. Still, I kept my eyes closed, relishing in every piece of her I took with me six years ago. Her long, chestnut hair was blowing in the breeze as she walked closer to me, her voice floating in the wind. I could feel her hand resting against my chest as she leaned in to whisper in my ear.

"I'm forever yours, Drew. Nothing can take me from you."

I could still hear those words she spoke to me that day at our house. Those were the last words she ever said to me and they haunted me to this day. It was a beautiful sentiment, but it didn't come true. She died a few days after she spoke those words to me. She was taken from me, and there was nothing that could ever bring her back no matter how hard I prayed. Believe me, I tried. For three weeks, I prayed that God would return her to me, but he didn't, and I couldn't stay there anymore. It was too painful to be around all her things and live in the house that we were supposed to grow old in together. I sold everything except our wedding rings, which now had a permanent residence on a chain around my neck.

I stood on my porch, basking in the feel of Iris, while the sun rose in front of me. It was our favorite time of day together. We would sit outside with a cup of coffee and I would watch her as her beautiful face lit up as she talked to me about the beauty of the morning. Iris was an eternal optimist and found a reason to wake up smiling every morning. I kept up our tradition even though she was no longer with me. It kept me calm, starting my day like this.

"Excuse me. Can you help me?"

With just those few words, my daydream shattered. Iris slipped away, leaving me cold and empty. I ground my teeth together as anger flooded me. Every moment that I got to spend with my sweet Iris was a moment I cherished. This intruder had ripped her from me when I was feeling closest to her once again. I spun around and cast an angry glare at the woman who had interrupted my thoughts. She flinched back at my harsh stare and then stuttered, trying to get out her sentence.

"I...I'm so...sorry. I just n-need a hand with my car. I need a...a jump."

She quickly looked to the ground, which only further annoyed me. She couldn't even maintain eye contact. She interrupted me when I had finally found my peace out here in the country. I found someplace that I could stand to stick around for more than a year, and now I had an annoying neighbor that would always be around to intrude on that peace.

I had been living in town with Harper, a woman I met when I first came to this town. She was in a hard place when I met her and I instantly felt a connection with her. We comforted each other when we had no one else. Eventually, she got back together with her ex-boyfriend Jack, and they now had a child together.

After Harper moved out of our rented house, I stayed until the lease was up. Since I'd decided to stick around, I thought it best to find my own place in the peace of the country. I found a nice, old farmhouse that dated back to the early 1900's on fifty acres of land. I was a country boy at heart and always had been, but these last six years of running had left me lost. I was beginning to lose sight of my Iris until I found this place. I had her back for brief moments in time that I wouldn't give up for anyone.

Iris and I met in my hometown in Florida, right by the Alabama border. We both grew up in the country and had always dreamed of buying a house in the country with a ton of acreage that would be all ours, where we could enjoy the solitude and watch the sun rise and set. That's what this place gave me.

After a minute of staring the woman down, I finally started walking back toward the house, pulling my keys out of my pocket and getting in my truck. I didn't wait for her to hitch a ride with me. I wasn't offering. I drove over to her car and hooked everything up, then leaned against my truck, waiting for her battery to charge.

I had the unfortunate luck of sharing a driveway with my neighbor. Apparently, the people that owned the property before me were brothers. They both lived in my house and farmed the land together. They had a falling out, but couldn't split up the land without ruining their income. So, they continued to farm the land together, but one brother moved out and built the small house on the other side of the driveway. There was never a need for another driveway, so they continued to live on the same land, farm the same land, and share the same driveway, but live in separate houses. When the brother in the smaller house decided to retire, he bought his parcel of land from his brother. I, of course, assumed that it was all part of my property.

Her house was to the left of the driveway and it was an old, rundown one story that looked like it should just be bulldozed. The yellow paint was peeling off the siding and the roof was sagging from years of neglect. The houses had been abandoned for quite some time when I purchased the property. Luckily, she only owned about a half acre of the land, mainly where the house was situated. At least I didn't need to worry about her wandering over to my property. She had a small yard in the back with a few trees that looked like they were as old as my house, but she had space for herself.

The woman moved in shortly after I did, and since I had assumed that the house was part of my property, I was completely shocked when she pulled in and started unloading. I had been so entranced by the view that I hadn't heard everything the realtor had said. I had just signed on the dotted line and moved my stuff in with the intention of bulldozing the monstrosity next door.

She walked up next to her car, looking like a kitten would scare her. I hadn't meant to be such a dick, but... well, maybe I did mean to be a dick. She pissed me off. It wasn't really her fault. I hadn't been listening to the realtor, but still, it pissed me off that this woman had the nerve to intrude on my peace and quiet. Every time I saw her, I was reminded this was supposed to be my land with Iris. I wasn't supposed to be sharing my land with a woman who could barely string together a sentence without squirming under my stare.

I watched her shuffling around by her car. Her slender frame looked like it would blow over in a stiff breeze, which around here was very likely. She had dull, brown hair that she had haphazardly thrown up in a knot on top of her head. Her dark brown eyes widened when she looked up at me, and her small nose looked like it would get lost on her face. Her mouth was about the most attractive thing about her. She had nice, full lips with a nice set of teeth. *Wow.* Pretty bad when you're describing a woman's best quality as a nice set of teeth. Her boobs and ass were way too small. Overall, she was just a tiny woman that did nothing for me. No woman had done anything for me since my wife, but still, this woman couldn't get me hard if she was completely naked. In fact, it would probably make her less appealing.

She mumbled something and I assumed she was trying to talk to me, but I couldn't understand her when her head was facing the ground.

"Did you say something to me?" I snapped. I didn't have patience for meek people. That was partly why Harper and I got along so great. Although, based on how we met, things could have been different, but she always tried for a smile. This woman looked like someone ran over her cat five or six times and she would never smile again.

"I said, I appreciate the help. I have to be in town in a half hour. Thank you."

When she was done speaking, she looked back at the ground, willing it to swallow her up. I stepped toward her and she instantly stepped back like I was going to attack her. Rolling my eyes in annoyance, I walked to her car and turned the key. The engine started with a putter and finally got going. It was a piece of shit, but that wasn't any of my business. I got my stuff and drove back over to my house without another word.

My two story farm house was in need of some fixing up, but was exactly what I had pictured when I started looking for a place. There was a wrap around porch that currently had one white rocking chair. The porch on the back was large and extended out further than the front and side porch. It was obviously built on at a later date than the original porch. It gave me space for grilling in the summer. The outside was painted white, but was peeling badly. I'd have to paint it this summer, along with staining the deck.

I went inside my house and stared at the sparse state of my new dwellings. I definitely needed something to make this look at least a little lived in.

Pulling out my phone, I dialed Harper, hoping she could help me.

"Hey, Drew."

"Hey, buttercup. I have a favor to ask."

"Sure. What's up?"

"I need furniture for my place. You got time to do a little shopping with me?"

"Drew, are you asking me to decorate your house?"

"No. No, I'm not. I'm asking you to help me pick out furniture. I don't need any decorating, just a few things so I actually have a place to sit."

"Really? I mean, the living room is great. With a few small decorations, it might actually be nice to sit in there."

"There's nothing wrong with the living room."

"I'm not saying that, but hell, you have those gorgeous built-in bookcases. You know, if you put some actual books in there, it might spruce up the place."

I rubbed at my eyes, already regretting calling her.

"And then you have those built-in cabinets that divide the living room from the study. I could get just a few things to put in there, maybe some knick knacks to make it more homey."

"No knick knacks," I said firmly. "I don't need any of that."

"And don't get me started on your kitchen. While I think it's great that all your old appliances still work, they're avocado. Do you understand that, Drew? Nobody needs avocado appliances."

"They're fine," I sighed. "I just need furniture—"

"And that little table you call a coffee table looks like something out of a reject thrift store."

"Harper—"

"And you should really fix those stairs. They creak so badly."

"It gives the house character," I argued.

"And what about the bedrooms upstairs? How is anyone going to sleep in them with no beds? Not to mention the lack of decoration. Just empty rooms sitting there, plain as can be."

"Nobody is coming to stay with me."

"Then why did you buy that gigantic house? Honestly, Drew, if you're going to live there, you should try and make it look nice."

"I'm working on it," I grumbled.

"Well, it's a good thing you called me. Now, I won't go crazy, but adding a few small touches won't kill you. Maybe we'll even go wild and get a picture for your walls."

I groaned, shaking my head. This was a disaster. "Maybe I should ask Jack to come instead."

She snorted. "Yeah, the two of you might pick out a recliner and call it a day."

"That sounds fine to me," I mumbled under my breath.

"Drew, I'm not going to let you continue to do this."

"Do what?"

"Live like a man who doesn't care about anything." I swallowed hard at her words. I did want to be better, but I just couldn't find the motivation to move on. "Drew, I don't know what happened, and I won't pressure you to tell me, but at some point, you have to start living life. What you're doing isn't living."

I knew she was right. I could do this. I could let her help me fill the house with...things. What was holding me back was that it all made everything so permanent. It wasn't as easy as just selling the house and leaving once I filled it up. Then I would create memories and start dreaming of a different life, and slowly my life with Iris would disappear. I wasn't ready for any of that, but I could at least buy some furniture.

"Come pick me up. I'll leave Ethan with Jack."

I sighed, knowing Harper wouldn't let this go now that I brought it up. "On my way, darlin'."

I hated the idea of settling down somewhere. It felt disloyal to Iris somehow, but now I had Harper and she was the closest thing I had to family. I couldn't stand the thought of leaving her. But decorating a house, filling it with things to make it a home felt like the final nail in Iris's coffin. It didn't matter how long ago she died. Doing this was admitting to myself that she wouldn't be coming back to me, but I knew it was time. Iris would be pissed at me if I spent any more of my days drifting. I grabbed my keys and walked out of the house.

I drove over to Jack and Harper's house, but I waited in the driveway. That irritating neighbor interrupting me had put me in a foul mood. Harper got in the truck and scooted directly over into the center seat to sit next to me. I wrapped my arm around her and pulled her in close, then waved to Jack as we pulled out of the driveway. Jack was a good guy, and an even better man for allowing me such close contact with his wife. He knew that Harper and I had a special bond that couldn't be broken and he gave me a lot of leeway.

When I first came to town, Harper and I were so instantly connected that we slept in the same bed the first night. There was no chemistry between us. It was just two lost souls being there for one another. I found comfort holding her in my arms, something I hadn't done since my Iris passed away. Harper was devastated from her break up from Jack and needed me just as much. We were still just as close today and I often found myself taking a nap with her on a Sunday, unless her son, Ethan, needed her. I had to admit, sometimes I was jealous of the little guy.

"I just love this store," Harper said, practically bouncing in the seat beside me. "We're going to have so much fun."

"I think you and I have different ideas of what fun is."

She stuck her tongue out at me. "That's because you never have any."

She hopped out of the truck and dragged me inside. Her face lit up as she saw all the furniture laid out for us.

"First, we need to find you a kitchen table and chairs."

"I already have that."

"Yeah, and every time I sit down, I feel like I'll fall on my ass. Seriously, that old man that lived there didn't buy furniture to last. You need something different."

Groaning, I let her pull me through the store until we found dining sets.

"Oh, this is beautiful," Harper said with a smile as she looked at one set.

"No, it's not at all my style."

"Well, your style consists of something cheap and forgettable."

"Harper," I moaned.

"Fine, fine. What about something more rustic?"

"I thought you said my stuff was too old?"

"Well, but we'll find something that's made to look old, but is really strong."

"So, you want me to pay for someone to make a new table, but make it old looking."

"Exactly!"

"That's like buying jeans with holes in them. It doesn't make any sense."

She dragged me over to another table that I had to admit looked pretty nice. "It's a farm table. And look at this bench seat. It would be great for entertaining."

"I don't entertain," I said in a bored tone.

"Yes, but you might someday. You have to think of the future."

I shook my head with a sigh. "Fine. We'll take this one."

She grinned and wrote down the product number, then dragged me off to look at living room furniture.

"Okay, you should definitely get something that's comfortable for you. I'm thinking a leather recliner."

I actually liked that idea and started trying out different recliners until I found one I liked. "This one."

She grimaced, but wrote down the number. "I think the one over there would be better."

"I don't need cup holders in the chair."

"You might. What if you were watching the game with the guys—"

"What game?" I asked, grinning internally.

Flustered, she shook her head. "I don't know. A game. *Any* game. Don't you want something that will be most convenient?"

"No, I want the most comfortable chair, and that's this one."

"Fine," she huffed. "But you also need a couch. I know that's maybe too much of a commitment for you right now, but you can't have people sitting on your floors."

I repeated the process of trying out couches, hating every minute of it. Meanwhile, Harper was trying out a chaise, relaxing in it like she was ready to buy it.

"I think you should definitely get this."

"When would I ever sit in that?"

"Well, you wouldn't. I would. I can just imagine lounging in this every day—"

"I'm pretty sure Jack would draw the line at you coming to my house every day to lounge around."

"Maybe you're right."

"Besides, I like this couch, and you said I just had to get a couch."

"And a coffee table, an entertainment center, and a TV. I mean, let's face it, it's hard to watch the game without one."

"You know, you sure are making a lot of plans for me."

"Hey, you need to crack open that shell and live a little."

"I bought a house. Give me a break."

"Not until you buy the furniture."

The day didn't end until she also roped me into buying a furniture set for my bedroom. I didn't go with the canopy bed that she thought would be *so amazing*. Instead, I went with the simplest thing I could find and called it quits.

"What about stuff for your back deck?"

"Harper, no. I've already bought way more than I ever intended too, but I draw the line here. I'm tired. I hate shopping, and now I want to go home and drink until I forget this day."

"You don't have to be so moody."

"Yes, I do. No man wants to spend hours shopping. It's just wrong."

"Jack takes me shopping."

"Jack gets laid at the end of the night."

"So, what you're saying is we need to find you a woman."

I cringed at the thought. The last thing I needed was a woman.

"Okay, so that's out, but we at least got you furniture."

"Lucky me," I grinned as best I could.

After dropping Harper off at home, I headed back to my house. I didn't feel bad about spending so much money today. Since Iris passed, and I basically lived like a nomad for years, her insurance money was still burning a hole in my pocket. Not to mention that I sold the house we lived in. Money wasn't an issue. Thankfully, all my furniture would be delivered tomorrow, and I could put this whole debacle behind me.

As I pulled in my driveway, I saw my neighbor unloading groceries from her car. I wasn't sure why, but I watched her for a moment after parking my truck. A big bag of groceries broke and the contents spilled on the ground. She knelt down and started to pick up the groceries, but then stopped and sat down on her butt with her head in her hands. I could see her shoulders shaking, I assumed from crying. Everything in my gut told me to leave her sitting there on the ground, but if it was Harper, I would want someone to help her. So, I headed over that way and started picking up her groceries and placing them in the other bags. I stalled when I picked up a bottle of prenatal vitamins.

Irrational anger surged through me, so I lashed out at her, angry that she was here alone and pregnant. "Knocked up, huh? You know who the father is?"

Her face jerked up to mine and her eyes blazed in fury. She pulled herself up off the ground and grabbed them from my hand. I grabbed two bags and hauled them inside, then returned for the rest. I ignored her as she glared at me. Whatever; my good deed was done and I was going home. She didn't even thank me. Although, I guess I did insult her, so maybe I didn't deserve a thank you.

I walked back to my place and tried to figure out what it was about her that had me being so nasty to her. Maybe it was because she was the total opposite of Iris, and I wanted my Iris back badly right now. Shaking my head, I decided she wasn't worth my thoughts. I wasn't gonna dwell on her or her problems. I walked in and fixed myself dinner, then sat on my back porch drinking beer as the sun set. My mind drifted to our first night in our house in Florida.

"I'M EXHAUSTED, Drew. Don't make me do any more work today."

"I got it, baby. I think we're mostly done anyway. Why don't you go take a bath and then meet me out on the back porch."

"Oh, that sounds like heaven right now."

I went to the garage and grabbed the table and chairs, and set them up on the back porch. Then I went back and got the loungers. One of them broke when I tried to pull it out, so I just brought the one over. I grabbed some cereal, milk, and bowls and headed outside. We didn't have much unpacked yet, so this would have to do for dinner. Iris came outside and sat down at the table in shorts and a t-shirt.

"Sorry, baby. This is all we have available to eat right now."

"It'll do. All I need is you and I'm set for life."

"Baby, you say such sweet things." I poured us each a bowl and we ate in silence as the sun set. Then we went to snuggle on the lounger. She laid between my legs, rubbing her hands over my knees.

"Drew, I have a move-in surprise for you."

"Baby, that's so sweet. I didn't get you anything. Now I feel like an ass."

"No need. This is something you gave me."

I looked at her in confusion. She got me a present, but it was something I gave her. I was wracking my brain trying to think of gifts that I had given her that she could give back to me, but none came to mind.

"Drew, I'm pregnant. You're gonna be a daddy."

My world stopped right then and there. My throat closed up and I felt like my heart would beat right out of my chest. I was going to be a daddy. There were never sweeter words than that.

"Baby, that's the best news I've ever gotten." My smile spread across my face so big that my cheeks hurt.

"So, you're not mad?"

"Not one bit." I kissed her and made sweet love to her that night under the stars.

TEARS ROLLED down my face as I stared at the sky. Out here it didn't matter if I cried. No one could see me in the dark. That was one of the best nights of my life, but it was short lived. We never had that baby. I never got to meet him or her. My life was torn away from me less than a year later and I still couldn't fathom how God could be so cruel. We had only been married for a year when she told me she was pregnant.

I pulled out my phone and put on Elton John. He had always been her favorite artist, and I put him on whenever I wanted to feel close to her. I didn't even like him, but she always sang along to his music, her favorite being *Your Song*. She said it was one of the most romantic songs she had ever heard. When it came on, the tears came faster and I totally lost it there in the darkness. My chest hurt so bad, aching to hold her again. I wanted one more kiss from her, one more "I love you". I needed more time with my sweet Iris.

When the song was over, I turned my phone off. That was enough for one night. Any more and I would need a strong drink to get through the night. I looked up to heaven and said a prayer for my Iris and our little one.

"Goodnight, sweet Iris. Until I hold you in my arms again."

Work flew by this week. I had been working at Ryan and Logan's construction company for about a year now and I found the work somewhat satisfying. It wasn't my dream job, but it kept me busy, which was the main purpose of me having a job. I didn't need the money, but I needed to keep my mind busy. I could probably find something to do with myself that would be more satisfying, but I honestly didn't have the ambition. I was still too wrapped up in my own grief to do anything else with my life.

My furniture had been delivered Sunday, and I had to admit it was nice to finally have something of my own. The guys invited me out for drinks tonight, and I really didn't want to go, but the thought of sitting around my house doing nothing with nobody was depressing. We met down at The Pub that had been newly renovated after the fire at New Year's, and I ordered tequila. It was probably not a good idea, but moving into the new house had been hard on me.

The guys laughed about things going on at work and they took turns ragging on each other about their significant others. Ryan and Sebastian didn't have girlfriends, so they were doing most of the teasing. Me, however, I drank. Hearing them all talk about their girlfriends and wives depressed me. By the time we had been there a few hours, I was way past drunk.

Sebastian had left about an hour ago with a woman that had come over and blatantly flirted with him. Jack left also to go home to his wife. Apparently, he couldn't stand to be away from Harper for the night. I should have gone over to see Harper instead of coming here.

"Drew, right?"

A mousy brunette stood in front of me, and even in my drunken state, I could see it was my neighbor.

"What the fuck do you want? And why are you in a bar if you're pregnant?"

She blushed furiously and looked down at her hands.

"Dude, what the fuck is your problem?" Ryan asked.

"I actually just came in to fill out an application."

Cole spoke up. "I think they're still looking for someone since Alex isn't here anymore."

"Who's Alex?" the neighbor lady asked.

"My girlfriend," Cole answered. "She got hurt, and she can't work right now. I'm sure they'll be grateful for your application. I'll introduce you to the boss."

She gave a small smile and said her thanks as Cole guided her away. I slammed back another shot of tequila, and was waving down the waitress for another when Ryan cut in.

"Don't you think you've had enough, Drew?"

"Not nearly enough," I slurred. Normally I didn't get drunk, but all this talk about girlfriends had fucked with my head, and I just wanted to forget.

"Come on. I'll drive you home."

"I can take him home if you want. He's my neighbor. I'm Sarah."

Ryan shook her hand and introduced himself. "That's fine by me. Are you sure you can get him in the house?"

"Yeah, we'll be fine. It wouldn't be the first drunk I've dealt with."

She blushed as she said it and looked down, like she hadn't meant to reveal that. Ryan grabbed my keys and then grabbed me by the arm, dragging me out to her shitty car. I barely fit in the front seat because I was so large. I was a tall guy and I worked out, so I was quite muscular. This was like fitting a block of cheese into a toilet paper roll.

"I'll bring your truck in the morning," Ryan said as he walked away. I flung my middle finger up, hitting the door frame and jamming my finger.

"Son of a bitch."

I saw Sarah roll her eyes at me before peeling out of the parking lot. She drove like a maniac, making my stomach swirl with nausea. She was going to kill us tonight, but at least I would see Iris again. Thank God I was numbed from the alcohol. I wouldn't feel a thing. We were pulling into the driveway when *Your Song* came on the radio.

"Not again," I grumbled.

"What?"

"Why the fuck does this have to be on the radio?"

I stumbled from the car and threw my hands up toward the sky. I was angry and drunk off my ass. I didn't care right now that I was humiliating myself or that my neighbor was witnessing it. "Are you trying to give me a fucking message?"

"What are you talking about?" I turned around to see Sarah looking at me in confusion. "What's going on?"

"She fucking left me, that's what's going on. Now I hear that fucking song everywhere I go."

My words were slurring and trying to walk was even worse. I'd be lucky if I got in the house at this rate. Sarah grabbed my arm and helped inside, plopping me down on the couch before disappearing. I closed my eyes and my sweet Iris appeared before me.

"Drew, what are you doing? You're better than this."

"Why did you leave me, Iris? I'm so lost without you," I whispered to her. She looked so beautiful, so real that I reached out for her, sure that I would touch her sweet face. I smiled as her hand caressed my face, the way she used to. "Iris, why'd you leave me?"

"Drew, I'm forever yours. Nothing can take me from you."

Tears streamed from my eyes as her hand slowly slipped from my face. God was torturing me by allowing me to feel her. I let out a tortured groan, wanting her soft skin touching mine again. My mind drifted to blackness as she faded from my vision.

CHAPTER 2

SARAH

I stood in front of him as he spoke about a woman named Iris. I could barely understand him, but I knew he was asking why she left him. Given his current state of drunkenness and his surly attitude, I could see why staying with him was less than desirable. I held out my hand to give him some ibuprofen, but he shifted and I fell against him, barely catching myself as my hand grazed his face. He started crying, his face twisted in agony. I had no idea what transpired, but I could only imagine he was hurting badly. He passed out a few minutes later, and I thanked God that he had because I didn't know how much more I could take of this.

I was exhausted and I needed to lie down, but I was afraid to leave him in this state. Not only had he been extremely distraught, but he was so drunk he could barely walk. What if he had to throw up? I really shouldn't care. He had been rude to me last week and again at the bar tonight. I'd barely spoken a full sentence to him, but that was all it took. He'd judged me already and handed down my sentence as a worthless piece of shit. He assumed that I was crying because I didn't know who my baby's father was. He couldn't be more wrong. I knew, which just made it even more devastating. I just found out a few weeks ago that I was pregnant, and when I moved here, I immediately found a new doctor for my prenatal care. It hit me when I got home that I was all alone in this. It felt like my whole world was collapsing around me and I was helpless to stop it.

Sighing, I grabbed a blanket and decided to sleep in the recliner. At least I could keep an eye on him. I laid there thinking about how different my life was from a month ago. Everything had changed in the blink of an eye, and I did my best not to break under the circumstances. My hand lay across my belly as I tried to imagine what it would feel like when my little bean sprout started to kick. I couldn't help my thoughts from drifting to Todd and the life we would have had, but thinking about that wouldn't do me any good right now. I had to focus on the present. I needed to find a job and have a way to provide for my little one. I hated that I felt so alone. This was my life now and I had no one to share it with. Even if my neighbor had been a friendly guy, I could never divulge what was truly going on to him. It was safer this way.

"S*ARAH, WHAT ARE YOU SAYING?*"

"*I'm saying you're going to be a daddy.*"

He placed his hand on my stomach and looked into my eyes. "I can't believe it's finally happening. We've waited so long for this. How far along are you?"

"*It's still early. Maybe five weeks?*"

He bent down in front of me and talked to my stomach. It was a little weird, but I went with it. "Hey, little man. You don't know me yet, but I'm your daddy, and I promise that I will do everything possible to protect you. No one will ever hurt you as long as your momma and I are around."

He leaned forward and pressed a kiss on my stomach before standing and wrapping me in his arms. He pressed kisses all over my face before lifting me and laying me down in bed with him. I thought he was going to make love to me, but instead, he wrapped his body around me and held me. His hand ran circles over my belly for a while.

"*Let's go out to dinner tonight and celebrate.*"

It had been a wonderful suggestion at the time, but turned out to be the biggest mistake of our lives.

I WOKE EARLY the next morning with my stomach churning. I got up quickly from the chair and ran around the first floor, hoping to find a bathroom before my stomach heaved up whatever was bothering me. When I found it, I wasted no time spilling the meager contents of my stomach and then sat there for a few minutes waiting for it to pass.

"Morning sickness?"

The voice made me jump and caused the nausea to come roiling back. I threw up again and then laid my head against the toilet, hoping that was the last time. My eyelids fluttered closed as exhaustion hit me. Not only was I not sleeping well, but the nausea combined with stress was really killing my appetite. I was running on empty.

A wet cloth was placed on my neck and I was grateful for the kind gesture. Drew reached around me and flushed the toilet. I knew it was gross to be that close to flying water, but I couldn't care less at the moment. When I finally felt well enough to get up, I removed the washcloth and started to stand, his hand wrapping around my arm and helping me up.

"Thank you."

"You want to tell me what you're doing in my house at five a.m.?"

I was momentarily taken aback by his harsh tone. He stood in front of me with his arms crossed over his bare chest. My eyes ran over his body, taking in the hulking man that stood before me. He was huge, extremely tall, and wide. He had muscles on top of muscles and with his arms folded in front of him, he looked like the Hulk, minus the green skin. He had short, dark hair and scruff over his face that made him look very dangerous. I subconsciously took a step back to get some space from him. He was radiating irritation and anger right now, and I didn't want to further upset the beast. He sighed in irritation and backed out of the bathroom. Then gestured for me to leave.

He walked in the direction of the kitchen. I wasn't sure if I should follow or not, but my feet went in that direction anyway. He pulled out some crackers and pushed them across the counter to me. It didn't sound that appealing to me at the moment, but I took them and nibbled on them.

"So, are you going to answer me?"

I looked up into his pale, scruffy face and saw that his night passed out on the couch had done nothing to improve his looks or his attitude. He was a handsome man, but his heavy drinking last night left him looking like he was still drunk.

"I was here because I brought you home last night and you were acting out of your mind. I was worried that you were going to choke on your vomit if I left, so I slept on the recliner."

He studied me for a minute before scowling at me. "I don't need or want your help. Next time, just leave me alone. Better yet, don't get involved at all."

"You don't have to be an ass about it. No wonder she left you."

I meant that last part to be said under my breath, but I was louder than I meant to be and he exploded at me.

"What the fuck did you say?"

"Who's Iris?" I asked before I could think better of it.

"She's none of your fucking business. How do you know about her anyway?"

I smirked. It looked like there was something about him that he didn't want anyone to know about. Maybe his friends didn't know he had been left by his girlfriend.

"You were crying over her last night, asking why she left you. Although, after seeing what an asshole you really are, I'm not surprised she left you."

He moved so fast around the counter that I barely registered his movements until he grabbed my arm and yanked me toward the front door. His fingers dug into my skin, reminding me that sometimes it was better to keep my mouth shut. He threw the front door open and dragged me to the porch.

"She didn't leave me. She died. Now go home and don't ever step foot on my property again."

He walked back inside and slammed the door in my face. I stared at the door for a moment, taken aback by his admission. My bad behavior left a sinking feeling in my stomach. I wasn't normally a bitch. I was a nice person, kind to everyone even when they didn't deserve it. But Drew brought out the worst in me. That and the fact that I had just lost everything in my life. Still, I was ashamed at my words to him. He was obviously hurting and I had thrown it in his face. He was still grieving for her and that's why he was so drunk; to forget. I didn't have that option. I was forced to be sober so I didn't hurt my baby, the only piece of Todd I had left.

MORNINGS SUCKED. What used to be my favorite time of the day was now something I dreaded. I hated waking up every morning puking my guts out. The nausea seemed to settle down by midday, which was a good thing because I got a job working at The Pub at night. I had been in this town for two months and I still didn't have a single friend. Most people looked at me like I was something they scraped off their shoe. I couldn't really blame them all that much. I wasn't the friendliest person. I rarely spoke for fear that I would say the wrong thing. There was nothing about my past that I could share with anyone, and frankly, I didn't know anyone worth sharing that information with.

I walked around the house that I now called home, looking at the current state it was in and decided that if I was going to live here for the foreseeable future, I needed to spruce it up a bit. Grabbing my keys, I headed into town and picked out some paint colors at the local hardware store. While the paint was being mixed, I wandered around the store to get the supplies I would need. I grabbed a roll of painter's tape, an edger, paint brushes, a drop cloth, and paint stirrers. This was probably going to send me over budget, but I needed to put some life in that house. I was expecting my paycheck in two days, so I should be fine until then.

When I went back to the paint counter, everything was ready and I put it all in my cart, then pushed it up front to pay. I was handing over my cash when Drew walked in the door, drawing my attention to the permanent scowl that seemed to be on his face. He walked past me and then paused when he saw what was in my cart.

"You're painting?"

"You're quick," I said sarcastically. He didn't seem to appreciate my comment, as he turned a glare on me.

"You shouldn't be painting. The fumes are bad for you."

"Well, I'll just go call my husband and tell him to come take care of it for me." Sarcasm dripped from my words, but inside it really hurt to say that. He didn't know how much I wished I could call my husband right now, but I never allowed myself to think about him that much. I had too much else to worry about and I couldn't let myself break down. Crying wouldn't bring him back, and it wouldn't help my baby either.

"Maybe you should have thought about that before you went and got yourself knocked up."

He walked away with a scowl on his face. I turned back to the cashier, not missing the scowl on her face as she looked down at my belly, then looked back up at me, pursing her lips and shaking her head at me. There was nothing I could do to change people's minds about me. It was what it was, and telling them that I did have a husband was out of the question. They would want more answers that I couldn't give.

I took my change and headed out to my car, loading my supplies in the back. I drove out of town, tears threatening to spill down my face, wondering how life had gotten so messed up. I just wanted my old life back. I wanted to go back in time and change all the shit that had happened. My vision blurred and I briefly thought of pulling over, but then I took a deep breath and wiped the tears away, just in time to see a deer run out in front of me. I jerked the wheel to avoid hitting it, but the deer was faster and my car plowed right into it.

I heard something hit the car, which I assumed was the deer, but nothing else really registered. The crash happened so fast that I didn't even know what happened until my head was whipped back from hitting the air bag. I felt the strain of the seat belt as it held me back, keeping me from flying through the windshield.

My head fell back at an awkward angle and my neck felt strained under the heavy weight. My whole face felt like it'd been smashed in. I wanted to get out of the car, but I couldn't have moved if I wanted to. Nothing on my body seemed to function at the moment. Instead of trying to move anymore, I laid there hoping that someone would find me soon. Fear started to seep into my brain as I thought about someone else hitting me if they didn't see me right away. I had no idea if my car was on the road or in the ditch.

"Sarah, don't stay there. It's not safe."

I shook my head slightly, careful not to shake too hard in case I hurt my head. I must have hit my head because Todd's voice was calling to me and telling me what to do, but that couldn't be. Todd was dead.

"Sarah, come on. Wake up, baby. You have to get out and get moving."

I must have slipped in and out of consciousness because I remembered it being light out when I crashed, but when I opened my eyes again, it was getting dark. I was trying to think back to what time I left the hardware store and I thought it was early afternoon, but my thoughts were too jumbled to be sure.

"Sarah, you've been outside too long. Come on, baby. Get out of the car for me and get moving. You know you can't stay here any longer."

The cold from outside had seeped into my car and my whole body shook. My head felt a little clearer than the last time I woke up. I knew I had to move. It was dangerous to just sit here. With a shaky hand, I unbuckled my seat belt, but as soon as I tried to open the door, pain shot through my left hand. Hissing, I reached across with my right hand and shoved the door open. My chest ached with every movement, and as I stumbled out of the car, I wondered how the hell I was going to make it home.

Leaning against the side of the car, I tried to remember where I was. I looked back in the direction of town and then back toward my house. I was on a deserted side road, which meant I was almost home. I didn't have a phone, so there would be no calling anyone for help.

"Just get someplace safe, baby."

I closed my eyes and let Todd's voice wash over me. I wanted to feel his arms wrapped around me. I wanted him to hold me and whisper that everything would be okay. But I knew that wouldn't happen. I was on my own, and the only person that was going to save me was me.

I started back toward my house, stumbling along each step, counting footsteps as I went. After every ten feet, I told myself that I had ten feet down and was that much closer to home. Despite it being absolutely ridiculous, it helped keep my hopes up that I could make it home.

When I got to my driveway, I almost cried. I was so close, but it still felt like my house was a million miles away. My body ached, my head pounded...I just wanted to sit down. I briefly considered sitting down and taking a rest, but I knew if I did that, I would never get back up. Pulling on my last bit of strength, I stumbled down the long driveway, only realizing when I got to the door that I didn't have my keys on me.

A sob tore from my throat as I frantically jiggled the handle. I was hoping I had just forgotten to lock the door, but I hadn't. I cupped my hands around my eyes, pressing my face against the window. The couch was just within view, waiting for me. I slammed my fist against the window, but all that did was hurt my hand. I found a rock and threw it through the front window. I stared at the hole, shaking my head slightly. For some reason, I assumed that the whole window would shatter, but it didn't. I looked around for anything to use to break the rest of the glass. A rock would only get me so far, but there was nothing close by.

Looking over at Drew's house, it felt like a million miles away, but it was my only option right now. I needed something to help me. Spotting a shovel that was leaning against the porch, I grabbed it and went back to my house, breaking the rest of the window. I dropped the shovel, gingerly climbing in through the window. It was difficult with my body hurting so much, but my need to lie down pushed me farther than I was willing to go. When I finally got all the way inside, I dragged my tired body down the hall to my bedroom and plopped down in bed.

"Good job, baby. Rest now. I'll watch over you."

It wasn't more than a minute before I was asleep.

MY BODY FELT like it was being thrown around like a rag doll. I slowly opened my eyes to see a dark figure looming over me. My instincts kicked in and I raised my arm, punching the intruder in the face. I screamed, hoping Drew was home and heard me. I grabbed the light off the nightstand and smashed it down on the intruder's head. I heard a grunt before he collapsed on the bed. I backed up against the wall, staring at the lifeless figure. Blood pounded in my ears as I tried to think of what to do next. My hands were shaking and my breathing was ragged.

A man appeared in the doorway, flicking on the light. The badge at his waist had me immediately raising my hands in surrender so I didn't get shot. He looked down at the bed, swearing before holstering his weapon and moving closer to me. I pushed myself further away, sagging in relief when he went to the person on the bed.

"Drew, you okay?"

"What?" My eyes flicked back to the bed, and now with the lights on, I could clearly see that it was my neighbor. "Drew? Oh my God!"

I ran over, brushing my hand over his forehead to see if he would wake up. His eyes fluttered, and that alone sent relief flooding through my system. He groaned before rolling over and grasping his head.

"What the fuck did you do that for?" He sat up rubbing his head, squinting at the light.

My hackles immediately stood on end. How dare he yell at me. "Don't you know better than to break into someone's house in the middle of the night? You scared the shit out of me."

"I didn't have to break in. The window was already broken. I thought something was wrong, especially since your car is abandoned on the side of the road with a deer stuck to it."

As I calmed down, I began to see how that could be disturbing and he would come check on me, but my objective when I walked away was to get somewhere I could lie down.

"Sorry. I wasn't thinking." I ran a tired hand over my face. This was all too much to take in at whatever ungodly hour it was.

"Why didn't you call a tow truck or something? Did you walk home? That was two miles away."

"I don't have a phone, and I was closer to home than I was to town, so I came here."

"Why don't you have a phone?"

I stayed silent, refusing to tell him the ins and outs of my reasons for not having a phone. "I just don't. I don't need one."

"Really? Tonight would suggest otherwise. What if something happened to the baby? What would you have done then?"

My face burned red at the implication that I couldn't take care of my child. "People never used to have phones and still had babies." I snapped at him because he was pissing me off. I knew it was better to have a phone, but I couldn't. It was too risky. This was how I protected my child.

"There was also a higher mortality rate."

The police officer cut in, putting an end to our bickering.

"Ma'am, my name is Officer Donnelly. I'm a friend of Drew's. You can call me Sean."

He held out his hand to me, but I was reluctant to take it. I wondered if he knew about me, though I was told that no one in the local police department would be informed. I took his hand and gave it a small shake.

"Sarah."

"Sarah...?"

"Sarah Anderson."

"It's nice to meet you Ms. Anderson. It looks like you got hit pretty good with the airbag. Are you hurt anywhere else?"

"Nothing that won't heal."

"Drew said that you're pregnant. I think it would be best to take you to the hospital and check to be sure the baby is okay."

"I don't think that's necessary. I'm sore, but otherwise fine."

"You are so damn stubborn," Drew growled. "Do you care at all about your child? Just go to the hospital and make sure it's okay."

Drew was practically yelling at me, scaring the hell out of me with his booming voice. I instinctively took a step back. I wasn't necessarily scared of him, but he was a big guy.

"Fine. Let me change and I'll be out."

I went over to the dresser and slowly pulled off my pants. I started pulling off my shirt, but the pain was excruciating. I slowly worked my arm out of one sleeve and then the other, but getting it over my head hurt too much. Dipping my head, I tried to pull it off with less movement, but the cry that tore from my lips had a huge alpha male bursting through my door a second later.

"Are you alright?"

He was staring at me with what looked like disgust on his face. I looked away, realizing a moment too late that I was completely naked, except for my undergarments. I grabbed a blanket from my bed and held it up in front of my body. My face flushed with embarrassment. I knew I wasn't the most attractive woman. I was extremely thin, I had small breasts, and my ribs protruded from my body. I couldn't help it, though. I had always been petite, but after Todd died, eating was difficult. Then the morning sickness kicked in, so now I looked like a scarecrow.

I held back the tears as I stared at the ground, hoping Drew didn't see how much the look on his face wounded me.

"Jesus. Look at your chest. Why didn't you tell us you were hurt that bad?"

He came over and yanked the blanket down, staring at my chest that was now covered in dark bruises. "You didn't think this warranted a trip to the hospital? Do you have any concern for your child or do you really care so little?"

His words were a slap in the face and I did my best to steel my spine against his harsh outburst.

"I care a lot about my child, I just…"

"You just what? Didn't think you needed to check if the baby was alright?"

Tears pricked my eyes and I wanted to defend myself, but I was having a hard time with that right now. I knew he was partially right, but I had been so tired, all I could think about was getting home and going to sleep.

"Drew," a harsh voice came from the doorway. "That's enough. Can I see you a moment?" Sean turned to me with a gentle look on his face. "Honey, why don't you put on something comfortable and I'll take you in to be checked out."

His kind voice had me nodding my assent. After he closed the door, the tears finally fell down my face. I was such a failure. It seemed like everything I did was wrong. I needed Todd. I needed someone on my side.

"What the fuck is your problem?" I heard through the closed door. I stepped closer, listening to the hatred in Drew's voice.

"She's being an irresponsible mother. Who on earth would let a woman like her have a baby. She got in an accident and didn't even bother to go to the hospital to be checked out."

"Do you hear yourself? She got in an accident. Did you miss the sizable lump on her head? She probably has a concussion and isn't thinking clearly. How long ago did you leave her at the hardware store?"

"About two this afternoon."

"Okay, so she could have been out there for hours, disoriented and not thinking clearly. You need to lay off and stop being an asshole. I've seen this enough to know it didn't even register what she had been through. It probably still hasn't."

I looked down at my body as I grabbed my clothes. When I saw the bruising on my chest again, something painful took hold of my heart, because I finally realized that my baby was in danger and I had done nothing to make sure she was okay.

Squeezing my eyes shut, I fought back a sob. "Todd, I promise I'll do better. I'll protect our child. I won't let you down," I whispered.

Funny, I had only thought of the baby as a fetus until now, but I could almost see her beautiful face right now. For some reason, I saw a girl and imagined her with Todd's eyes and his beautiful smile. I would do better for Todd. He didn't let us down, and now I needed to pull myself together and do the same for him.

I finished dressing and opened the door to my bedroom. Sean was sitting on the couch waiting for me and Drew was on the phone. Sean stood as I approached, his hand guiding me toward the door.

"Let's get you checked out."

"I'll take her," Drew's gruff voice called out.

I didn't want to spend one more minute with him than I had to, so I turned to Sean with a pleading look.

"Please, I just want to go with you."

He nodded and turned back to Drew. "I'll take her. Why don't you clean up that window and see about getting a replacement."

We walked out the door to the police car, and as I got in, I saw Drew standing in my doorway with a scowl on his face. I don't know what I did to make him hate me so much, but I vowed to stay as far away from him as possible. I just needed to focus on taking care of my child.

CHAPTER 3

DREW

That woman pissed me off so much. I didn't really know why, but something about her made me want to wring her neck. After Sean put her accident into perspective, I calmed down considerably. My words had been harsh and I'd hoped she hadn't heard them, but based on the fact that she asked Sean to take her to the hospital, I would guess she had.

I went back to my shed and found a piece of plywood that would cover her window, and then nailed it in place. As I took the measurements for the window, I became more frustrated when I started checking the other windows and the doors. They were all crap. She shouldn't be living like this. I'd have to talk to her about that later. Spring was getting closer, but she was going to need to replace her windows before next winter. Her doors should be replaced before then. Someone could break in with a good boot to the door. I called Ryan and gave him the window measurements and hoped he had something in our inventory.

I walked through her house and did a more thorough examination of her house, noting the roof was leaking. That would be another thing we would be discussing. Other than that, her house was mostly in decent condition, it just needed some updating.

Then I thought about her car still sitting on the side of the road. It needed to be towed, and I wasn't sure if Sean had already taken care of that. Pulling out my phone, I called Jack.

"Drew, please tell me you're not calling to steal Harper."

"No," I grunted. "I need a favor."

"A favor? From you? No way. Holy shit, I'm gonna have to call the guys."

"Why would you do that?"

"Because you never want help or need anything. Now you're calling me," he laughed. "Oh, this is just too good."

"Are you gonna help or not?" I growled.

"Alright, alright. What do you need?"

"My neighbor hit a deer. Her car is on the side of the road and it needs to be towed. Can you take care of that and then check it over? I'll need to know if it's salvageable. Also, check the car over to see if—"

"Seriously? Are you telling me how to do my job? Because you can come down here and do it yourself if you think you can do it better."

I rolled my eyes and sighed. "Just do it."

"Isn't this the neighbor that you claim to hate?"

"I don't hate her. She just...irritates me."

"Irritates you in a good way?"

"Is there a good way to irritate someone?"

"I don't know. Harper irritates me all the time, and then I fuck it out of her."

I scoffed in disgust. "I don't need to know about how you deal with Harper."

"I'm just saying, maybe you need to approach this situation differently. It could end pretty well for you."

"Not gonna happen," I said, ending the call before he could spout anymore bullshit.

Sighing, I ran a tired hand over my face. I didn't know why I was still over here worrying about her house. She annoyed me and I didn't really have any desire to be a friendly, helpful neighbor. I grabbed my keys and got in my truck, driving back over to my place. When I got out and went inside, I found myself looking around for something to do. I should go to bed, but my thoughts kept drifting to Sarah. I wondered if the baby was okay and if she was hurt any more than she was letting on. Against my better judgement, I gave Sean a call.

"Hello." His voice said, yeah, I was expecting your call.

"How's Sarah doing?"

"She's back being examined now. I don't know anything more than that."

"Shit. Well I feel like a complete asshole now."

"What is it about this girl that makes you such a growly bastard?"

"I don't know. Something about her is deceptive. I can't put my finger on it, but I don't trust her, and when I met her, I instantly disliked her. I really don't know."

"They're calling me back. I'll check in with you later."

I hung up the phone and waited for the next half hour for him to call me back and give me some news, but he never did. I considered calling him, maybe demanding that he tell me what was going on. But then, why did I care? She was nobody to me. She was the neighbor, and not a very good one at that. I didn't even like her. Stomping upstairs, I got undressed and headed to bed. I didn't need this shit in my life. I didn't need to worry about a woman that meant nothing to me. Harper was the only woman in my life now. The only one I needed to consider. Worrying about a woman that didn't bother to take care of herself was not something I needed. I was trying to get my life together here and finally start living again. In order to do that, I needed to focus on myself.

AFTER MEETING with a rancher the next morning and finalizing a deal where he could use part of my property for horse breeding in exchange for a fee, I sat down and thought about what else I wanted to do around the house. With Iris, we'd always talked about having a vegetable garden, and since this house was in part for her, I decided that was exactly what I was going to do. I didn't have a greenhouse yet, but with spring coming, I could get started on building one. I wouldn't have everything I needed for this year, but next year, I could get started earlier. I headed into town for supplies, ready to get to work.

I was just driving past Jack's garage when I remembered Sarah had been picking up paint supplies from the hardware store yesterday. They had to be in her car still since she had walked home. I shouldn't care. It wasn't my problem that her stuff was still there. But it would be the neighborly thing to take them to her, whether I believed she should be painting or not. Turning around, I headed back to the garage and headed inside to see Jack.

"Drew, stopping in to see me now? Harper's gonna think you want to spend more time with me than her."

"I'm just here to get Sarah's paint supplies."

He grinned. "So, you're helping her out now."

"I live right next to her," I said with a glare. "I'm just being nice."

He snorted. "Yeah, that's you, Mr. Nice Guy."

"Are you gonna get them for me or not?"

"Sure." He stood and made his way to the door. "That was some accident she had. Probably scared the piss out of her."

I grunted in reply. I didn't want to get into how scared she was because then I would have to admit that I was an ass to her.

"So, does she have someone living with her or is she living out there all alone?"

"She's by herself."

"Huh. Pregnant and alone. You seem to find yourself in this situation yet again."

"What the fuck are you talking about?"

"Well, when Harper was pregnant and alone, you sure were willing to step in and take the reins. Is that what you're doing here?"

When Harper and Jack were broken up, Harper went to England to visit her father and thought that having a one night stand would help her get over Jack. She ended up pregnant and was facing being a single mother. I told her I would be there for her no matter what, and I would have been. Harper meant everything to me and there's nothing I wouldn't do for her. In the end, Jack and Harper reunited, and Jack gladly stepped into the role of the father of her child.

"That was different. Harper was special to me. I would have done anything for her, and I still would. I don't even know this woman. Hell, I just learned her last name last night. This woman... she can't seem to do anything right by herself. She's gonna end up dead somewhere."

"Yeah, I used to feel the same way about Harper, but she proved me wrong."

"No. It's different with this woman. Harper was fiercely independent. This woman looks like she just ambled into the country and said, *I think I'll live in the country now*. She doesn't even have a phone. She has a kid on the way, an unreliable car, no phone, and from what I can see, unreliable income. She got herself knocked up and she's gonna have to deal with that."

"So, where do you draw the line at who deserves help? Harper got herself knocked up. It wasn't like she was with someone for years and it was an accident. Harper had a one night stand and wound up pregnant. What happened with this girl?"

"I don't know."

"You don't know?"

"Not a clue." I shrugged. I didn't want or need to know.

"Pretty judgmental for not knowing what's going on in her life."

He gave me a sidelong glance that told me I was being an ass.

"Look, I don't want to know or need to know. I just want to be left alone on my property and not have to deal with her drama. I moved to the country for peace, not so I could look after a woman."

Jack held up his hands in surrender and took a step back. "Hey, it's no skin off my nose. You do what you want. I'm just saying, you don't know her well enough to cast her as the town whore."

I grunted and then followed him back to her car that looked like it was totaled.

"Shit. Is it salvageable?"

"I haven't finished going over it, but from what I can see, it's going to the junkyard."

"Perfect. She's gonna be wanting rides into town from me."

"Relax. I'm sure her insurance will allow for a rental until she gets a new one."

I grabbed her stuff, noticing her purse in the front seat, and loaded everything into my truck. I headed back to my place, thinking about what Jack said. Maybe I was judging her too harshly, but I wasn't going to think about that anymore. I had my own shit to take care of. I made one more stop before heading out to her place.

When I pulled up to her house, I thought momentarily about just dropping her shit on the porch and leaving, but I had her purse, so that wasn't really a good option. I unloaded the first set of paint supplies and brought it to her front door. I gave a hard knock and waited for a minute before she answered. When she did, I was taken aback. She looked horrible. She was leaning heavily on the door and she had a large, beige wrap sweater on that she was hugging to her chest as she slouched over. Her hair was pulled up in a messy knot on the top of her head, and her face was blue on the right side. If someone bumped into her, she'd probably face plant.

"Are you okay?"

"Yeah, I'm just tired. I haven't slept too much. There's not much I can take for pain without harming the baby."

I nodded. "Well, I brought your stuff from the garage. Where do you want me to put it?"

"Um, you can just set it anywhere." She waved her hand to the living room and then went and sank down in the couch. Her head immediately went to the arm of the couch and the cushions just swallowed her body as she sank into them.

I quickly unloaded the truck and then brought her purse over to her. "I picked up a phone for you. It's nothing fancy. It's just a flip phone, but at least you can call someone if you need help. I programmed my number in and Sean's also. Here's a prepaid phone card. You can add more minutes as you need them."

She stared at the phone for a minute as if pondering whether or not she really needed it. "It's not in my name is it?"

I furrowed my brow. That was an odd thing to ask. "No. I bought it with my card and the minutes can be added with cash."

She nodded and closed her eyes. I sat there looking at her trying to figure her out, but she was an enigma to me. Of course, I hadn't tried to get to know her.

"What rooms are you planning to paint?"

"All of them," she said sleepily.

"Before you go to sleep, you should really try to eat something."

"I'm not hungry. I just want to sleep."

"Sarah, that's really not good for the baby."

"Really? What do you know about babies? Do you have one?"

A stab of pain shot through me as I thought of the child I should have had. "No, I don't have any kids."

"Well, then how about you leave me alone and let me take care of myself and my child. Do you think I don't know what you think of me? I know you've already made up your mind that I'm some trashy whore that got herself knocked up. You think whatever you want. I don't need to prove myself to you or anyone else in this town."

"I'm not judging you."

"Don't give me that bullshit. You've judged me since the day you met me. Just go away. I don't need anyone. I'm perfectly capable of taking care of myself."

I leaned back and watched her for a minute. Her eyes were

closed, and I could see the bruising around her eyes from the accident and probably lack of sleep. She looked so tiny lying on the couch. I subconsciously started rubbing at the ache in my chest. I wasn't sure why I hated seeing her like this, but suddenly I didn't like that she was lying here helpless, that she was all alone. I usually tried not to interfere in others' lives, but this woman was getting under my skin. Not that I wanted her, I just wanted to understand her.

After a minute, her breathing evened out and I knew she was asleep. I took a few minutes to look around her house. There was no TV, no pictures, no computer, nothing personal. It looked like she had moved in with clothes. I recognized it because that's what I used to do. I didn't want to have any attachments, so I didn't bring anything with me. She was going to have a baby, though. Shouldn't she have something that would show she was putting down roots?

I got up because it was none of my business what she chose to do. I went to her kitchen and saw her discharge papers. Being the nosy fucker that I was, I read over them. Basically, she had a bunch of bumps and bruises and since she was pregnant, she was on bed rest for the next week. She had been spotting in the hospital, but the baby appeared fine, so they discharged her. She was to call back if she had any cramping or bleeding.

After reading that, I decided it would be the neighborly thing to make sure she had some ready meals so that she wasn't doing shit she wasn't supposed to. She didn't have anyone helping. How was she supposed to get rest if she was all alone with no one to look after her? I set down the papers and rubbed a hand over my face. It didn't matter. I would make her some dinner and wash my hands of the situation. I wouldn't even check on her tomorrow.

∼

THE NEXT MORNING, I found myself walking over to Sarah's house. I wasn't sure why, and frankly, I didn't really have the time. I cursed myself as I checked my watch and saw I was going to run late if I didn't leave soon. I was supposed to be at work in an hour, but something was telling me to go check on her. I knocked on the door, but no one answered. I tried the door, but it was locked. I raised my fist and started pounding.

"Sarah!"

Pounding some more, I waited for an answer and still didn't get one. What the fuck was going on?

"Sarah, answer the goddamn door."

When she still didn't answer, I walked around the house, peering in windows to try and see her. I was passing the bathroom window when I finally saw her. She was lying in the tub, unmoving. I banged on the window, but got no answer. Shit. I ran around to the front of the house and practically broke the door down. I ran down the hall to the bathroom, flinging the door open. Thrusting my hands in the water, I grabbed her behind her back and under her legs just as a piercing noise hit my ears. It took me a minute to register that it was her screaming.

"What are you doing? Get out of my bathroom!"

I gently set her back down, but not before noticing that most of the bubbles were missing from the tub and I could see every inch of her body.

"I said get out! Stop looking at me."

I backed up and ran into her sink before turning and heading out the door. I waited for her in the living room, but it took a good ten minutes before she came out dressed in a robe. I stood and stepped toward her.

"I'm so sorry. I didn't mean to embarrass you."

"Embarrass me? Why would I be embarrassed? You're the one who came into my bathroom unannounced!"

Her face was red with anger and she was holding her side.

"Are you okay? Why are you holding your side?"

"Someone came into my bathroom and scared the crap out of me while I was trying to soak."

"I'm sorry. I came to check on you, and you didn't answer the door. I saw you in the tub through the window-"

"You were watching me through the window?"

"I was just trying to make sure you were okay. I pounded on the window, but you didn't answer, so I broke in your door and came in here right away. I thought you were unconscious."

"Do you hear yourself? You broke into my house because I was taking a bath!"

"You weren't answering!"

"I had headphones in!"

"How the fuck would I see that from the window?"

"Why the fuck would you be looking through my windows? Don't you know how to respect a person's privacy?"

"Look, I was just coming to make sure you're okay. I've done that and now I'm leaving."

I walked toward the front door and stopped at the sight of the door hanging off its hinges. Sarah came hobbling around the corner, yelling at me. She gasped when she saw the door.

"Wait! You broke down my door. What the hell are you gonna do about that?"

"I'll have someone from work come fix it."

"You'd better have someone out here in an hour. It's cold outside and I don't need my heating bill skyrocketing."

I held out my hands, trying to calm her down. Jesus, she was like a frickin' rabbit on steroids. "I promise. Just relax. I'll take care of it."

"Just relax? I'll relax when you leave me alone. Do not ever come over here again. I don't need you to play white knight and save the day, so next time you think I'm in trouble, turn around and walk away."

I clenched my jaw, mostly angry at myself. I had come over here, against every instinct to stay away, to check on her. And where did that get me? She was pissed at me for caring. "Don't worry, sweetheart. I won't step foot on your property unless I absolutely have to."

I walked out the door and trudged over to my house. I put in a call to Ryan and headed into work. I didn't need this shit. That ungrateful bitch could sit there and freeze for all I cared.

～

AFTER ROPING off a large portion of the land for the rancher, I still had about ten acres of land that wouldn't be farmed or used for the horses. I had started building the greenhouse further back on the property so I wouldn't have to look at it from my back porch. The garden was to the right of it, closest to the field.

When I wasn't at work, I was building the greenhouse and getting all the vegetables planted. I'd also bought some trees to act as a windbreak, and every once in a while, I glanced over at my neighbor's house and wished I could put some between us. Then I wouldn't have to stare at her house every day and wonder if she was okay. I shouldn't even be thinking about her. This garden was my dream with Iris. I was doing it for her.

We'd only had a garden the one year we lived in that house. She wasn't able to enjoy it very much, but I did it for her and she sat out in a chair watching me work.

"YOU SHOULD REALLY BE *inside resting. It's too cool outside for you.*"

"*Pfft. Nonsense. I'm fine. I have a blanket around me to keep me warm. Besides, the view out here is better than anything I could see inside.*"

I glanced at her and saw her eyes trailing over my body. There weren't many days when she felt well, but on the days she did, she just wanted to do something to feel normal. I dropped my hoe and walked over to her, kneeling in front of her.

"*You see something you like?*"

"*You mean like the hot, sweaty man in front of me? Yeah, he's okay.*" *She smiled brightly before grabbing the cowboy hat off my head and setting it on her own.* "*What do ya think, cowboy? You wanna take* me for a ride?" She waggled her eyebrows suggestively at me, eliciting a huge grin from me.

"Well now, ma'am, my momma raised me to be a gentleman. I don't know that that would be proper."

"Why, my, my. You are quite the gentleman. I'm afraid my poor, southern heart couldn't take it if you declined to take me for a ride." She fanned herself dramatically while batting her eyelashes at me.

"Ma'am, I couldn't stand it if I was the reason your poor heart was broken."

I picked her up and carried her inside where I made love to her.

I SMILED at the memory as I stopped working and laughed at her playfulness. I looked over, thinking that I would see her sitting next to the garden in a chair, waiting for me to take her inside. All I saw was a lawn and a house that didn't have a thing to do with her. Just like that, the memories faded and I was brought back to the present, reminded that I would never get to take her inside and see her beautiful body.

That had been the last time I had made love to her. She was too weak after that to do much of anything. I hadn't cared. I just wanted her to get better so we could move on with life. I never once let myself think about moving on without her. I guess that's why it had been such a shock to me when she passed. I knew it was coming and I knew I had to prepare, but my mind wouldn't let me accept that she was going to be leaving me. I remember her mother calling the minister when she passed to come say a prayer for her. I had been too distressed to pray to God for anything other than for him to bring her back to me.

My hand went to the rings that were laying against my chest. Some days it felt like they were literally burning a hole in my skin, but I couldn't bring myself to take the chain from around my neck. So much of my life had been wrapped around Iris. The rings symbolized more than a marriage. They were reminders of a love that could never be lost, even in death.

After about a half hour of sitting in my garden, being swallowed up in memories, I finally picked up my tools and headed to the shed to put them all away. There was no point in working on the garden anymore today. It would only bring memories back that were better left forgotten.

CHAPTER 4

SARAH

A month had passed since my unfortunate incident with the deer. I was getting ready for work when the mail arrived and I went out to grab it. I was usually too tired after work to stop for the mail, so I tried to get it before work when possible. Today was not my lucky day, though. Opening the mailbox, I saw the letter I had been dreading. It was from my case manager, telling me that I was due in court next week and that someone would be picking me up on Friday. All the pertinent details were listed, including the fact that I should plan to be gone for a week. That was more than I wanted to take, but it wasn't like I had a choice in the matter.

When I got to work, I told my boss that I had a family funeral to attend and would have to leave on Friday, and I might be gone up to a week. There was a good chance I could lose my job over this. I hadn't been there that long, and I had already taken off due to my car accident. I had to look like the most unreliable employee ever. However, Hank was really nice and told me to take all the time I needed. It was very generous of him and I thanked him, giving him a big hug.

As the week went on, I tried to rein in my emotions, but the idea of going through that night all over again scared the shit out of me.

The prosecution already told me that I wouldn't be able to give my testimony via video, I would need to be in court. They couldn't give a written testimony because it wasn't as effective as in person. Besides, the defense argued they would not be able to properly cross examine, which the judge agreed with. I was going to be called to the stand on Monday at nine in the morning. There was no getting out of it. I had to do it if I wanted protection.

I was hoping that I could sneak out of town without anyone the wiser, but of course, my annoying neighbor didn't miss a thing. He came outside as soon as the black SUV pulled into the driveway and watched them as they loaded my bags into the trunk. Still, I thought I could escape, but then he started walking toward me.

"Sarah, you going somewhere?"

"Um...yeah. These are some family members of mine. My ...um... father died and they're taking me to his funeral. We're driving, so I'll probably be gone for about a week."

"Family, huh? Do all your family members carry multiple weapons on them at all times?"

The agents stiffened next to me and I started to feel panic creep up. My throat felt like it was closing up, but I couldn't allow him to suspect that anything was wrong. I let out a little chuckle.

"We're from Texas. Everyone carries a gun in Texas. Don't worry, they have permits."

"Funny. I didn't hear an accent."

"I haven't lived in Texas for a long time."

He didn't look like he believed me, but he nodded and walked back to his house.

We made the drive back to New York, my stomach churning the whole way. I couldn't believe I was actually going to do this.

"I'm going to check in, and the others are securing the perimeter. When I give the signal, we'll enter through the side door. Understood?" I nodded, taking a deep breath. I wasn't at all ready, but I didn't have a choice. I waited as he went inside, and when the driver confirmed that everything was clear, the agent returned and ushered me inside.

"Keep your head down," he murmured as we headed for a flight of stairs. I did as he asked, thankful when we reached the room and I was safe inside. The curtains were drawn, shielding anyone from seeing inside. At least, that's what I assumed.

The agent walked over to the window, peeking out the curtain. "Don't ever open these. A sniper could easily take you out with a bullet to the head, and we wouldn't even know he was there until you were lying dead on the floor."

I swallowed hard, feeling like I was going to throw up. This wasn't what I signed up for, was it? Was this really protecting my child? Suddenly, all I wanted was to be back in that small town in Pennsylvania where no one knew my name and I was free to come and go as I pleased without worrying about someone killing me.

However, the condition of being placed there was that I would return to testify when my husband's killer was shot. If I chose not to, I would no doubt have half the Italian mob hot on my heels to put a bullet in my head, because the government would not provide me with witness protection.

I settled in at the hotel, my nerves making me jump at every sound. My security was cool and calm, like this was just another job to them. But this was my life. Everything that happened this week held my life in the balance.

I'd never felt so alone as I did waiting to give my testimony on Monday. The agents were there for my protection only and I had no family or friends that I could talk to. This would be the rest of my life. I would never see my friends again, and I didn't have any family other than Todd's parents. He had never been close to them, so I really doubted they even cared what happened to me.

The agents gave me a blonde wig and made sure I had all the makeup necessary to look like my old self. I had switched to brown colored contacts when I was put in witness protection because my eyes were a distinctive blue. For the next few days, I had to remember to not put them in.

I spent all of Sunday preparing with the prosecution for taking the stand. I was nervous and my stomach was churning to the point I thought I'd be sick. The prosecution suggested I take something to calm my nerves, but there was nothing I could take while pregnant. I just needed to suck it up and do this before I chickened out.

I waited in a secluded room on Monday until I was called to the stand. My knees shook as I walked through the courtroom and took the stand, then was sworn in. I sat down and wiped the sweat from my palms on my skirt, hoping that I could give solid testimony that would get my husband's killer put away for life. As I looked at Marco Abruzzo, a hitman for the Italian mafia, all I saw was the promise of revenge. My body quaked in fear at the threat in his eyes. I forced myself to look away from him and focused on the agents that were there to protect me.

I closed my eyes and saw Todd's face in my mind. I imagined him in front of me, telling me everything would be okay. Todd had a strength to him that infused me as I sat in the chair in the witness box preparing to put his murderer in jail. He winked at me one last time before I opened my eyes. I could still feel him surrounding me, even if I could no longer see his face. When the assistant district attorney stepped forward, I braced myself for the next few hours of questioning.

"Mrs. Matthews, can you please tell us what happened the night your husband was murdered?"

"My husband and I were out celebrating and we went to Mama Lolita's for dinner."

"What were you celebrating?"

"I'd just found out that I was pregnant."

The ADA gave a sad noise. "Please continue, Mrs. Matthews."

"We were leaving the restaurant and had parked on a side street to the restaurant, so we decided to cut through the alley. When we got to the end, there was a second alley that formed a t with the one we were in. We were going to turn left down that alley to get to our car. We were about to step out when my husband heard someone rack a gun."

"And how did your husband recognize this sound?"

"He was former military and served for eight years. Then he worked at a security firm." My voice shook as I remembered what he had done for me that night. How he had done everything possible to protect me and our child. I took a second to pull myself together.

"So he was well acquainted with weapons." I nodded. "Please continue, Mrs. Matthews."

"We heard a man speaking to another man about making something happen or it wouldn't be good for him."

"Can you be more specific, please? Do you remember what exactly was said?"

I took a deep breath and replayed the events in my head, the harsh words spoken by Giuseppe Cordano to Police Chief Waters. Chills racked my spine and ADA Rayland had to ask me several times if I could continue. I shook the memories from my head and cleared my throat.

"Giuseppe Cordano was standing with Marco Abruzzo in the alley. Cordano was telling the police chief that if he wasn't willing to look the other way, things would turn out very bad for him."

"This is now deceased Police Chief Waters?"

"Yes."

"Did you know it was them at the time?"

"No. I was asked to look at photos at the police station and I picked them out from there."

"How can you be sure you identified the right people? Wasn't it night?"

"Abruzzo pulled a gun on the police chief when he refused to comply. It scared me and I made a noise. They...they turned and looked at me. There was a light off the back of the restaurant, and as they turned, I got a good look at their faces. Abruzzo turned his gun on us immediately, and the police chief yelled at us to run. Cordano pulled a gun and shot Police Chief Waters. He collapsed to the ground, and that was the last I saw of him."

"And why didn't you run as soon as you saw this meeting?"

"It happened really fast, and my husband had worked with the chief in the past. He was a good man, and my husband would never have walked away from someone in need."

"Okay, so Abruzzo pulled a gun and pointed it at you. What happened next?"

"My husband shoved me back down the alley and yelled for me to run. His face...he knew it wasn't going to end well. I could see it in his eyes. I turned and ran, but I turned back to see if he was behind me. He wasn't. He was fighting with Abruzzo. Abruzzo had dropped the gun, so they were using hand to hand combat, but my husband turned to make sure I was leaving, and when he saw I wasn't far enough away, he yelled at me to get out of there." Tears filled my eyes as I saw the final look on his face, the determination to keep me safe. "He was distracted because he wanted to make sure I was safe, and Abruzzo pulled a gun from his ankle and pointed it at me. Todd jumped in front of the gun just as it went off." A small sob escaped as I tried to hold it together. "My husband died protecting me. He died because of me."

Tears poured from my eyes at having to relive that night all over again. It took me a few moments, but I finally pulled myself together enough to finish the questioning.

"What happened after you ran, Mrs. Matthews?"

"I flagged someone down in the street and asked them to take me to the police station. I knew that I needed protection and that I wouldn't be able to go home."

"Thank you, Mrs. Matthews."

The judge had us take a short break so I could pull myself together. I had to go to the bathroom, and of course, my entourage followed me. I was walking into the stall when a hand grabbed me and shoved me up against a stall. My face was squashed into the stall by the hand holding my head in place and the stall handle dug into my side.

"Listen up, bitch. You'd better find a way to throw this case or you'll never see that baby inside you. I'll cut it right out of your belly. You understand me?"

I nodded my head quickly and a moment later was released. I didn't see where she went, but she was gone the next instant. I almost collapsed in relief, grabbing onto the stall door to steady myself. My whole body was shaking. I couldn't be alone. I needed the guards. I was just about to get them when I stopped and pressed my hand to my stomach.

I'll cut it right out of your belly.

If I didn't throw the case, I was risking my child's life. But if I didn't continue to testify and tell the truth, Todd died for nothing. He would want me safe, but he also believed in justice. I couldn't let him down, not when we'd come this far. I had to see this through to the end and pray that the agents could keep us safe.

Stepping to the door, I looked down the hall in both directions. The guard was watching me closely, his eyes showing concern. "Is everything okay, ma'am?"

I shook my head slightly and waved him inside. He followed, shutting the door behind him.

"A woman was just in here. She told me to throw the case or she would kill my child."

He immediately grabbed my arm and pulled me toward the door, checking in all directions before guiding me down the hall.

"I need the ADA in room fourteen ASAP. We've had a threat against Mrs. Matthews."

I was taken into a room where he quickly shut the blinds and pushed me into a corner, blocking my body with his. I was terrified and relieved at the same time. When the door opened, he immediately pulled his gun.

"Stop and identify yourself," he commanded.

"It's ADA Rayland."

"Alright, step into the room."

The door opened the rest of the way and the ADA walked inside, his gaze immediately finding mine behind the protection of the agent.

"What's going on?"

The agent stepped aside, allowing me to speak with the ADA. "A woman was in the bathroom and she shoved me up against the stall. She said I had to find a way to throw the case or she would…cut my child out of my belly."

The ADA's lips thinned as he stepped forward and rubbed his hands up and down my arms. "Are you okay?"

I gave a jerky nod, but I was on the verge of losing it. Tears built in my eyes, but I sucked them back, trying to keep it together.

"Do you know who the woman was?"

I shook my head. "No, I didn't see her."

"You can't identify her in a lineup?"

"No, I never saw her face."

He sighed, running his hand through his hair. "Alright, I'm going to talk with the judge. We'll see if we can get a continuance."

I nodded and waited for him to return. The minutes crept by, each making me more and more nervous. I wasn't sure what would come out of getting a continuance. I would rather just get this over.

The ADA returned looking more frustrated than ever. "I talked with the judge, but with no cameras showing proof of the altercation and without you being able to identify the woman, the judge has decided to proceed."

I nodded, knowing this was coming. "It's better this way. I'd rather get this over with."

He took a deep breath. "Well, let's do this then. Are you ready?"

"As I'll ever be."

We headed back to the courtroom for cross-examination and I took the stand again. This time, I stared right at Abruzzo, letting him know I would not be intimidated.

"Mrs. Matthews, you understand you are still under oath, right?" Roberts, the attorney for Abruzzo, was just as slimy as he was. He was tall with slicked back hair and an expensive suit that he no doubt could afford because of his ties to the mafia.

"Yes."

"Mrs. Matthews, do you have much interaction with the community down in Little Italy?"

"No."

"Have you ever seen Mr. Abruzzo before?"

"On the news."

"Would it be safe to say that your mind could have pulled his picture from a memory of a news story and that's how you identified him?"

"No. I recognized him from seeing him shoot my husband."

"It was dark out. Are we really supposed to believe that a terrified woman remembers the face of her husband's attacker? No doubt, you were more focused on your husband than on the person harming him."

"It was dark, but I could never forget such an evil face."

"How long would you say it took for all of this to occur?"

"Maybe a few minutes."

"So, from the moment you heard the voices to the moment you turned after your husband was shot was three minutes?"

"Probably."

"That's a lot to happen in such a short window. Tell me, why didn't you stop to try to help your husband?"

"He wouldn't have wanted me to. He didn't give up his life so that I could go back and get killed. Believe me, it killed me to walk away from him."

"Obviously, since you are still with us today."

Roberts smirked at me as my stomach roiled at his implication. The ADA stood and objected, but the jury had already heard what a coward I was, that I had left my husband to his fate to save myself and our child. Not a day went by that I didn't wish things were different. Many days, I wished I had died beside him so I didn't have to feel this pain, but I didn't, and I had to keep living for our child.

"Mrs. Matthews, did you and your husband ever fight?"

"Every couple fights."

"Has he ever hit you?"

"No."

"No? I have a police report here that says otherwise. Police were called to your residence in the middle of the night for domestic abuse."

"That's not accurate."

"It's not accurate that your husband hit you? Or that the police were called?"

"It was a mistake."

His questions were coming rapid fire now and he wasn't giving me the chance to explain.

"It was a mistake?" He boomed as he slammed his hand down on the stand. I flinched back at the look on his face. "Doesn't every abused spouse say that?"

"He wasn't abusive!"

"But he hit you. I think what really happened was that you were looking for a way out of an abusive marriage and you shot your husband, disposed of the gun, and pulled two suspected criminals out of the papers and blamed it on them."

"No! That's not what happened! They were there. They shot him!"

Air was barely getting to my lungs as he continued to accuse me of killing my husband. Tears were blurring my vision as they smeared my husband's reputation. He was a good and honorable man, but reporters would say differently. If only I hadn't made that noise. None of this would have happened. My husband would still be with me and we would be celebrating our child's birth in five months.

"You wanted your husband dead and when Police Chief Waters came upon you, you shot him to cover up murdering your husband!"

"No. That's not what happened."

I was practically in tears now and barely able to speak as this man accused me of murdering the police chief and my own husband.

"No more questions, your honor."

He sauntered back to his chair, knowing he had just shredded my world. ADA Rayland stood up and walked toward me with a determined face.

"Mrs. Matthews, what happened the night your husband attacked you?"

I took a steadying breath, knowing that I needed to calm down and answer clearly so the jury could see who my husband really was.

"My husband was suffering from PTSD at the time and I woke him from a nightmare. He didn't know who I was or where he was. He attacked me because he thought I was the enemy. That was two years ago and he has seen a counselor ever since. He never once laid a hand on me since that night."

"Thank you, Mrs. Matthews."

I was excused from the witness stand and ushered back into the room. When the ADA came in, I calmly stood.

"I'm done."

"You may be recalled—"

"No," I said firmly. "I've done what you asked. I testified to what happened, but I can't go through that again. I can't have my husband's name smeared through the mud for some criminals who—" I choked on a sob that was building and covered my mouth. I shook my head slightly, sucking back the tears. "I'm done."

He nodded slightly, knowing that was it. "Well, it was probably enough."

"Do you really think so?"

He didn't look so sure. "We're going up against organized crime. There are never any assurances. All we can do is our best and hope it's enough."

I went back to the hotel after that and closed myself in my bedroom after the guards checked out the room. I felt lost and alone, and longed for my little hideaway. But I knew as soon as I got there, I would feel just as alone as I did here. It didn't really matter what I accomplished here today. My husband was still gone. My child would never know him, and I would never be allowed to speak his name. It was like I was wiping him from the record, dismissing the wonderful life we had.

Stripping off my clothes, I ran a warm bath and sank down, trying to clear my head. But the longer I laid in the tub, the more my thoughts played on repeat. There was no way to forget. Todd's death would always haunt me, and I would always blame myself. I pulled the plug after an hour and got out, drying myself off. I was just stepping out of the room when the door opened.

The WitSec agent, Sanders, that I was working with walked through the door with a sigh. "Well, that could have gone better, but we were prepared for him to throw that stuff our way."

"He accused me of murdering my husband and the Chief of Police."

He waved his hand, dismissing what I said. "Don't worry about that. The defense needed a viable theory to get his client off. All he needed was to present reasonable doubt. It doesn't matter if the story is true or if the forensics match up. If he can get the jury to believe there could be another scenario, there's a chance they won't find him guilty. It's in the hands of the assistant district attorney now."

"What happens now?"

"You can go home."

"Back to my home in New York?"

He looked at me with sad eyes. "No. You'll never be able to go back there. With Cordano in jail, he already has a hit out on you. The whole mafia will be looking for payback. Especially if you manage to put away Abruzzo too. He was the nephew of one of the bosses. There's no way they'll ever let this go."

"So I'll never have my life back."

"No. Sarah Anderson is who you are now. We won't be keeping a detail on you, so my advice is to stay under the radar as much as possible. Don't put any information online if you don't have to. Social media is a great way to attract attention to yourself, so for the love of God, don't sign up for anything. Some information is already out there, but let's try to keep it to a minimum. That's the best way to keep you safe. Also, try to keep your picture out of the paper. If you think anything seems off, we'll move you and give you a new identity."

I nodded, trying to take in all the new information I was getting.

"We'll stop at a motel on the way home and give you a chance to rest. You'll also need to put in your contacts and make sure you aren't wearing any makeup. Maybe after you get home, you should cut your hair drastically. It will help conceal you better. There's one more thing that you have to keep in mind. You can't tell anyone who you really are."

"I understand that."

"No, I mean, if you were to get married, you could never tell your husband or your kids your true identity. If something were to happen, if you were to get divorced, they would know who you really are. From now on, no one will know you as Sarah Matthews. Your child will not get to have your husband's name, and it would be best if you didn't name him or her after your husband in any way. Now, your DNA isn't in the system, so you should be fine for having the baby in the hospital."

I gave him a curious look. "I don't understand."

"The mafia has a long reach. If you had DNA on file, they could hack into hospital records to scan for a DNA match. Since there is none on file, they won't be able to find you that way."

"Are you sure I'm going to be safe? You make it sound like they could find me a multitude of different ways."

"They could, but we don't believe that they'll be able to find you. We have never lost anyone that stayed in the WitSec Program. You're well hidden as long as you help us keep you that way. Any other questions?"

"Just one. What am I supposed to tell my child about his father when he or she asks?"

"You won't be able to tell him the truth. You'll have to say that he was a one night stand or something along those lines. Todd will never be able to exist for you or your child ever again."

Sanders was a good man and had done so much to help me feel safe, but the idea that I would be going through this alone was daunting. If I had been going through this with Todd, at least I would feel like I had someone watching my back. I had no one now. Worse, my whole life would be a lie. I would have to lie to my child about his father. He would never know what a hero Todd was. I would never be able to tell him or her about his father's time serving our country and would never meet his or her grandparents.

Sanders put his hand on my arm. "I know this seems impossible now, but you'll adjust soon enough. Remember that you are doing this for your child and yourself, and that should help keep things in perspective."

CHAPTER 5

DREW

I spent days thinking about Sarah. Something wasn't right. I knew it the moment those guys showed up at her house with guns. Texans or not, men didn't just show up with guns on them for no reason. And the way they dressed, like they were government agents or something...I couldn't shake the feeling that there was something else going on.

I wanted to ask her more about herself when she returned, but she would probably laugh in my face. I'd been a complete asshole to her from the moment she arrived. Not to mention that she was already closed off. She didn't want me to know anything about her, and since I had built a stellar reputation of being the worst possible human being on earth, I didn't see her suddenly opening up to me.

I walked out of my house on the way to work and looked over to her poor, dilapidated house, wondering when she would be home. Every morning I looked for her, and every morning I was disappointed. Sighing, I walked down the steps to my truck. She said she would be gone for a week, so I'd give her that, but if she wasn't home, I was going straight to Sebastian. He'd be able to help me out.

I practically laughed to myself as I headed to work. For a woman that I insisted was a pain in the ass, I sure was spending a lot of time worrying over her. I didn't know what it was about her that had me so interested. I told myself it was morbid curiosity, but deep down, I knew that wasn't true. I hadn't been curious about anyone since Iris died, except Harper. Maybe that's all this was. She was another Harper in my life.

Determined not to go insane over this, I pushed her from my mind for the rest of the week. I didn't need to spend all my time thinking about her. So, I offered my services to the rancher that was building on my property. He needed a fence built, and I needed a certain woman off my mind. Somehow, Ryan, Logan, and Cole found their way over to my house and helped me build the fence for him. By Sunday, quite a bit of the fence was built.

We were sitting around eating pizza on my back porch after a long day's work when Sean pulled up. He wasn't in his uniform, but the look on his face said he was here on business.

"Sean, you're a little late if you came to help out. We already finished for the day, but you can come back next weekend to help," Ryan said.

"Yeah, I'm pretty sure I'll be working, but thanks for the invite." His eyes flicked to mine. "Drew, you got a minute?"

I stood and walked inside with Sean, crossing my arms over my chest as I turned to him. "What's going on?"

Running a hand through his hair, he sighed. "Look, I know you don't get along with your neighbor really well, but I'm asking that you look out for her."

"What do you mean look out for her?"

"Just keep an eye out for anything that doesn't seem right."

"Is she in some kind of trouble?"

"I'm not sure. I have a possible lead on her, but I don't know for sure. If she is who I think she is, she's in a lot of danger."

"Who do you think she is?"

He hesitated. I wanted so badly to push him to tell me, but I also was telling myself that I didn't need to know. She was none of my business. "I can't tell you that. Trust me, I would if I could."

"Sean, I just want to live my life in peace. I don't want any trouble, so if you think she's trouble, I prefer to stay out of it."

What a goddamn lie. I had just been worrying about her the whole week.

"She doesn't deserve what's happening to her. Trust me on this. She needs someone to keep an eye out for her. Please. I wouldn't ask if I didn't think it was necessary."

I took a minute to consider what he was asking. I didn't need this shit, but I was the one living next to her, so it made sense that he asked me. "Fine, but if shit comes my way, you better get here real fast."

"I promise I'll let you know if anything comes of this."

I walked back outside with Sean and sat down to join the guys. Sean left a few minutes later, and I contemplated why I had just let myself get talked into babysitting duty. And worse, I didn't have any more answers than before.

∼

A FEW NIGHTS LATER, I was dragging carpet out of an upstairs bedroom and out to a dumpster I had rented when an SUV pulled up to Sarah's house. There were three men with her, and they all got out to help her get her bags out. Two of the guys walked over to her house and seemed to be checking out the house. I wanted to walk over there, but I held back, not wanting to be the pushy neighbor that nosed in. I saw one man hand her a small packet before he gripped her shoulder and then walked back to the SUV, joining the other two and driving away. She stood on her porch watching the vehicle drive away, looking completely dejected. I wondered if she had been close with her father, or if the trip had just worn her out.

I grabbed a quick shower and then decided to bring some food over to her. I didn't want to be her friend, I just wanted to find out what was going on. If Sean was going to have me keeping an eye on her, I was going to do some digging and find out everything I could. Something was just wrong with her and her situation. She hadn't told me anything about the baby's father, but I couldn't blame her for that. I hadn't been the most welcoming. I assumed the baby was the product of a one night stand, but after this strange encounter with the men with guns, I wasn't so sure about that. She was hiding something, and I was determined to find out what.

I walked over to her house with a chicken dish I had made. I was planning on taking it for leftovers, but this was the perfect way to invite myself over. Otherwise, I wouldn't have an excuse. I knocked on the door and when no one answered, I knocked again harder.

"Sarah! I brought you some dinner," I shouted through the door.

"It's open!"

That shocked the hell out of me. I expected her to answer the door and then tell me to fuck off. I opened the door and about lost my shit at the sight before me.

"What the fuck are you doing?"

She turned to me from her position on the highest rung on her ladder and shot me a glare.

"Excuse me?"

"I said, what the fuck are you doing?" I made sure to say it nice and slow, in case she was having trouble hearing.

"I'm working on taping so I can start painting."

"I meant, what the fuck are you doing standing that high on the ladder? You're pregnant."

"Does that mean I'm not allowed to work on my house? Is being pregnant somehow an affliction that makes it impossible for me to do things I did in the past?"

"Jesus, woman. It's not safe for you to do that. If you fell, you could have a miscarriage. Don't you think at all before you do this shit?"

Putting a hand on her hip, she cocked an eyebrow at me. "I am well aware of how high I'm standing, which is why I'm being careful. Besides, someone has to get this house ready for my child, and it looks like I'm the only one to do it." She turned back around and started taping some more around the molding.

"Maybe you should ask the father for help."

She stiffened as I said it, and I took that to mean that she really did have a one night stand. Either she didn't know who the father was, or he had already told her he wasn't interested.

"If I wanted your advice, I'd ask for it. Was there some reason you stopped by, other than to give me shit about taking care of my house?"

"I came by to bring you some dinner." She stopped and looked at me questioningly. "I figured that since you were gone all week, you probably didn't have food in your house. I made extra, so I thought I'd offer it."

She came down from the ladder and walked over to me, lifting the foil and sniffing the food. "It doesn't smell half bad."

"Well, I can cook some things. Come on, let's go eat."

I walked into her kitchen, ignoring how her mouth dropped open at my statement. I didn't care. If I was going to find out anything about her, I was going to have to play nice.

"You can just leave it and go home. I'll eat later."

"I haven't eaten yet, so we can eat together."

I put down the dish and started going through her cabinets looking for plates. I grabbed two and then went through her drawers looking for silverware. I dished out two helpings and then sat at her table, all the while she stood in the doorway staring at me in disbelief. Finally, she shook her head and sat down to eat. We ate in silence for a few minutes before I started in.

"So, how many rooms are you painting?"

"All of them."

"All of them?"

"Well, I want to paint before the baby comes. I doubt I'll be up to it after the baby is born. You know, working and taking care of a baby full time." She stopped speaking suddenly and dropped her fork with a clatter. "Excuse me," she murmured and then shot up from the table and ran to her bathroom. I followed behind her and stood at the doorway listening to her break down.

Something hurt inside to listen to her so broken up. I wasn't sure why I had given her a hard time before. I had practically offered to help Harper raise her child, but I couldn't squeeze an ounce of consideration for this woman, until now. I couldn't stand to listen to her cry, so I went back to the living room and started taping where she left off. After ten minutes, she walked out and stood in the entry to the living room.

"What are you doing?"

"I'm finishing the taping."

"Why?"

"Well, it's not okay for you to do it by yourself. If you fell and hurt yourself, I would feel like an ass knowing that you had been over here doing it and I had let you."

She rolled her eyes at me and crossed her arms. "I'll let you finish this room, but then you can leave. I have a lot of work to do, and I don't need your help with it."

I climbed down from the ladder and walked right up to her. "Oh, I'll be here to help you with all of it. There is no way I'm letting you paint this whole house by yourself. I don't want to think of you climbing ladders, and the fumes aren't good for the baby."

"We work opposite schedules. There's no way we can work on this together."

"I'll give you jobs that you can do during the day and I'll come over and work at night. Together, we'll have this place done in no time. You just have to let me know what rooms you want painted in which color."

"There's no way that I'm letting you into my home when I'm not here."

"Then we'll have to work on the weekends."

"I work on the weekends."

"But not during the day. I can be over here bright and early to get started."

She stared at me for a moment in thought. I could see the wheels turning, how she really didn't want to let me in, but she also knew how much work had to be done. I held my breath, waiting for her answer. If she agreed, this would be so much easier.

"I'll think about it, but for now, you can go home."

"I'm not done with this yet. I'll finish up and then head home."

"Look, Drew, I don't know what inspired this sudden change of heart that made you feel that you should come over here and barge into my life, but I'm tired. I've had a long day, so I'd appreciate it if you would go home so I can go to sleep."

"Just sit down on the couch and I'll finish up here."

She sighed and walked over to the couch, sitting down and pulling a pillow onto her stomach. I turned back and did some more taping. When I turned around five minutes later, she was passed out on the couch. Now that she was relaxed, the bruising under her eyes was more prominent, probably from all the traveling. I hadn't thought to ask her about the funeral, and I was sure it weighed on her also.

Since she was asleep on the couch, I decided to do as much taping as possible. I finished the living room and then moved on to the kitchen and her bedroom. When I finished, it was after ten at night and I had to work in the morning. I walked back into the living room and was about to leave, but my more considerate side said it wouldn't be nice to let her sleep on the couch.

I picked her up and carried her into her bedroom. I was surprised at how little she weighed, though it should have been obvious. She weighed maybe a buck ten, and she was a few months pregnant at least. I laid her down on the bed, then brought her blanket up to her shoulders. I was about to leave when she moaned.

"Todd."

It was quiet, but I was pretty sure that's what she said. I frowned, wondering who the hell Todd was. Could it be the father of her child? And if she knew him enough to call for him in her sleep, why the hell did he leave? I looked down at her again and that's when I noticed that her left ring finger had a white line where a wedding band should be. So, she was married at some point. Maybe she was so private because the marriage ended badly. Maybe he walked out on her when he found out she was pregnant. Some people could be assholes like that.

Standing here wasn't going to give me any answers. I'd have to figure out a way to get her to talk to me, but I wasn't sure how. I struggled to talk about my own personal life, so I had no clue how to get someone to talk to me about theirs. Knowing that she wouldn't want me to witness her talking about someone else in her sleep, I snuck out, locking the door behind me.

Lying in bed that night, I found my thoughts drifting once again to my sweet Iris. We had been looking forward to the day our baby arrived. She was three months pregnant when she felt the lump in her breast. The doctor told her it was probably a clogged milk duct, but after further testing, it was discovered that she had breast cancer that the doctors said had probably been growing for years. As we sat in the doctor's office in stunned silence, he explained our options to us.

"Mrs. Whitaker, your test results show that your breast cancer has already spread to your liver. We need to start treatment as soon as possible if we are going to get ahead of this. We need to be as aggressive as possible."

Iris was holding it together better than I was. That is, until the doctor said his next thoughts.

"You need to consider terminating your pregnancy." She immediately shook her head. *"We can't give you proper treatment if you're pregnant. The fetus wouldn't survive. So either we terminate or we delay treatment until the baby is able to be delivered."*

"Then we wait. There is no way I'm killing my own child. Don't ask me to do that."

"It's very possible the pregnancy will wear you out even faster, and you may not survive until delivery. There's no way to predict how this pregnancy will go for you. You'd be taking a huge risk with your life."

"No. I won't do it. I could never live with myself if I did that." She was on the brink of tears, so I asked the doctor to step out of the room.

"Iris, I know this is a tough decision.."

"Don't you start, too. I can't do it, Drew."

"Baby, I don't want to live without you. Please don't ask me to do that. We can make another baby, but I can't make another you. Please. At least consider what he's saying."

"Drew, you're asking me to kill a part of myself. You're asking me to kill my own child!"

"I understand that, and I know it isn't fair of me to ask, but this child isn't here yet. You are, and I will fight for you even when you aren't willing to fight for yourself. You need to look at this from my perspective. If you don't do this, I will lose both of you. You heard the doctor, there is no guarantee you would even survive the pregnancy."

She cried for a few minutes before looking up at me with resignation on her face.

A FEW MONTHS AFTER THAT, the cancer spread to her brain, and it wasn't long after that that I lost her. It had been painful for her. The medication helped, but unless she was constantly medicated, which made her drowsy, she was in some form of pain. Her parents helped the entire time, and we all took shifts staying with her. I would have spent every day with her, and I did for the first few weeks, but her mother came to me and asked for some time with her. She was their only daughter and they wanted to spend as much time as they could with her. I didn't want to leave, but I couldn't deny them the little time they had left with her. I continued to work, and my boss was very understanding about giving me time off when I needed it. I eventually went down to part time, and then the final month, I hadn't worked at all. I could tell she was slipping away from me.

That final month went by fast. At first, she had trouble with balance, and then walking was difficult. Then, moving at all was hard. Pretty soon, even talking was a challenge, which was why it surprised the hell out of me when she said those final words to me. *I'm forever yours, Drew. Nothing can take me from you.* She said it so crystal clear that it about tore my heart out. I knew that was the end for her. It was as if God had given her the strength for one final message to me. After that, she fell into unconsciousness. I spent every last minute by her side, holding her hand until the end. She passed on the third morning as the sun was rising. The windows were open and the breeze was blowing through the window just as she liked. The sun shone across her bed, lighting her beautiful face one last time.

When the nurse came in to pronounce her dead, I swear I lost my mind. I sat at her bedside begging God to bring her back to me. I couldn't live in a world without my sweet Iris. It took me several hours to finally accept that she was gone and that I needed to let her go. When she was taken away from the house, her parents were with me, and many of the neighbors stood outside with sad expressions on their faces. Iris was loved by everyone because she was a friendly and caring person that made everyone feel like they were special. For days, I went to our church and prayed to God to give Iris back to me. I knew it was crazy, but my grief had become too much for me to handle.

Iris had wanted to be cremated and spread in the wind. Though not legal, I took her to our favorite lake at sunrise and spread her ashes in the breeze. Her parents weren't with me, and they never forgave me for taking away their last chance to say goodbye. The next few weeks were absolutely horrible for me. I locked myself in our bedroom, but people kept stopping by to see how I was. After the second week, I knew that I couldn't stay in that house with Iris's memory any longer. I sold everything in the house to anyone that wanted it and informed her parents they needed to come get anything they wanted of hers. I asked her mother to take care of all of Iris's personal effects, as I didn't have the stomach for it. An offer was accepted on the house within the week, and I was in my truck and on the road a few days later. I hadn't spoken to her parents since.

Thinking about that day and the after effects sent me into a depression for the next week. Ryan and Logan asked me if I needed anything, but they knew me well enough to know when to leave me alone. One of them must have called Harper, because she showed up on my porch Friday night.

I pulled her into my arms, my breath hitching as she held me close. I needed my best friend so much right now. She didn't ask me what happened or if I wanted to talk, she just pulled me back to my bedroom and laid down in bed with me. That was the great thing about Harper and Jack. Harper always knew when I needed her, and Jack always allowed her to come to me without question. There was no way I could ever repay Jack for that kind of understanding. Most men would never allow their woman to go spend the night with another man, but this had been our relationship from the beginning.

I never told any of my friends about Iris. I found it too painful and I went into a tailspin if I thought about her too much, so I couldn't imagine what talking about her would do to me. I'd never even told Harper, even though she had opened herself up to me when we first met. She never pushed, and I took that as a sign that I had truly found my best friend. If it hadn't been for my grief over Iris, Harper would have been a woman I would have pursued, but as it was, I just didn't have the heart to move on.

I fell asleep holding Harper in my arms and feeling my heart finally start settling again in my chest. The ache lessened and I didn't feel so much like I had just lost Iris. In the morning, Harper was still wrapped in my arms when the bell rang. I knew it was Jack coming to collect Harper. There was only so long he would allow me to keep her and I was alright with that. I woke her up and we walked down the hall together. I gave her a hug and thanked her for coming over, then opened the door and ushered her into Jack's arms. Jack gave me a chin lift and turned to leave, but stopped at the last minute.

"Get some rest. You look like shit."

Words of encouragement if I ever heard them.

CHAPTER 6

SARAH

"You're so stupid," I said as I stared at myself in the mirror. "Why did you think he would come over?"

The girl staring back at me was sad and pathetic, and I had never been sad and pathetic in my life. I didn't recognize myself anymore, moping around because my neighbor didn't come over during the week. I wasn't even sure why I was expecting him to. We had different schedules, and it wasn't like he was my boyfriend or even my friend.

I sighed and set the brush down on my dresser, wishing the picture of Todd and me on our wedding day was sitting in the corner where it was supposed to be. But it wasn't and never would be again. As the marshall said, I couldn't have him as part of my life anymore. I needed to act like he didn't exist, but that was easier said than done.

With no one in my life that cared about me, it was impossible to distract myself from thoughts of my dead husband. When Drew came over the other night, angry that I was taping my own molding, I was pissed. But then he was all sweet in his own way, offering to help me out. I had hoped that Drew might be someone I could lean on. I didn't need him to come paint my house or feed me, I just needed someone that could be there for me as a friend. Which honestly, was a lot to ask considering that I couldn't tell anyone the truth about who I was. It was silly, honestly. Drew didn't want to get to know me. He just didn't want to be the asshole that didn't help.

I stared at the dark circles under my eyes and thought back to how easily I had fallen asleep with Drew in the house. I never felt safe anymore, but with him here, I was able to let go a little knowing that I wasn't alone. It had been the first time that I had been able to sleep since I went back to testify.

By the time we headed home, it really began to sink in that this was my new life. There would be no going home when the trial was finished. My life in New York was so much different than here. We had lived in a town house on the upper west side in Manhattan. It was pricey, but we both made good money, so that was one luxury we indulged in. Todd worked at an elite security agency that catered to high end clients that favored anonymity. I worked as the manager of one of the most prestigious art galleries in Manhattan. We had a completely different life there, one that I would never see again. I was a city girl at heart, and now I was living in the country where I rarely even heard a car drive by.

When I came here the first time with the Marshals, I had to leave all traces of my old life behind. Todd and I saved a lot of our money in cash because Todd always wanted to be prepared in case we had to move fast and didn't want to be traced. I called him paranoid and told him he was spending too much time with his clients, but as it turned out, his security net in cash had really helped. The WitSec program allowed me so much money a year until I found a steady job, which at this point was difficult considering that I was pregnant, but I had no idea when that money would dry up, so I was trying to be as frugal as possible. The one small thing I allowed myself to buy was the paint supplies.

When I packed to come here, I didn't know exactly where I would be going, but my case agent told me to pack things that were casual and would help me blend in. Luckily, I had plenty of jeans, t-shirts, and sweatshirts, so packing was easy enough. However, I also had a lot of art at my house and all of my old stuff. The case agent said the agency would see to selling all of our belongings and then transfer the money into an account in my new name. Since we only had Todd's parents, there was no one to leave anything to. They were doing fine on their own and wouldn't care about any of our stuff. I supposed I should be grateful that I got the money, but what I craved the most was some trinket of my time with Todd.

I was able to keep my wedding ring, but I wasn't allowed to wear it because it didn't go along with my new identity. I had an idea to turn it into a heart pendant. It was a simple band because we couldn't afford anything else when we first got married. I'd married Todd when we were twenty-one and he was in the military. I was just out of school and working in a small gallery, not making much money, and he was living off the meager salary from the army. I didn't care, though. Todd was all I needed. We waited to have kids because he didn't want to have any while he was overseas, and then he wanted to wait until he was settled in his new job. That night at dinner, after I told him I was pregnant, he told me he wanted me to consider moving to the suburbs where we could have more space to grow as a family. I was one hundred percent willing to go along with it because I had Todd with me. Now, living out here all alone left me feeling isolated from everything I knew. I could never work in a gallery again, and I wasn't sure what I could ever do in this town that would leave me satisfied.

So here I sat, early on a Saturday morning, stirring paint to get started on the next room. Not being able to sleep, I'd accomplished a lot. The walls were white, or dirty white from years of neglect, so I didn't have to use as much paint as I thought. I wanted bright colors to keep me feeling happy. Blue would make me sad, and though it was my favorite color, it would do nothing for my down days. I painted the kitchen a bright yellow that reminded me of baking with my grandmother when I was little. I stuck with white in the living room, since I hadn't decided yet how I would decorate. I had decided on lavender for my bedroom, because I have never been allowed to use any pretty colors with Todd. Everything needed to be masculine. If I was going to start over, I needed to make this place mine.

I still hadn't decided on a color for the baby's room yet. Not knowing what I was having, I decided I would wait on that until I found out the sex of the baby. According to the doctor, I would do an ultrasound in two weeks. It seemed like such a long time to wait. Right now I was hanging on to any small piece of information about my baby to keep me going. My child was all I had right now, so every month, when I got my exam, my baby's heartbeat reminded me that life does go on.

I was brought out of my thoughts by a knock on the door. I put down the paint stick and walked to the door, peeking through the peephole. A small flutter swept through me when I saw my neighbor on the other side.

"Good morning," I said in a small voice.

"Good morning," he said hesitantly, swiping a hand through his hair. He looked uncomfortable or unsure of himself. "I didn't know if this was too early to come over or not, but I was up, so I thought I'd come over and get to work."

His gaze swept over my body and a scowl appeared on his face.

"Aren't you fucking eating? You've lost weight since the last time I saw you. And when was the last time you slept?"

My smile immediately dropped from my face as he snapped at me. I didn't need this shit. I was doing the best I could, and him pointing out my flaws wasn't what I needed. Instead of responding, I slammed the door in his face and walked back to my can of paint. I tried not to let what he said bother me, but my chest tightened as I held back the tears that threatened to fall. Pulling myself together, I poured the lavender paint in the tray as I listened to banging and yelling coming from the front door. I ignored it and got out my roller and started painting my bedroom.

After I finished with the first wall, I moved on to the wall that my dresser was against. I would have to move it by myself, which would have been easier if Drew was here, but he wasn't and I wasn't going to rely on anyone else to help me out right now. The room took me half of the day to paint, and by the time I was finished, I was completely exhausted. I had to be at work in a few hours and I hadn't eaten very much today, so I grabbed some food and then started getting ready for work.

My stomach had been feeling off for a few days now. I didn't feel sick, but I got dull pains that I assumed were caused by the stress I had been under. They had been getting progressively worse throughout the week and it was starting to make me think that I needed to make an appointment with my OB-GYN. I sat down and considered calling off of work, but it was too late to get someone to replace me. Besides, it was a Saturday night and the best time for tips. I pulled myself together and headed into town. When I arrived at The Pub, I clocked in and got to work waitressing. Every step was hell on my body, and I finally accepted that I had over done it and needed to slow down.

About ten o'clock, Drew came into the bar with another man I didn't recognize. They sat down in my section and I reluctantly went over to take their order.

"What can I get for you?"

"Water. I'm Sebastian. I don't think I've seen you around before."

"I'm new to town. I'm Drew's neighbor actually."

Sebastian looked over at Drew and raised an eyebrow. "He didn't mention he had a new neighbor."

"Well, I haven't been there that long. What can I get for you, Drew?"

"Beer. Whatever's on tap."

I nodded and turned to walk away, but Drew caught my wrist and pulled me back toward him. "Look, I'm sorry about earlier. I didn't mean to be such an ass. You just don't look like you're feeling all that well."

"You know, some people would say *how are you?* or *are you feeling okay?*. Next time, start with one of those."

I walked back to the bar and put in my order, then grabbed the tray with the drinks and made my way back to their table. I was just lowering the tray when pain shot through my belly. My hands shook and I squeezed my eyes at the pain, hoping that it would pass and I could get to the back room to rest. The pain got worse and the tray slipped from my hands as a wave of dizziness washed over me. I barely registered the drinks falling to the floor or the glass shattering at my feet. Hands caught me as the world spun around me, sending me into a tailspin. A moment later, I was picked up and carried out to a truck. My heart beat wildly and I tried to calm my breathing. This wasn't normal.

"Hang on, Sarah. I'm getting you to a doctor."

"Sarah, it's okay. You're going to be okay. Just hang on and trust Drew. He's a good man."

I looked over and for a minute, I could swear that Todd was sitting next to me. My head lulled against the seat as I stared at my husband who couldn't be here because he was dead.

"Todd, how are you here?"

He looked at me funny and when he spoke, his voice didn't sound like Todd's. "We're almost to the hospital, Sarah. Just hang on."

Drew. It was Drew talking to me. I closed my eyes and when I opened them again, Todd was gone. I breathed as calmly as I could, tears burning my eyes with every breath. I was all alone.

"You're not alone, sweetheart. I'll always be watching over you."

Drew drove frantically to the hospital, making me more nervous we would wreck than the fact that something was wrong with my body. We pulled up to the hospital and someone came out with a stretcher as Drew carried me to the ER doors. My body jostled as I was laid down, and the lights were spinning above me as they wheeled me down a corridor. I didn't understand what was happening to me and the pain was getting too intense. I let go and hoped the doctors would be able to save my baby from whatever was happening.

"Well, you had kidney stones and we were able to remove them, but you have to drink more water. You were extremely dehydrated, which probably caused the kidney stones. Water will help keep you and your baby healthy, so you need plenty of that and rest. Now, before you go, let's take a look at that baby of yours and see how it's doing."

Dr. Walsh instructed me to lift my shirt for the ultrasound. The only problem was that Drew was in the room with me, and it felt way too personal to show off my belly in front of him. He had come in after I got out of surgery and hadn't left since. He insisted that someone needed to be around to make sure I took care of myself, and since he lived next to me, he argued that he was the best candidate. I didn't understand why he would help. He never seemed to like me very much, so I didn't really understand his concern.

"Um, Drew? Could you please step out of the room?"

He gave me a hard look and barely shook his head as he narrowed his eyes at me. "I'm not going anywhere. I'll stay here while they check on the baby."

His look said not to argue with him, and frankly, right now all I wanted was to see my child and know it was safe. I shrugged at the doctor and lifted my shirt as instructed while trying to maintain some sense of privacy with the blanket.

I didn't hear anything at first and dread filled me at the thought that I had lost my child. Drew must have thought the same thing because he grabbed my hand and gave me a reassuring squeeze. A moment later I heard whooshing through the speaker and an image appeared on the screen. I had no clue what I was looking at, but it filled me with joy.

"Well, I have some interesting news for you."

"What? Can you tell the gender already?"

"No. I can't see that yet, but I am happy to tell you that *both* babies look good."

My head snapped around to the doctor's smiling face.

"Huh? Um... I mean...can you say that again?"

"You are going to have fraternal twins. Congratulations, Ms. Anderson."

My brain was still trying to catch up with what the doctor had just unloaded on me.

"I'm sorry. I don't understand. There are no twins in my family or in...I just don't understand how this is possible."

"It really isn't about whether they run in your family. If it runs in your family, it can increase your chances of having them, but fraternal twins means that you dropped two eggs and they were each fertilized by a different sperm cell. They each have their own placenta and amniotic sac, so it's pretty safe. Now that we know the babies are fine, you'll be seen more often for ultrasounds starting at six months. We like to monitor twins more closely to make sure both babies are developing at a normal rate. I'll put it in your notes and you can give the clinic a call on Monday to schedule an earlier appointment."

She pulled the wand from my body, leaving me feeling sad for not getting more time to look at them.

"What special instructions does she need to follow now that she's carrying twins?"

I wanted to roll my eyes at Drew for taking over like he had a say in this pregnancy. He was nothing but my annoying neighbor who only liked me when it was convenient for him.

"For the next week, you need plenty of rest and water, but after that, just resume your normal activities. If you're feeling tired, take a break. You just have to recognize your limits and follow that. Everyone's pregnancy is different, so it all depends on your body. I can tell you the easier you take it, the easier your pregnancy should be. Or at least there's a better chance of an easy pregnancy. Also, I see that you haven't really put on any weight yet. In fact, you seem to have lost some weight. Have you been sick a lot?"

"No. Just under a lot of stress. I had to go home for a tr...funeral."

"I see. Well, try to eat some more. You need to put on a little more weight with this pregnancy. I'll have one of the nurses bring in some paperwork for you to review about fraternal twins and your diet. Look it over and we'll discuss any questions at your next appointment."

"Thank you, Dr. Walsh."

She smiled at me and then left me alone with Drew. I noticed I was still holding his hand and quickly removed mine from his grasp. An uncomfortable silence fell between us as I tried to process what had just happened. I couldn't believe that I was pregnant with twins. It figured that I would have two babies. Todd always said he had super sperm and was going to fill our house with noise. I started to laugh as I thought about the day he said that to me. He was such a goofball and always knew how to make me laugh. Pretty soon I was laughing so hard that Drew started to look at me funny. It didn't last long though, as I thought about my kids never knowing their father, and the fact that I had to raise them on my own. It wasn't fair. Todd should be here with me.

Sobs wracked my body the more I thought about him and all our wonderful times together. I could still see his gorgeous smile with the stubble always on his jawline. I covered my face and cried into my hands for what felt like forever. Drew came over and held me at some point, but all I noticed was my heart breaking all over again. I hadn't let myself truly grieve over the loss of my husband yet. I had cried a little, and it killed me when I saw him shot, but this was the first time I had truly let it all out.

"Shh. Sarah, you have to calm down. You're crying out all the water they just pumped into your body."

Laughter bubbled up inside me. It didn't seem like a very Drew-like thing to say, but I guess I didn't really know Drew all that well. He rubbed my back as my breathing hitched with every cry that I tried to hold back. I finally calmed down to the point that I could breathe normally again, but I was ashamed at my reaction and I couldn't look at Drew.

"You're not alone, Sarah. It'll be okay."

"That's where you're wrong, Drew. I'm completely alone, and none of this will ever be okay."

∼

I SPENT the next few days imprisoned at Drew's house. He insisted on taking me back to his place so he could make sure that I rested and I was properly taken care of. He was driving me nuts. I wasn't allowed to get out of bed unless it was to use the bathroom or take a shower. Every meal was brought to me in bed—his bed—while he slept on the couch. I couldn't take much more of this. It might be sweet if he was my husband or at least if these were his babies, but that wasn't the case. He mostly growled at me to stay put and to drink more water or eat more food. He was practically shoving meals down my throat, and while I did feel better, I really wanted to be on my own. I didn't feel like I could think around him. He just wanted to make everything better for me, but the truth was, I needed to be able to do this on my own. The babies weren't even close to being born yet and he was hovering like they would be delivered at any moment. He hadn't even been to work because he *needed to take care of me.*

After breakfast on the fourth day, I got out of bed while he was in the kitchen and got dressed. I started packing up the few things I had to bring home with me and was just turning around when he walked in the room.

"Where do you think you're going?"

"Drew, I really appreciate you taking care of me, but it's time for me to go home."

"You're supposed to be on bed rest for a week. How are you going to manage that if you're alone?"

"I'm fine. I feel a lot better, but this isn't working. You aren't my husband and you're not the father of my children. Hell, we aren't even friends. You're just my neighbor, who for some reason, feels the need to look after me."

"We are too friends."

I stopped what I was doing and stared at him in shock. "Really? When was the last time that you looked at me and smiled?"

"I don't like to smile," he said with a shrug.

"Drew, I have to do this on my own. I'm all these kiddos have, and I need to be sure that I can do it alone. Leaning on you won't help. I can't rely on other people to help me when they're born."

He frowned at me, like he truly didn't understand what the problem was. "Why not?"

"Well, first of all, you're the only person I know and you rarely have anything other than a scowl on your face when you look at me."

"Maybe if you'd listen once in a while," he murmured under his breath.

Walking over to him, I placed my hand on his arm. "Thank you for everything."

I ignored the hurt look on his face and told myself this was for the best. I was beginning to like Drew, even if he was a pain in the ass, but I had to face reality. Playing house with my neighbor wasn't going to help me prepare for the future. I walked out the door and went back over to my house and relaxed on the sofa for the rest of the day.

∽

I CALLED my boss the next day and talked to him about my current predicament. I really wanted to keep working there, but working nights wouldn't last much longer before I got completely worn out.

"Hank, I was wondering if you could put me on days? I don't think nights are going to be feasible after a few weeks."

"Well, days don't make very good tips. Are you sure you want to do that?"

"I think I need to. Maybe I could work during the dinner shift and get off earlier? I know that might put you in a bind, so if that doesn't work, I could just do days."

"Honey, you are one of my hardest workers. I know this is hard for you, but we'll work it out. Just one last thing. What do you plan to do when the babies are born? Will you be coming back to work?"

"Um, I hadn't really thought about it. I know I'll need to find a sitter for them so I can work."

"Well, let me know your plans, because I was actually thinking of hiring a day manager that could help me out with inventory and such. How about we see how you do on days and take it from there? If it looks like it'll be a good fit, we'll see about that management position."

"That would be great, Hank. I won't let you down."

For the first time since I moved here, I finally felt the slightest weight lifted from my shoulders. Everything so far had been so stressful and I felt like I would crack under the pressure. This opportunity would go a long way to help me out. The next step would be finding reliable daycare for the babies. I would take maternity leave, but I wouldn't be able to do that for long.

CHAPTER 7

DREW

I don't know why I cared that she left. I helped her out for a few days and now she could go home and take care of herself. It wasn't like I was responsible for her or anything. If she didn't want my help, then I certainly wasn't going to go out of my way to help her anymore. She was right. She needed to be able to raise those kids on her own. Obviously, I would help if she was in a bind, but I needed to get back to my life and forget about her. She wasn't anything special anyway.

Still, I kept going back to a few days ago when we were in the hospital. There were several times that she started to say something and then stopped herself. I couldn't help but wonder what it was she was trying not to say. It bugged me, and a part of me wanted to go over there and demand answers, but I knew she wouldn't give them to me. She was right. I never even smiled at her. I basically treated her like shit the majority of the time.

I ended up working the weekend at Jackson Walker construction. Since I had taken most of the week off, when they called and said they needed to work Saturday to finish a job, I gladly offered to work. It would help keep my thoughts off my neighbor.

Sunday night, I sat on my back porch, watching the sun set. Again, my thoughts drifted to Iris. I closed my eyes and listened for her. A warmth passed over me as her sweet voice drifted over me. I smiled as the sun set, content again with only having this piece of her.

No matter how much I tried, I couldn't erase Iris from my memory. I wasn't sure I wanted to, but some days, I wondered if my life would be easier if I could just forget about her. However, the thought of never hearing her voice again or seeing her smiling face in my dreams was more than I could stand. I just had to keep moving forward.

When I finally got up, I glanced over at my neighbor's house. It hadn't escaped my notice that she was going to have twins all on her own. She didn't wallow in grief, or whatever she went through. She pushed on because those babies needed her. She had more courage than I did. She pushed on while I barely lived. I shook my head in disgust. Six years later and I was still a fucking coward.

∽

Over the next two months, I worked on putting my life back together and moving forward. I finished fixing up a lot of the upstairs and had a few ideas for what I wanted to do with the downstairs. It was now mid-summer, so working around the house was a pretty sweaty job. Still, with every room I finished, I felt more and more like I was finally doing something to move on.

I was outside getting vegetables from the garden when I saw Sarah outside working in her flower beds. Over the past few months, she'd finally put on a little weight, and was now sporting a small basketball belly. We exchanged pleasantries every once in a while, but mostly kept to ourselves. I'd watched over her house and kept an eye out for anything suspicious, but so far, I hadn't seen anything of concern.

I thought it would be the neighborly thing to take her some vegetables from my garden, so I went inside and grabbed a basket.

After I picked what was available, I divided it up between us, because there was way more than I had expected. I grabbed the basket and headed over to where she was planting flowers.

She was sitting on her knees in a pair of shorts and a t-shirt and she had on a straw sun hat. I had to admit, she looked adorable. I studied her as I walked closer and noticed that her color looked a lot better, and she didn't look so tired anymore. Her breasts had filled out also, and I felt a bit like a pervert for ogling a pregnant woman. She looked good, even I had to admit that. Those early months when she was facing this alone had taken its toll on her, but now she was glowing. She looked beautiful.

I almost stopped in my tracks when I realized that I was attracted to her. I wasn't sure why I was noticing now when before I hadn't been able to stand the sight of her. Maybe it was because she really didn't look that great when she first moved here. No doubt that was due to her pregnancy. But I had a feeling that I was still too caught up in my grief to really look at a woman in any way. But that day I realized what a coward I was being, when she was pushing on, something changed in me. I still missed Iris desperately, but the desire to move on had at some point overcome the need to wallow in self-pity. And that was almost as hard to swallow as the fact that Iris would never come back.

As I stepped up next to her, she looked up at me with a big smile on her face. "It's a beautiful day, isn't it?"

"Yeah, it is." I couldn't help but smile back at her. The look on her face was pure contentment. It was infectious.

"Is that a smile I see on your face? No way, Drew. You never smile."

"Like you said, it's a beautiful day. And I do smile."

She raised an eyebrow at me. "I don't think I've ever seen you smile."

I would definitely have to work on that, especially if it brought that beautiful smile to her face. "I brought you some vegetables from my garden. It turns out, I planted way too many and now I have more than I know what to do with."

"Oh, thank you." She started to stand and I held my hand out to help her up. Her left hand slipped into my hand and my gaze lingered on the thin silver band on her ring finger. When I looked up into her eyes, she quickly diverted them and clasped her hands together. "Let's go inside. I need something to drink."

I followed her inside and set the basket down on her kitchen table. She walked over to the fridge and took out a large pitcher of tea. She poured two glasses and handed one to me as we sat at the table. I about choked on my first sip.

"Shit. Is there any tea in this?"

"You don't like it?"

"It's just...all I taste is sugar."

"It's sweet tea. I'm trying a few things now that I'm living in the country. I saw a recipe from a southern magazine about sweet tea being this really big deal. I don't really like sweet tea, but it's supposed to be pretty popular, so I wanted to try it."

"I think I prefer regular tea with just a touch of sugar."

"Me too. Besides, I don't think all that sugar is good for me."

"Probably not."

My gaze flicked to her left hand again, but the ring was gone, leaving only a thin, white line in its place. Obviously, I was not meant to see that. That led me to wonder, was she divorced? Maybe the guy had just up and left her when he found out she was pregnant, or perhaps she was like me and was a widower. Although, I couldn't understand how any of that would warrant such secrecy. Maybe she'd had an affair and the pregnancy was a result of the affair.

She stood from the table and dumped the rest of the tea, then retrieved two water bottles from the fridge. "Ya know, if you have too many vegetables, I could can them for you."

I raised an eyebrow at the suggestion. "You know how to can?"

"No, but it's another thing I read about and thought I'd try."

"Well, if you do it, it wouldn't be for me. We can split them, and you let me buy the supplies."

She narrowed her eyes as she studied me. "Deal, but I have to warn you, I know very little about canning, so this might not turn out very well."

"I used to help my mom can, so I can help you."

"That's so cute that you used to help your mom."

"Yeah, well, she only had me. She always wanted a girl, but it wasn't in the cards for them."

"You're an only child?"

"Yep. What about you?"

I saw the moment she hesitated. It was getting personal and she didn't want to answer. "No brothers or sisters."

I didn't understand why that was so hard to answer, but I figured if that was difficult for her, I wouldn't get too much other information out of her. Silence fell between us and I wasn't sure what more to say to her. Luckily, she stood up, taking the decision out of my hands.

"I'd better get back out and finish my garden."

"Okay. You'd better put the broccoli in the fridge so it doesn't wilt."

"Oh, thanks." She picked the basket up and unloaded it in the fridge, then I followed her outside.

"You look like you're doing a lot better. Is everything going okay?"

"Yeah. It's been good so far. I uh...I found out the sex of the babies last month."

A shy smile spread across her face and I found myself returning it. "What are you having?"

"A girl and a boy."

"Wow. That's great. One of each, huh?"

"Yeah. You're the first person I've told. It feels so good to finally say it to someone else."

That was a sucker punch to the gut. How sad was it for her that I was the first person she had told such great news to? I couldn't imagine how lonely that had to feel. I walked over to her and wrapped my arms around her, surprising both of us. I just couldn't let her go on any longer feeling like she was the only one that cared about this pregnancy. I knew her pregnancy didn't involve me in any way, but I would be there for her when she had good news to share. I couldn't give her a lot of me, but I could give her that.

"I'm glad you told me." Her hands gripped me tighter and I heard a slight catch in her breath. I waited until she let me go before pulling back and smiling at her. "You know, you can come talk to me if you want. I know we got off to a rough start, but I can be your friend."

I swore I saw tears in her eyes for just a second, but I must have imagined it because when she looked up at me, her eyes were bright and clear.

"Thanks, Drew."

"Do you want some help with your garden?"

"No. It's good therapy to do it alone."

I nodded and waved goodbye as I headed back to my own place. I kept thinking about the fact that she didn't have anyone to talk about this pregnancy with. I remembered when Iris found out she was pregnant. She called about every single person she knew to tell them the good news. Every time I walked in the door, she was on the phone with a girlfriend talking about her pregnancy and her plans for the house.

I thought back to what Sean had said about how I had been willing to help Harper, but I was treating Sarah like dirt I scraped off my shoe. He was right. It didn't matter what I initially thought of Sarah. She was alone and needed some good people in her life. I was fortunate enough to know some great people that could be a part of her life.

∼

THE NEXT WEEKEND, I walked over to Sarah's house and knocked on the door. I waited a minute, then heard her walking across the floor and checking the peephole before opening the door.

"Hey, Drew. What's going on?"

Sarah was wearing a tank top and striped, blue pajama bottoms. Her hair was pulled up out of her face and she looked a little tired, but still beautiful.

"I came to invite you over for a cookout tonight. I'm gonna be grilling and some friends are coming over. Everyone's bringing a side dish and it's gonna be a lot of fun."

"Oh, well I don't have anything to bring."

"That's okay. You can just bring yourself. I'll have some veggies from the garden."

"Um....maybe another time."

I frowned, sure that she would have been excited to come over and meet some new people. "Why?"

"Why what?"

"Why don't you want to come?"

"I just don't know anyone, and I don't want to intrude on your company."

"Well, you're not going to meet anyone if you don't come over to meet them. You see how that works?" I grinned. "Besides, I'm inviting you over, so you aren't intruding. Oh, and Harper will be there. She has a kid, so you two can talk all about girly shit."

"Who's Harper?"

"My buddy Jack's wife. She's really awesome. She was the first person I met when I came to town. I actually lived with her for a while before she married Jack."

"I didn't really sleep too well last night. I think I'm just going to stay home and get some rest."

"Look, why don't you take a nap, then come over around five."

"I just don't—"

I knew she didn't want to meet people, though I wasn't sure why, but she needed this. She couldn't continue to live out here all alone without friends. "Sarah, these are good people, and think of all the good advice Harper could give you."

She fidgeted for a minute, and I saw the gears turning in her head as she tried to think of some excuse not to come over. I wasn't going to give her the chance to back out though.

"Well, I'll see you around five."

I turned and walked off her porch, heading back to my place. I glanced over my shoulder to see her standing uneasily on her porch. She'd come around. The idea of talking to another woman about motherhood would be too much to resist. At least, I really hoped it would.

I brought the grill out and set up the tables and chairs on the back porch, then went to the fridge and took out the meat for grilling. I seasoned everything and stuck it back in the fridge until everyone came over, then went about the rest of my day. I still had quite a bit to fix up around the house, but that would have to wait for another day. I cleaned up the messes that I had left from my latest project and then got cleaned up.

I was just getting out of the shower when I heard the first knock on the door. Throwing on some shorts and a t-shirt, I headed downstairs and pulled the door open to the most beautiful sight I'd seen in a long time. Sarah was standing at the door holding a delicious smelling pie, but that wasn't what caught my attention. She looked... different. Her brown hair was shiny and slightly curly, and she had put on some makeup. Not a lot, but enough to make her eyes really stand out. She was wearing a tight, yellow sundress that showed off her growing baby bump. I had to admit, pregnancy really agreed with her. Now that she wasn't sick all the time, she really did glow.

But as I looked at her, ogling her like some dumb jackass, it also hit me that I had been so horrible to her. Right from the start, I was a jerk, and why? Because she had the dumb luck of being my neighbor? God, I was an asshole, and now I was an even bigger asshole because despite the fact that she was carrying someone else's kids, I was attracted to her.

She cleared her throat, and I finally dragged my eyes back up to her face, seeing a slight pink in her cheeks. "I made homemade apple pie. I've never made one before, but I found a recipe online and it had great reviews, so I hope I didn't screw it up."

"I'm sure it'll be great. Come on in."

I moved aside and grabbed the pie from her, guiding her back to the kitchen.

"I'm early, aren't I?"

"That's okay. You can give me a hand getting everything together."

"Sure. Just tell me what to do."

"Can you go to the pantry and get out the paper plates, forks, spoons, and napkins?"

She nodded and walked over there. Like the asshole I was, my eyes perused over the curves of her body. She was gorgeous. Still, I couldn't fathom how I hadn't seen it before. For the first time in years, I felt something stirring below the belt and I cursed my bad luck. Of course, now that everyone was going to be over here, I would get a chubby that I wouldn't be able to hide. I started thinking of anything to get my body under control, but then I glanced back at Sarah and saw her bend over as something fell to the ground.

"Fuck," I groaned.

She turned around with concern on her face. "Is everything okay?"

"Uh..." I cleared my throat. "Yeah, I was just remembering something I forgot to do. I'll be right back."

I walked out of the kitchen and headed upstairs to my bathroom to pull myself together. After a few minutes of thinking about anything other than the woman downstairs, I finally got myself under control and went back down where Sarah was sitting at the kitchen table.

"I'm gonna get the grill started. Can I get you something to drink before we head out?"

"I'm gonna stick with water today."

I grabbed the cooler I had brought out this morning and loaded it up with ice, beer, and water. We went outside and I got the grill started.

"So..." I cleared my throat, trying to come up with something to say other than *you have a really gorgeous body*. "How is it working at The Pub?"

"I actually switched to days a while ago. Hank is training me for daytime management."

"Really? That's great. It'll be a lot easier for you when the twins come."

"Yeah, I just knew I couldn't keep going at night. It was just too much."

"I can see that. And you like it?"

She shrugged. "It's not my dream job, but it's okay. It pays the bills."

"And what is your dream job?"

A shadow cast over her face momentarily, but she quickly put a smile on her face. "To have a million dollars and live on a remote island."

I smiled. "Wouldn't we all like that."

"The job is fine. It's—"

She gasped, bending over slightly. I was out of my seat a moment later, kneeling next to her.

"Is everything okay? What's wrong?"

I was struck once again when a big smile pulled across her face. "The babies kicked. Here, put your hand here." She grabbed my hand and placed it on her stomach. I waited, but nothing happened. I was about to pull away when I felt the slightest bump against my hand. I stared at her stomach in awe and swallowed thickly. That's what I would have felt if my baby had survived. I quickly pulled my hand away and stood, walking over to the grill.

Out of the corner of my eye, I saw her frown. I didn't mean to be so abrupt with her, but I needed a moment to myself.

"I'm sorry if that was weird. I didn't mean to make you uncomfortable."

"No. I'm just gonna start grilling."

She was about to say something, but a few trucks pulled up and people started making their way up to the back porch. Soon everyone was sitting around drinking beer and introducing themselves to Sarah. I made sure to keep myself occupied at the grill while they all caught up.

"Everything okay, Drew?"

I swear, Harper always knew when something was wrong.

"I'm good."

"Yeah. I've said that enough in my life to know when it's not true."

I looked over at Sarah and saw her smiling at Cece, Vira, and Anna. They were laughing about something and I found myself wanting to know what that laugh sounded like.

"You know, you've never told me what happened, and I'm not asking, but it's okay to move on. It doesn't mean you've forgotten, it just means you're choosing to live your life."

"I'm not moving on, I'm just..."

"Staring at your neighbor like she's everything you want right now?"

"I wasn't staring at her," I grumbled, getting back to the grilling.

"Right. If you want to keep lying to yourself, go ahead, but you won't be able to hide it from everyone. One look at you and we can all see that you're smitten with your pretty, little neighbor."

She walked back to the group of women and I turned back to the grill. I focused on finishing the meat, and then put it on plates on the table. Everyone else had set their food on the table and we all started digging in. I chose to forget my attraction for now and just enjoy everyone's company.

CHAPTER 8

SARAH

I had no clue what I said to make Drew close up so quickly. He was quiet the rest of the day and he barely glanced my way. Maybe he thought I was trying to reel him in when I put his hand on my belly. I wasn't looking for a surrogate daddy for my children. I was just so excited that I was feeling the kicks more often and I wanted to share that with someone.

He was right, though. I did have a great time talking with Harper, Anna, Vira, and Cece. Alex, Cole's girlfriend was still recovering from her attack and wasn't up to visiting today. It felt almost like I had girlfriends again, which was something I desperately needed at this point. I had been here for months and had no friends, unless you counted Drew, which on most days I wasn't sure about.

"So, Harper, you're with Jack, right?"

"Yep. We've been together for a couple of years now and we have a son, Ethan."

"How old is he?"

"Gosh, he's almost seven months old now. He's over at his grandma's so that Jack and I could have a date night. We don't get those very often, so this is like our second date in six months."

"Wow. That's nice that you have that."

I bowed my head as I said that, so that no one would see my face. I wouldn't have that. There wouldn't be anyone to go on a date with, let alone a family member to watch my children. That seemed awfully daunting at the moment, and I felt tears prick my eyes. I quickly got up and left the porch before I broke down in front of everyone.

I walked inside and headed toward the bathroom where I locked myself in. As soon as the door closed the tears started falling. I wasn't even sure what I was crying about anymore. There was the fact that I was going to be raising twins alone, Todd was dead, I had no family, I had no support system, and the biggest one at the moment, I was a pregnant, hormonal mess. A knock on the door had me quickly wiping my eyes and calming my breathing. When I swung the door open, I expected to see Drew, but instead I saw Harper. She pushed her way inside and leaned against the counter.

I tried to ignore the pang in my chest when I saw it wasn't Drew. I didn't need a man in my life, but still, Drew had somehow become something of a friend, and part of me wished that he was the one here to check on me.

"Are you okay?"

"Yeah, I'm totally fine. I was just having a little hormonal me time."

"I remember those days, crying over every little thing that made me sad."

She waited for me to say something, but I had no clue what to say. I didn't know this woman and I couldn't say anything even if I wanted.

"So, I'm assuming the dad is no longer in the picture?"

"No."

She nodded in understanding. "Well, I won't push for details. If you want to tell me, I'm here to talk."

"Thanks."

She didn't say anything, but then grinned at me. "That actually meant that I'm going to get it out of you one way or the other, so you might as well give in now and tell me everything."

I laughed at her bold statement as she handed me a tissue.

"Seriously, though. You can come to me anytime you need to talk. I know what it's like to not have the father in the picture."

"Jack wasn't in the picture?"

"Ethan isn't Jack's son. I mean, biologically. He's never treated him differently, but Ethan is the product of a one night stand while I was trying to get over Jack. It didn't take him long to come around, though."

"Wow. That's...That's something else for a man to step in and take care of someone else's child. What happened with the one night stand?"

"It happened over in England. I don't even remember his name. We didn't exactly exchange particulars. I just wanted to feel something and move on. It didn't end as I hoped, but I got Ethan and Jack in the end, so it's all good."

"Yeah, I don't think that'll be the way my story ends. Drew barely can stand me most days."

She grinned at me. "So, you have a thing for Drew?"

"No," I said a little too quickly. "It's not like that. I just mean, he's the only man that I even consider a friend in this town, and now that I'm pregnant with twins, I doubt I'll be reeling in the guys. Besides, I'm not looking for anyone right now."

She reached down and grabbed my left hand, running her finger over the faint white line that was still on my ring finger. Even though I wasn't supposed to, I still wore my wedding ring when I was at home. It felt so wrong not to wear it, and for just a little while, I could pretend like Todd was just on a business trip and would be home soon.

"Well, no one says that you have to move on right away, but you have the girls and me now. We'll be here to help you with whatever you need."

"That's a nice offer, but I need to do this on my own."

"You know what? That's the same thing I said to Drew when he told me he would be there to help me with my baby. Do yourself a favor. Don't push away the people that are willing to help you. We could be really good friends if you give us a chance." I nodded as she ran her hands up and down my arms quickly. "Come on. Let's get you cleaned up and back outside before they get to wondering what we're doing in here."

"Thanks, Harper. Believe me, I will take you up on your offer at two in the morning when I'm not getting any sleep."

Harper laughed and then helped me fix my makeup. We headed back outside and I sat down with the girls who pretended nothing was wrong. I listened to Harper and Anna tell stories about each other for the next half hour. They were hilarious together. It seemed like all they did was get into trouble together.

"Harper, just face it. You're a walking disaster. It's not so much that you get into trouble, it just seems to appear whenever you're around," Anna said.

"Oh, come on. That's not fair. Name the last time that I got into any trouble."

Jack walked over and interrupted. "How about a few weeks ago when you thought you'd plant some flowers and you dug into the ground before talking to me. You hit the sprinkler line and flooded the backyard."

The girls all burst out laughing and Harper crossed her arms and huffed. "That wasn't my fault. If you had helped me like I asked weeks before, I wouldn't have had to do it myself."

"Wait. Were the sprinklers running when you hit the line?" Ryan asked.

"No. I had started digging and didn't realize I had hit the line. Then Jack's mom called and asked me to go over with Ethan and I left it for the next day. When I woke up, I got my coffee and went to sit out on the back porch. By then, the sprinklers had already started running and all the water was pumped out into the yard."

"Yep, and why don't you tell them what happened after that," Jack said, crossing his arms over his chest.

Harper shot him a death glare. "I saw the water coming up and I went over to try to plug the hole before Jack saw, but I ended up getting all wet. It created this giant mud puddle around me and I was covered in about two minutes. Jack heard the baby crying and was wondering where I was, so he came outside to find me and saw me slipping and sliding in the mud. He just stood there laughing at me!"

Everyone was making fun of her, but she took it in stride.

"See, the thing you gotta understand, Sarah, is that Harper here could find trouble sitting in her own living room," Jack said as he continued to laugh at her, but then he walked up to her and gave her a big kiss. "I swear, one of these days I'm gonna have to wrap you in bubble wrap."

For the next hour, everyone shared their favorite Harper stories, to which she good-naturedly laughed along. After about another two hours, I decided it was time for me to head home. I'd had a great time, but I was getting tired and my bed was calling my name.

"It was great to meet everyone, but my back is killing me and I'm ready for bed."

Drew stepped forward and spoke to me for the first time since his friends arrived. "Why didn't you say so? I could have gotten you some pillows or something."

I quickly peeked around the group. Everyone was watching Drew like he was a wild animal at the zoo. "It's fine. I was fine. I'm just ready to call it a night. Thanks for having me over."

I started to head to the steps when I heard someone's boots on the steps behind me. I turned to see Sebastian following. Maybe he was leaving too. I continued to walk toward my house, but when he should have turned to go to his truck, he continued to follow me toward my house.

"Um...did you need something?"

"Nope. I'm just walking you home."

"Okay. Well, thanks. So, Drew tells me that you run a security firm?"

"Yeah, I started it after I got back from the war."

"Where were you stationed?"

"Afghanistan and Iraq. I served for thirteen years, then I got injured and was discharged."

"I'm sorry. Do you mind me asking how you were injured?"

"I got too close to an insurgent strapped with explosives. They went off and I lost some of my vision in my left eye. It's not too bad, but I couldn't pass the eye exam to get back out there."

"So how does that work, you having the security company?"

"Most of my job is administrative. I can still do some field work, but I mostly delegate to the teams now. It sucks, but there really isn't much opportunity for me to be involved when I'm the boss."

"I bet you miss it."

"Yeah, I do."

"Once a soldier, always a soldier."

He looked at me funny and I quickly snapped my mouth shut. I had to learn to think before I spoke or I would give myself away. But it was hard to pretend like I didn't understand what he was going through. I already knew the mindset from Todd. When he was discharged for PTSD, he had a difficult time adjusting to being home. Even after he got better, he wanted to re-enlist, but I begged him not to. I wanted to start living with him and not through him. Luckily, he'd had an offer from a security firm that he was very interested in and he decided to take it.

"Yeah, something like that. Anyway, I figured if I couldn't serve anymore, I needed to do something that put my skills to use. I opened my firm six months after I got home and we've been slowly building ever since."

"How do you get clients way out here?"

"We're only about an hour from Pittsburg, so that's a pretty easy commute for setting up meetings. Then, when I get a job farther away, I send a team with everything they need. It actually works pretty well with today's technology. If things go well, we might be setting up another office out east, maybe New York."

I stumbled when he said New York and he grabbed my arm to steady me. There were plenty of places to set up a firm in New York, but if he went there, the chances of my identity staying hidden would become substantially less.

"Are you okay?"

"Yeah. I'm fine. You know, pregnant people have horrible balance."

He didn't look like he bought a thing I was saying, so I climbed the steps to the porch, hoping to escape his scrutiny. Unfortunately, he followed me right to the door.

"Thank you for walking me home. It was nice to meet you."

"Sarah, I know you're running from something and if you ever need help... please let me know. I can help you.

"What? I...I don't know what you're talking about. I'm not running from anything."

"Really? I did a background check on you. It's very...thorough. None of it makes sense though. It says you were born and raised in Texas."

"Yeah, that's right."

"But you don't have an accent, not even a hint of one, and Drew told me that you looked up a recipe for sweet tea because you had never tried it, which is funny since Texans love sweet tea. Also, you dye your hair and wear color contacts. It's almost like you're trying to look like someone else."

"Did you ever think that I did my best to drop the accent because I didn't want to sound like I was from the south? Or maybe that I was too poor for sweet tea growing up? Maybe I just like to feel like someone else every once in a while and that's why I color my hair."

"And wear colored contacts?" He stepped forward, his gaze penetrating. "And most Texans would never say they were from the south. They would just refer to themselves as Texans."

My heart was thundering in my chest. I didn't know quite what to say to this man. I couldn't let on who I was. It wouldn't be safe for him or for me, but I didn't know how to convince him that I wasn't on the run. If he figured me out, I was going to have to run again and I was just settling into my new life here.

"You paid for this house in cash, which either means that you have a lot of money laying around or you didn't want a money trail. You didn't carry a phone on you until Drew gave you one, and you have no online activity, which means you don't want a big online presence. You don't even have a bank account. You pay for everything in cash."

I needed to find a way to shut him down. He was calling me out on every single thing I was doing to protect myself and my child.

"Where do you get off talking to me like this? You think that because you're in security you know everything about me? I don't like credit cards, so I don't use them. I'm a Luddite, so no, I don't go online, and what is wrong with paying cash for what I need? You're just picking apart my life, trying to find something about me that you don't like. Do you want me to move? You don't like me in your town? Just say the word and I'll leave. It's not like there's anything holding me here."

He stepped in close, trapping me against the wall. My heart started to pound in fear. What if he worked for Cordano? I needed to leave. It was no longer safe here.

"I don't want you to leave. I want to keep you safe. All of those things separately don't mean a whole lot, but when you put them all together, it looks very suspicious. It adds up to someone who is running, and I know who you are."

He stared at me for a minute, letting that little bomb drop on me. My food threatened to come back up if I didn't calm down. I grasped for the handle behind me, hoping that I could slip inside away from this man that was supposedly Drew's friend. He must have read my mind because he reached for the handle and opened the door, ushering me inside. He steered me toward the couch and then sat down next to me. I did my best to avoid his stare, certain that if I looked at him, I would give myself away.

"Sarah, look at me."

Slowly, I turned my head to stare into his knowing eyes. They softened slightly and he reached out to grasp my hand.

"I know you're scared, but I can help you if you'd just trust me. I won't share your secret with anyone. No one at my company knows who you are, and I won't tell them unless it's absolutely necessary."

I still didn't know what to say. He might be guessing and looking for me to confirm his suspicions.

"Sarah Matthews testified and helped put away Giuseppe Cordano and Marco Abruzzo. You disappeared for a funeral the same week that Sarah Matthews testified against Abruzzo. I know from Drew that men came to pick you up that were heavily armed, probably WitSec. I know you have all the same facial features, height, and weight as Sarah Matthews. When I suspected who you were, I ran you through a facial recognition program and changed your hair and eyes. Guess what? It looked just like you do today, minus the baby bump."

I couldn't listen to this anymore. I got up and raced back to my bedroom, pulling my suitcase out and throwing clothes inside. I heard him approach me, but I couldn't spare any time for him right now. I had to move fast before the mafia found me.

"Sarah, you don't have to leave. I'm here to help you." I couldn't. I just kept packing. "Sarah, just sit down for a minute and listen to me." He grabbed my arms and gave me a slight shake. I finally looked up at him with tears in my eyes. He gently pushed me down on the bed and then sat in front of me on his haunches. "I know the rules of WitSec. I'm not asking you to admit anything, but I'm going to give you my cell number, and you use it day or night if you feel like something's off. I can get here faster than any agent and I can protect you and your children."

I shook my head slightly, tears falling down my face. "Why would you do that?"

"I would do it for anyone that was in danger, but mostly because Drew considers you a friend. I know that you can't tell him what's going on, and that's a heavy burden to bear. I can help you keep up appearances so it doesn't get overwhelming. Just trust me to help you."

"If you found me, so can they. I have to go before someone else recognizes me."

"I found you because I'm trained to look past disguises. I've also been following the case, so it didn't take much for me to link the two. I promise you, the average person is not looking at you and saying, *oh, there's Sarah Matthews*. Sean is suspicious, but he's a cop. He's suspicious of every newcomer. I can help you with him also. You don't have to uproot the life you've started here."

I still wasn't sure. It wasn't just my life at risk, and I didn't know this man. Despite the fact that he seemed very nice, that didn't guarantee that he could keep me safe.

"Look, I wouldn't have approached you, but I can see you're struggling with keeping everything straight. I know what you've lost, and I know what you're facing. I wanted you to know that you're not alone. I want to be someone you can come to if you're struggling. I know that you can't talk about things when they get tough, but you can trust me and you can call me when you're feeling overwhelmed. I promise, I only want to help."

I looked at him warily. "You promise not to tell anyone?"

"I swear it. I won't say a word."

I really didn't want to call WitSec and ask to be relocated right now. It would be difficult to move half way through my pregnancy, and finding a job would be even harder. Who would hire me so close to my due date? Besides, I had really started to like living here. It was peaceful away from all the chaos of the city, and without Todd, all the hustle and bustle just felt empty. Where would they stick me if I had to be moved? And if I said a word to them about Sebastian knowing, they would uproot me in a second.

"I'll stay, but I'll be moved if WitSec finds out that you know. I'm content here, so please don't mess this up for me."

"I won't. Here, get me your phone and I'll give you my number."

I got up and grabbed my phone, handing it over reluctantly. I wanted to trust him so badly. I just hoped I didn't get burned.

"Alright. You keep your phone on you at all times, and if something is off, even if it's just a feeling and you don't have proof, call me and I'll be here as fast as I can. I promise, I will keep you safe."

I nodded and felt a little relief for the first time since this whole ordeal had begun. I finally had someone that was in my corner and sticking around. Better yet, he was a friend of Drew's, and his friends had already made attempts to accept me into their circle. Now I just had to focus on these babies and pray that Sebastian could really help me through all this. He was the only one I could really rely on now.

CHAPTER 9

DREW

Sebastian had walked Sarah back to her house a half hour ago and I was still waiting for him to return. What the hell could he be doing over there for this long? Everyone else was sitting around bullshitting, but all I could do was watch for any sign that Sebastian was on his way back over. Maybe she wasn't feeling good and Sebastian was taking care of her. Or maybe she was finally opening up to somebody, but shouldn't that somebody be me? I was her neighbor after all, and I was the one that invited her over today. The thought that really turned my stomach was that Sebastian might be over there flirting with her and asking her out. It wasn't that I wanted to go out with her. I was still way too screwed up for that, but I had come to think of her as mine in some weird way.

Finally, after another fifteen minutes, Sebastian emerged from her house and started back over. He hadn't even made it halfway back to my house before I was off the porch and up in his face.

"What the hell were you doing?"

"Excuse me?" His brows were knitted in confusion.

"Don't give me that shit. You were over there for forty-five minutes. What the hell were you doing?"

"Shit, Drew. Relax. I walked her home and then we talked for a little bit."

"Were you hitting on her? Because she doesn't need that shit right now. She's got two babies on the way to think about."

"I wasn't hitting on her, but maybe you should rethink what she needs. Do you really think she shouldn't look at the opposite sex because she has kids on the way? Maybe she needs a good man to help her out."

"And I suppose you think you're that man?"

"No. That's not me, but now I'm starting to wonder if that's you."

"If what's me?"

"If you're the good man that could help her out."

My brows slanted in confusion. "Why the hell would you think I'm the man that could help her out? I'm not in any place to take care of a woman and two kids. Besides, I know nothing about her. She doesn't share anything. I couldn't be with someone that hid herself from me."

A look of disappointment crossed his face, but I couldn't figure out why. He didn't know anything about her, so why would he care if I wanted more from her or not. Besides, I wasn't exactly an open book, and I wasn't planning on becoming one anytime soon.

"You could just be a friend to her. That's really all she needs right now. You don't need to know all about her to do that for her."

He walked past me and headed back to the party. I stood staring at Sarah's house and considered what he said. He was right. I could be a friend to her. There was plenty I could do to help her out that didn't involve any sort of romantic attachments. I walked back to my party and considered what I would need to do and how to put my plans in motion. By the end of the night, I had a solid plan and had the guys all in to help out next weekend.

∽

THE NEXT SATURDAY at precisely seven in the morning, I walked across the property with my tools to Sarah's house. I had wrangled Cole, Sean, Ryan, Logan, Jack, and Luke into helping me do some work on Sarah's house. Sebastian wasn't able to make it because of an important job he had. We were going to be replacing her roof and all her windows today. She just didn't know it. I had come by during the week and taken measurements of the windows, and Ryan had placed the order for me. The windows arrived yesterday and he was bringing them with him this morning. I walked up to Sarah's door and knocked. The look of surprise on her face morphed into confusion when she took in my tool belt.

"Um...morning, Drew. What are you doing with all those tools?"

She glanced behind me just as I heard all the trucks pulling into the drive and up to the house. I figured that it would be best to wait until we were supposed to meet up to tell her what our plans were. She was much less likely to nix my plans if all the guys were there to help. I knew she wouldn't like the fact that I was paying for this, but I had the money to help out, and she needed the help.

"What are they all doing here, and why are they coming to my house?"

"We came to do some work on your house. We're gonna replace the roof and all the windows today, and you're going with the girls."

"Going with the girls where?"

Luckily, I heard Harper behind me. If I told Sarah what the plan was for her, she'd probably laugh in my face. Or yell at me. Probably the second.

"Hey, Sarah! Are you ready for our spa day?"

"Spa day? Drew, what is she talking about?"

"Well, I didn't think you'd be very relaxed if you were sitting around here all day while we're working, so you're going with Harper, Vira, Cece, and Anna to the spa." I decided now was the time to throw on the pleading. "Please do this for me. Harper hates the spa, and she'll go crazy if she has to sit and do girly shit with the others. They all love that shit."

I pulled out the puppy dog eyes and did my best to look really distraught. A small smile played at her lips and she quirked an eyebrow at me.

"Nice try. I know what you're doing, and I'll play along, but only because you've basically railroaded me into it."

She grabbed her purse, then walked out to one of the trucks, but turned as she stepped off the porch.

"Drew, I can't...I don't know how I'll ever repay you."

"You don't have to. I'm just trying to help you out."

"Thank you." Her smile lit a fire in my chest, filling me with something I could only describe as happiness. Sebastian was right. I didn't need to be romantically involved to help her out. And much like Harper, I enjoyed knowing that I was doing something good for her.

⁓

"So, what inspired this little project today?" Logan asked.

"Have you seen the windows? They won't work for shit next winter. That won't be good for the babies, and the roof was leaking like a sieve."

"Are you sure that's the only reason why?"

Now that Logan and Cece were officially together, he seemed to have grown a vagina and thought it was okay to try to 'figure me out'. All of which included talking about potential love interests and questioning me on past relationships. Usually I just ignored him, but today I felt particularly irked by his line of questions.

"Now, why would there be another reason? She's my neighbor and friend. She's having twins and has no one to rely on. Why is it so hard to believe that I would help her out just for those reasons?"

"It's not, but you have to admit, she's very pretty."

"Yes, she is, and what exactly would that have to do with anything?"

"I'm just saying that since you've been here, you haven't put your dick in anything that I'm aware of. Unless, of course, Harper and you have something on the side that we're all unaware of. In which case, I wouldn't let that little piece of information reach Jack's ears. I don't think he'd take too kindly to that."

"What wouldn't I take too kindly to?"

Jack walked around the corner of the house with Sean in tow.

"Drew and I were discussing whether or not he was sticking his dick in anyone at the moment."

"Well, not that I've seen. The only woman he ever goes near is Harper, and we all know what would happen if he touched her," Jack said with a smirk.

"Yeah, you'd beat the shit out of him," Sean replied.

"No, Harper would grab a turkey and beat him with it," Logan cut in.

"Uh-uh. Harper and I already had a nice, long conversation about staying away from all large meat products that could be seen as a potential weapon," Sean said with a shake of his head.

"Guess you're in the clear then, Jack." I couldn't help but get in on the ribbing.

Jack glared at me, but shrugged off the comment. "You know what they say, it's not the size of the ship or the motion of the ocean. It's whether the captain stays in port long enough for all passengers to get off."

"How many passengers are we talkin'?" Sean asked.

"Two. Just two. I'm not into that kinky shit. Besides, Harper's a handful all by herself. I don't need to add anyone else to the mix."

We got to work replacing the windows in the back of the house as the guys continued to rib one another. Sometimes, I just didn't need to hear the shit that came out of their mouths.

"There's nothing wrong with kinky shit. Cece can be quite wild in the bedroom."

"Yeah, I walked in on that shit." Sean turned to me, telling me a story from when he first met Cece and Vira. "So Cece texted Vira, telling her to send me over to Logan's place to 'release him'." He shook his head as he recalled the events of that day. "That was something I definitely didn't need to see. I walked up to his bedroom to see him buck ass naked on the bed, handcuffed to the headboard, and he had a coffee filter over his dick. She just left him there."

"In her defense, it was part of her scheming to get back at me," Logan said defensively.

"In her defense? Now you're defending her revenge? Man, you are pussy whipped," Jack said as he pulled out the old window.

"Have you ever had revenge sex?"

"Can we just get the windows installed? Jesus, are we just gonna talk about your women all day?"

"Hey, I don't have a woman," Sean insisted.

"Really? Vira's not your woman?" I asked.

"Don't listen to him. I've heard them fucking in the next room. Believe me, if her pussy is as magical as he tells her it is, he won't be looking anywhere else." Logan shuddered like he was trying to shake off the images.

Sean just shrugged. "She's not into relationships, so no, we're not together. But that doesn't mean I can't fuck her until I find someone else. And believe me, she does have a magical pussy." He waggled his eyebrows and grinned.

I had enough of this shit. I didn't need to sit around and listen to them talk about pussy all day. I came here to do a job, and I just wanted to finish it so I could go back home and relax. I walked away from the guys and headed for the ladder to the roof. I would just help Cole, Ryan, and Luke for the rest of the day.

∽

WE FINISHED with the house around seven that night and everyone was headed into town for dinner. The girls had gotten back around three, and I told them they could hang out at my house until we were done. I was in no mood to go out for dinner. I liked hanging around with everyone, but I still wasn't as social as the rest of them. No matter how hard I tried, I just wanted time to myself with Iris.

After making myself a few sandwiches, I headed out onto the back porch with a few beers. I sat out there enjoying the peace and quiet for a good hour when footsteps drew me out of my thoughts. I turned to see Sarah walking up the steps to my back porch, carrying a six pack of beer.

"I see that you already have beer. I picked this up for you today as a thank you. I know it's not really enough, but I didn't know how else to thank you."

"You don't have to give me anything. I was just doing it for the babies."

The last thing I needed was her thinking I did it out of affection for her. After Logan's ribbing today, I started to worry that he wasn't the only one that would think I was helping her because I liked her or wanted more from her. I hadn't thought about that when I started planning this. Sebastian had convinced me that I could be a friend to her, but what if she thought I was offering more?

"Well, either way I appreciate it. Can you let me know how much I owe you?"

"You don't owe me anything. I didn't do it with the intention of being paid back."

"Well, I would at least like to pay for the supplies."

"Look, I don't know about you, but I think it would be pretty shitty if I decided to fix your roof and windows and then asked you to pay for it after I had already done it. I took care of it and it's done. Let's just leave it at that."

"Well, maybe I can cook you dinner and make you dessert or something."

"I already told you, you don't need to pay me back."

"I don't want your charity, and I'm not going to sleep with you." She practically shouted at me. I finally realized that she was just as nervous as I was that this meant something more.

"Look, I'm not expecting anything from you. I did it because you're my friend and I was trying to find some way to help you. That was something I could do to help. I'm not looking to sleep with you, and I'm definitely not at a place in my life where that even sounds a little tempting."

She looked a little stricken with that last comment, but did her best to hide it. "I know that being pregnant doesn't make me the most attractive prospect, but you don't have to be an ass about it."

Shit. That wasn't how I meant it at all. "That's not what I meant. I'm just not in a place to be tied to any woman, let alone a woman that is about to have kids. That requires responsibility, and I can barely take care of myself most days. Like I said, I was just looking for some way that I could help you."

The sun was starting to set, and the more I talked to Sarah, the less time I had with Iris. She needed to go now. My chest was starting to tighten at the thought of missing out on my time with Iris. This was my ritual, my special time with her and Sarah was intruding.

"I never asked you to take care of me or my kids. I just came to say thank you."

"Well, you said thank you and now you can go the fuck home and leave me alone."

"Good Lord, you run hot and cold more than any person I know. Fine. I said thank you and now I'll leave you to your brooding."

"Thank fuck!"

She stomped off the steps and I dismissed her from my thoughts the moment she hit the driveway. I closed my eyes and leaned back in my chair, waiting to feel Iris wrap her warmth around me. It was like this every night. I would watch the sunset and wait for Iris to show. No, she wasn't actually here, but I'd swear that I could feel her spirit. I was still hanging on to every last piece of her. No matter how much I chose to move on with my life, this was the one thing I could never give up.

I had made the decision to stay in this town, to get a job here, to open myself up to friends, to buy the house, to buy things to fill the house. I had moved on as much as I could, but I would hold on to this time with Iris as long as she continued to show.

I cleared my mind of all the bullshit of the day and finally allowed my mind to drift to better times with Iris.

"Drew, where are we going?"

"We're going dancing. Get your cowboy boots on and let's go."

I was practically shaking with nerves. Tonight was the night. I would make her officially mine and we were gonna start our life together. She was back at the door a moment later with brown cowboy boots that had teal stitching all over them. She was wearing a knee length dress that flowed from her waist and had small flowers over it. She exuded innocence, but she was a temptress deep down.

"Come on, cowboy. I can't wait to dance with you."

We headed out to my truck, and after I helped her inside, I walked around to my side, patting my pocket one more time to be sure the ring was still there. We pulled up to the club ten minutes later and I ushered her inside and right to the dance floor. Going line dancing was one of our favorite things to do on the weekends. I spun her around the dance floor for a few songs. We two stepped to "Chattahoochee" by Alan Jackson and "A Good Run Of Bad Luck" by Clint Black. She threw her head back and laughed as I stepped on her feet occasionally. I was generally a pretty good dancer, but there were times I was too caught up in her beautiful smile to keep my feet moving in time to the music.

When "Any Man Of Mine" by Shania Twain came on, I begged off for a drink at the bar while she line danced with the other ladies. I didn't mind at all. I sat and drank my beer while I watched her shake her ass on the dance floor. I hadn't quite decided yet when I was going to propose to her tonight, but the next song had me headed to the dance floor and pulling her into my arms. "I Cross My Heart" by George Strait played over the speakers as I pulled her close and rested my chin on her head. Her hand rested on my chest with my hand holding it there. I sang softly to her as I twirled her around the dance floor before stopping and looking into her eyes. She was completely shocked when I got down on one knee and pulled the ring from my pocket.

One of the DJs must have seen me because he turned down the music so she could hear me.

"Sweet Iris, I cross my heart and promise to give all I've got to give to make all your dreams come true. In all the world, you'll never find a love as true as mine." I sang along with the music, but stopped for the next part. "Marry me, Iris. There will never be anyone but you for me. You are my love and my life. Say that you'll share the rest of your life with me."

She knelt down and flung her arms around my neck as people started clapping. I didn't give a shit about them, because the most gorgeous girl in the world had just given me the best gift of my life. I pulled back and slid the simple diamond ring on her finger. She smiled up at me and I pulled her back to her feet to finish dancing to the song with her. When the song ended, I didn't want to release her yet, and I still would have slow danced even to a fast song with her. Luckily, "Cowboy Take Me Away" by The Dixie Chicks came on and I got to hold my sweet Iris a little longer.

SHE WAS THERE with me as the memories washed over me. Like every other time, her perfume lit my senses and I could almost feel her arms around me. I kept my eyes closed as the tears pricked my eyes once again.

"My sweet Iris, I'm forever yours. Nothing can take me from you."

The warmth of her started to fade and I opened my eyes to the sun setting low on the horizon. She was gone for tonight and I was once again alone. There would never be a time when I would be used to the feeling of her leaving me. I got up from my chair and headed inside to go to bed alone like I did every night.

CHAPTER 10

SARAH

I couldn't figure Drew out. One minute he was doing the most amazing things for me, and the next, he was practically shoving me out of his life. I could only guess that I had crossed some imaginary line. The problem was, he never talked about anything personal and I didn't know which lines I couldn't cross. If I was going to have any kind of friendship with him, I was going to have to talk to him and find out how to stay on his good side. For now, I would give him a few days to calm down.

I knew I didn't have any right to ask him to open up to me when I wasn't allowed to do so myself. I supposed that I could make up a version of the truth and give him that much, if he ever asked, which I doubted he would. Drew didn't strike me as the kind of guy that got to know his friends on a deeper level. Except maybe Harper. When we went for our spa day, Harper filled me in on how she met Drew. It was a funny story, but the way she described Drew at the time broke my heart. I could see it in him from time to time, like last night. It was like he was lost and needed to be alone. But I was sure if Harper had been there, he wouldn't have asked her to leave.

I wasn't sure why that bothered me. Harper and Drew had a

connection, and anyone could see how strong it was. But me? I didn't have a connection with anyone. No one looked at me like I was the one person they needed in their life more than air. Well, not anymore. Todd had been that person to me and I had been that to him. When he was discharged from the military, he tried his best to fit back into society. He hid his reactions well, but I saw when anxiety was creeping up on him. I did my best to divert his attention to something else, and for the most part it worked.

After a few days of letting my anxiety over the situation stew, I walked over to Drew's with a casserole. I didn't know how else to break the ice with him and thought maybe dinner would be a nice thank you for all his work the previous weekend. Walking up his front steps, my nerves took over and I started to wonder if this was really a good idea. I knocked on his door, but when he didn't answer right away, I set the casserole down and quickly turned to head back home. I was on the bottom step when I heard his door swing open.

"Sarah? Is everything okay?"

I turned to look at him and for some reason couldn't find the words and fumbled over everything. "Yeah, I made food... dinner, I mean... casserole. It's there." I pointed at his feet like an idiot. "On the porch. Just...you know...thank you for everything and..."

"Thank you. That was very nice of you. Have you already eaten?"

"Me? No, I...at home...I was going to..."

God, I sounded like such an idiot, stuttering and stammering over all my words. I couldn't figure out what my malfunction was tonight. I had to clear my throat several times so that sounds would actually leave my throat. Though, grunting and throwing out word vomit wasn't exactly making me all that attractive at the moment. Attractive? Was that what I was hoping I would be?

"Why don't you come in and join me?"

He turned and walked inside with the casserole, leaving the door open. I didn't really have a choice but to follow. I walked inside fidgeting with my summer dress and running my fingers through my hair. I had no idea why I was primping for Drew. He was my neighbor, and most of the time didn't like me. Still, I found myself wanting to look presentable to him.

When I finally reached the kitchen, Drew already had plates and silverware out and was serving both of us. I sat down at the table and fumbled my fork twice before I was finally able to take a bite of food. I caught him looking at me out of the corner of his eye with a confused look on his face. Why wouldn't he be confused? I was acting like an idiot.

"Is there something you want to tell me? You're acting a little strange."

"No, of course not. I'm just...well, I...I mean." I stopped and took a deep breath. Maybe I just needed to clear the air with him and then everything would go back to normal. "I'm sorry about the other night. I feel like maybe I crossed a line and I don't know what that line was, but I'm sorry. I want to be your friend, but I don't know what things will make you mad, and I feel like I make you mad a lot."

"You didn't do anything." I gave him a look that said I was calling bullshit.

"It's not you, it's just, when you came over..." He blew out a harsh breath and looked away in irritation.

"It's okay. You don't have to say anything. I'm sorry, I shouldn't have come over." I stood to leave because I'd never felt more like an intruder in my life. It felt like I was always barging in on him, and I knew at any moment he would get tired of me and tell me to leave him alone for good. I couldn't stand to lose the only friend I had made, so leaving him alone would be best for now.

"No, wait. Don't go."

"Drew, I really like you, as a friend, and I don't want to push you. If you ever want to talk, I'll listen, but I shouldn't be inserting myself into your life, especially when you don't want me there."

He grabbed onto my arm, stopping me from leaving the house. He looked really irritated or angry, I wasn't sure which, but I didn't like that I was the one doing that to him.

"I don't want you to go. There are just things that I haven't told anyone, and I don't know how to even begin to talk about it. Just sit down and finish your meal. We can talk about it after dinner. I'm gonna need something stronger for this conversation."

I hesitated, but if he was going to try and open up to me, it would be rude of me to walk away. "Okay."

I returned to the table and sat down, picking up my fork once more. We continued eating in uncomfortable silence for the next ten minutes. I wracked my brain trying to figure out what he could possibly need to say that was so difficult. Yeah, like I couldn't think of anything that would be difficult to tell another person. I almost snorted to myself, but stopped myself in time.

After we finished eating, we brought our plates over to the sink, and Drew grabbed a water bottle for me and a glass of whiskey for himself. He ushered me outside and we sat on the deck chairs for several minutes before he finally spoke.

"I haven't told anyone this, not even Harper."

He was quiet for a minute and I almost told him to forget about it. It was obviously painful for him to talk about.

"I used to be married," he said quietly, staring off into the distance. "She was beautiful and the most special person I've ever met. She could light up a room just walking in. She was everything to me." My eyes were riveted on him. I saw his throat work as he fought to keep control of his emotions as he told me the story. "She died about a year and a half after we were married. She got pregnant about a year in, and that's when she felt the lump. The doctors said it was probably a clogged milk duct, but testing showed that she'd had a slow growing cancer for a long time. For some reason, the cancer took off when she got pregnant. She had to either keep the baby and wait for treatment or terminate the pregnancy. The doctors didn't give her very good odds if she kept the baby."

"What did she do?"

He turned and looked at me with sad eyes. "I begged her to terminate the pregnancy. They said it would probably kill her. I didn't want to lose her."

He looked off into the distance and stared at the setting sun for a long time. I didn't want to interrupt him because he looked like he was finally at peace. He closed his eyes and a smile touched his lips. I wanted to know so badly what caused him to get that look on his face. I sat in silence for the better part of an hour, not sure if I should stay or go, but he wasn't asking me to leave, and I didn't want to intrude on his thoughts.

As I waited for him, the breeze picked up and despite the cooling temperature, I felt warmth wrap around me. It was a strange, yet peaceful feeling.

"Can you feel her?"

I looked over to see Drew looking at me curiously. I crinkled my eyebrows, not understanding what he was saying. "What do you mean?"

"She was here. Could you feel her? It was like..." He closed his eyes as he tried to figure out how to describe her.

"Warmth," I said and he snapped his head back to me. "I felt her. It was like peace was settling inside me."

His eyes held an understanding, and I could swear I saw a tear slip from his eye in the darkness. "That's why you wanted me to leave the other night."

He nodded sadly. He had just shared something very personal with me, and I wanted to reciprocate. Maybe I couldn't say everything, but I could let him know that I understood.

"My babies' father is dead. He died right before I moved here. He talks to me sometimes, like when I had the accident. He kept telling me to get out of the car, that it wasn't safe to stay there. He urged me to keep moving. When I got home, he told me to sleep, that he would watch over me." I looked over at him and saw no judgement on his face. "It's the best and the worst gift, isn't it? I can hear his voice and it brings me peace, but it doesn't make it any easier to move on. At the same time, I can't imagine what it would be like if I no longer heard him, you know?" He nodded. "How long ago did your wife die?"

"Almost seven years ago."

I nodded thoughtfully. "You've been lucky, I mean, to have her with you for so long."

"She fades a little more each day. I think the more I move on, the less I feel her. Maybe that's why I refuse to make too many changes. I mean, I settled here and bought a house. I made friends, but I haven't moved on from her. I don't know if I'll ever be ready to date someone else."

We sat for a few minutes in the dark in silence. It was nice to know that I wasn't the only one going through this. I was about ready to head home when Drew asked me something I couldn't answer.

"The father, was he your husband?"

My breath caught in my chest as I contemplated my answer. I couldn't bring myself to lie, but I also knew I couldn't tell Drew the truth. There was nothing in my new identity about being married, so I couldn't tell him that Todd was my husband, but the thought of denying it was like a knife to my chest. Instead of answering, I sat there in the dark and wallowed in the reality of my new life.

Drew didn't ask any more questions after that and neither did I. We sat in silence for so long that I dozed off, only waking when the babies started kicking me. The urge to use the bathroom was strong, so I got up and walked over to Drew, placed a kiss on his cheek and headed home.

∼

THE NEXT WEEKEND brought more of the same around my house. I spent most nights curled up on the couch watching cooking shows and reading books. After many months of not having a TV, I finally broke down and got myself a small one.

My weekends were spent in the garden and finding little things that needed to be done around the house before the babies came. I'd painted the babies' room white with an accent wall in a pretty blue. Most of the decorations were wild animals. I wasn't much of a decorator unless there was expensive art involved, so the room didn't look like much. Overall, it was pretty plain, but that was okay. I didn't need the room to look like something out of a Martha Stewart catalogue.

I still needed to buy all the furniture for the babies' room and, well, everything else. I was probably the least prepared mother in the history of the world. I had eight weeks until the babies were considered full term. The doctor told me that most twins were born around thirty-six weeks, but they considered twins full term at thirty-eight weeks. She said that if I didn't deliver by then, they would induce because of additional risks that could present themselves at that point. I was doing well though, and aside from some Braxton hicks contractions, everything was going great.

I was still searching for a daycare provider for the twins, though I didn't really want to do that. Ideally, I would like to find someone that could come to my house and take care of the twins during the day, but I wasn't sure if I could afford that. Harper said she'd heard of someone that could potentially be a live in nanny, but I wasn't sure I was okay with that, and I didn't have the space either. She was going to get me the information so I could contact the woman.

My little basketball stomach had gotten quite large over the past month, and I now looked like I was about to pop any day. I had gone shopping after work one day this week because all my clothes were too tight on me. I now had a new wardrobe of summer maternity dresses that I absolutely loved. I stayed away from flowy dresses though. They made me feel twice as large, and I constantly worried about my dress blowing up with a strong breeze.

I asked Drew if he would take me shopping this weekend for the furniture I needed. I would have gone by myself, but I wouldn't be able to lift the boxes or get them home in my little car. Drew said he would pick me up after lunch to go shopping, which I was fine with because I enjoyed sleeping in as much as I could before the babies came. Most nights I would wake up to go to the bathroom and then be up for hours afterward. I didn't have the luxury of sleeping in during the week because I was the day manager at The Pub, but the weekends were all mine for the next two months.

I was just sitting down for a second helping of lunch when Drew knocked on my door. Holding my sandwich, I walked to the door and pulled it open as I took a huge bite.

"Did I miss lunch?"

"Come on in. I'm just eating my second helping."

"Second helping? I thought you weren't supposed to take that whole 'eating for two' thing literally?"

"I'm not eating for two. I'm eating for three. I think my son is taking after his daddy in the eating department."

"How do you know it's not your daughter?"

"Because she's sitting lower and he's higher. All the kicks are up in my ribs. Every time I'm hungry, he starts kicking me, which leads me to believe that he's hungry too."

Ever since I told Drew about the twins' father, I had felt more comfortable mentioning him in conversation. I never gave away anything that happened, but over the last week I had opened up to him a little more about general things. Drew had made it a habit to stop by and see how I was when he got home from work and make sure there was nothing I needed. It was a relief to know that someone cared enough to stop in.

"Have you thought about names yet? Maybe some family names?"

"I don't have any family that I would name them after."

"What about your son? He could take his dad's name."

How did I explain that I couldn't give my son his father's name? Everyone would question why.

"No. I think I'll give him something that's all for him."

In truth, Todd and I had talked for a long time about giving our future son his grandfather's name. He was a great man that Todd admired and loved very much.

. . .

"When we have kids, if we have a girl, I want to name her Charlotte."

Todd quirked his eyebrows at me. "Where does Charlotte come from?"

"I just like the name. I've always liked it, but now that we're thinking about having a baby, I'm putting my request in now so that you don't override my decision when I'm pregnant and can be swayed with food."

"Really? You think I could sway you with food?"

"You do it now, so what would make me think I could resist if I was pregnant?"

"Fine. I accept your choice if you accept mine."

"That depends. What's your choice?"

"Alastair. We could call him Ally for short."

I scrunched my nose in distaste. Ally? That kid would be teased as a child and an adult.

"I'm sorry. I can't accept that name. Ally? Really? Are you asking for your child to be bullied?"

"It was my grandfather's name. It would mean a lot to me if we named our son after him. My grandfather was a great man. My parents used to drop me off at my grandparents house and go to parties and go on vacation. The man practically raised me until I was seventeen when he died. He taught me everything I know about honor and respect. He taught me survival skills and how to shoot. The man guided me toward the future I had. It was a blessing because my parents would have sent me off to boarding school and washed their hands of me. I owe everything to him."

Well, how could I say no to that? "Alright. We can name him Alastair, but can we come up with a different nickname for him?"

Todd threw his head back in laughter. "I was just joking. We won't name our kid Alastair. That wasn't even his name."

"You made that all up? That's horrible!"

"No. I didn't make it all up. My grandfather really did do all that for me, but his name was Henry."

"Henry." I tested it on my lips and decided it wasn't that bad. "Alright, but under one condition. We make his middle name Jones."

"Really? We're going to name our kid after Indiana Jones?"

"Well, only partly. Henry for your grandfather and Jones just fits."

He gave a sigh, but agreed. "Fine. If we have a girl, we'll name her Charlotte and if we have a boy, we'll name him Henry Jones."

I smiled at him, not expecting him to actually name our son Henry Jones.

"Sarah. Sarah. Is everything okay?"

I finally pulled myself from the memory and looked up at Drew. His face was pinched in concern.

"I'm sorry. I was just thinking about something. I didn't hear what you were saying."

"It must have been painful."

"Why do you say that?"

"Because you're crying."

I reached up and felt the wetness on my cheeks, quickly wiping the tears away and pulling myself together. "I'm fine. Let's go get this shopping done or you're gonna have to take me to dinner too."

He smiled and pulled me in close. "Well, you'd probably spend more on dinner than you would on all the baby furniture, so let's get going."

We walked to his truck, but he stopped me when we got to the passenger side. "You know you can talk to me, right? I'm here if you need to vent or talk about anything."

"Thanks, Drew. I appreciate that."

I climbed into his truck and shut the door, effectively ending the conversation.

"Drew, where are we going? This isn't the way to Target."

"We're stopping by Jack's house on the way. Harper wanted to have you look at a few baby items she has first."

"Oh, that's nice of her. She doesn't need them?"

"I don't know. I don't really know anything about baby stuff, so you'll have to ask her."

We pulled into Jack's house a few minutes later and I got out, curious as to why there were so many vehicles there.

"Are they having a party or something?"

"I think they're having a barbecue this afternoon. You know, summer is coming to an end and they want to get as much grilling in as possible before the cold weather starts moving in."

"It's mid-August. That's hardly the end of summer. We still have a few weeks to go."

"Yeah, but it goes by fast."

"I guess you're right."

We walked up the steps and Drew pushed open the door, then placed his hand on my back and guided me through the door.

"Surprise!"

Startled, I took a step back and bumped into Drew as he steadied me. All of his friends were gathered in the living room smiling at me. There were baby banners and some kind of cake made out of diapers. Boxes and bags were scattered through the living room, overflowing with tissue paper. In the corner of the room was a giant teddy bear sitting in a rocker. Before I had time to process what I was seeing, women were walking toward me and wrapping me in warm hugs. Some people I didn't even know.

It was a little weird and I couldn't understand why people I barely knew were here throwing me a baby shower. My stupid hormones took over and I ran from the room crying and headed for where I hoped the bathroom was since I had never been in this house before. After locking myself inside, I pressed my hands to my eyes, willing them not to water. A knock sounded at the door before I was ready to see anyone, but the voice was reassuring.

"Sarah, are you alright, sweetheart?" Drew asked.

I opened the door a little and allowed him to come in. He pulled me into his arms, and I immediately melted into him. I cried into his shirt for the better part of five minutes before pulling myself together. He leaned back, brushing his thumbs over my cheeks. He looked so concerned, which just made me want to cry all over again.

"I don't know what happened. These stupid pregnancy hormones have me crying at the drop of a hat."

"You don't have to lie to me. You know more about me than anyone else in that room. You can tell me what's bothering you."

"The thing is, I don't know what's wrong. I should be happy. All these people are here and they brought presents for my children. I should be so grateful that these people thought enough of me to do this for me, but..."

"But it's not who you wish was here."

I dropped my head in shame. "That's so selfish of me."

"It's not selfish to wish the father of your children was here. I don't know anything about your life before you came here, but I'm sure you wish there were people from that time here to celebrate with you. That's not selfish."

I gestured toward the hallway, completely embarrassed that now I would have to go out there and face them all. "They're going to think I'm crazy."

"Maybe. You seem to always end up crying in the bathroom, but we've all been around hormonal, pregnant women. We're well aware of the idiosyncrasies of a pregnant woman. You don't have to tell them what you're feeling, though they would all understand. You just say you were overwhelmed by the support and you needed a moment to pull yourself together."

"Okay." I nodded and took a deep breath, finally ready to go out and face the music.

"Come on. I'll introduce you to everyone. I'm sure there are people here that you've never met before."

We walked out of the bathroom after I did a quick check in the mirror and went back to the living room where everyone was chatting as if nothing happened. Harper made her way over to me and wrapped me in a big hug.

"I acted a little crazy when I was pregnant, too." Harper whispered in my ear, but apparently not quietly enough.

"A little? Woman, you drove me up the wall when you were pregnant. In fact, we're not having any more kids cuz I'm not sure if I can deal with that particular brand of crazy again."

"Really? So what am I supposed to do with the little one currently residing in my belly?"

The whole room went deadly silent, and Jack stared at her like he was considering whether what she was saying was true. After a long pause, an older woman ran forward and started kissing Harper on the cheeks and patting her tummy, rambling on about getting another grandbaby. Jack, finally pulled from his reverie, stalked toward Harper and pulled her into his arms and kissed her with so much passion my face turned red. When they finally came up for air, the rest of the group gathered around giving their congratulations and well wishes.

"I'm so sorry, Sarah. I didn't mean to announce that at your party."

"It's okay. It takes all the pressure off me!" I gave her a hug and stepped back looking at all the happy faces around me. I didn't know all of them, but they were all so friendly and seemed like a great group of people, like a family. They couldn't replace those that weren't here with me, but it wasn't a bad place to start.

Everyone took turns pulling me around the room and introducing me to those I didn't know. Harper's mother-in-law, Agnes, gave out hugs and kisses and promised me homemade lasagna. She was Italian and made everything from scratch. She promised to teach me all about cooking someday, and I was overjoyed since I no longer had a mother to teach me that stuff. Alex was sitting on the couch smiling and when she tried to get up, I stopped her. She was still recovering from her attack, and although she looked fine, Drew told me she was still struggling to do physical activities.

Cece, who now sported a slightly rounded belly, stood next to Vira who was glaring at someone across the room. I followed her gaze to see an equally upset looking Sean, glaring back. I didn't want to know what was going on there. I had enough to deal with. Anna was also there, and her baby was toddling around somewhere by the guys. Cole's mother, Patricia, was also there. I had never met her, but she was just as motherly as Agnes. My heart hurt the more I thought about the fact that I was alone, but I pushed it aside as I continued around the room. Cole's cousin Kate congratulated me and gave me her card, making me promise to call her if I had any questions. She was a physician and though OB-GYN wasn't her area of expertise, she promised to help me with anything I needed. There was one more woman that stood off to the side, not really engaging in any conversation. Cara, Sean's sister, was sipping water and pretending to blend into the wallpaper. It felt as though I had found a kindred spirit in her.

"Hi, I'm Sarah."

"Cara. I'm Sean's sister."

"Yeah, he's mentioned you."

"Oh really? What did he tell you?" She had a snarky attitude, and I could only guess that it was a defense mechanism of some kind.

"Nothing, he just mentioned who you were."

"Well, I'm not really someone worth knowing, so you should just go join the sorority girls over there."

"Um...I'm not...I mean, I don't really fit in anywhere. I just moved here and I've only met them a handful of times. They're really nice, but I'm not quite as..."

"Bubbly?"

I laughed at her assessment. That wasn't really what I would consider them. They weren't bubbly. They were just full of life, and I wasn't. I had a feeling Cara felt the same way.

"Maybe you could help me get through this party without feeling like a total outsider."

She nodded and grabbed my hand, pulling me over to a seat that I gladly sat in. I had only been standing for about a half hour, but it was already too long. As I sat down, I noticed Sean looking intently at Cara and me. He had a look on his face that I didn't quite understand, but he wasn't objecting to me being around his sister, so I sat down and waited for the party to commence. I looked out at the sea of gifts and blew out a breath. This was going to be one long party.

CHAPTER 11

DREW

The guys all hung around the back porch and the kitchen, but I kept mostly to the kitchen where I could keep an eye on Sarah. When she broke down in tears, I thought maybe I had misstepped, but I really thought this would be good for her. No matter what happened before she moved here, she needed friends around that would support her when the babies were born.

Sean seemed to stick close by also. I noticed him watching Cara and Sarah a few times. He seemed nervous at first, but then relaxed as he saw the two women interacting. I never would have thought Cara and Sarah would hit it off. Cara was so abrasive after what happened to her and Sarah seemed way too emotional to deal with that. For some reason though, it worked.

There were so many gifts that Sebastian and Ryan had to help haul stuff back in their trucks. I didn't even know what half this crap was, but Harper, Anna, Agnes, and Patricia all insisted it was all necessary, while the other girls looked on in curiosity. I had to admit, it was fun watching Sarah open all the presents. Most of them, she had no clue as to their function, but she smiled and thanked everyone anyway.

"Where do you want the rocker?" I asked after Sebastian and Ryan left.

"I think we should just leave it for another day. I'm exhausted and I just want to go to sit down for a while and relax."

"How about this? Let's watch a movie and I'll order a pizza."

"We just ate two hours ago. Don't tell me you're already hungry?"

"I'm not, but I know you are. Don't deny it."

She bit her bottom lip and looked guiltily at the couch as she rubbed her belly. "Alright. Yeah, pizza sounds really good right now."

I guided her over to the couch and then ordered a pizza for us. We looked through movies on the TV to find something to watch. After much arguing, we finally settled on *Red*. She had never seen it before and I promised she would like it. She did and actually laughed during most of it. It was probably the most relaxed I'd ever seen her before. I'd also never seen her laugh so much in all the time I had known her. When the pizza arrived, she put away half of the family size pizza, and I ate the other half.

When the movie was over, I got up to leave and Sarah grabbed my arm. She looked vulnerable and unsure of herself as she tried to ask me something. I couldn't take it anymore.

"Sarah, whatever it is, just ask."

"I was wondering if you could stay with me tonight."

At first I thought she meant it as something more and I was about to tell her no, but then I realized that nothing about tonight would point to her feelings being more than friends. Knowing that, I couldn't refuse her. She'd had a hard day and obviously needed a little comfort tonight.

"Sure. Why don't you go get ready for bed and I'll lock up. I can sleep on the couch."

"No. Can you...I want you to...to stay in bed with me. Strictly platonic. I just don't want to feel alone tonight."

I wasn't sure that was a great idea, but I'd done it with Harper. Why not with Sarah? "Okay."

I went to the kitchen and cleaned up, then made sure all the doors were locked. I took my time, making sure she would have plenty of time to get ready and in bed. I didn't want to make her uncomfortable. When I finally went into her bedroom, she was getting in bed in a short pair of shorts and a tank top that stretched over her belly. She didn't see me, so I watched her for a minute from the doorway. She was beautiful. She was so strong, dealing with the death of her babies' father and impending motherhood that she would be facing alone. She fluffed the pillows all around her and spent a good few minutes getting everything in place. When I saw how long it was taking her to get situated, I decided to step in and help.

Walking over to the bed, she finally saw me and laughed at her predicament. "It gets harder every night to get comfortable."

"Why don't you give me a minute and we'll try something."

I walked to the bathroom and made quick work of getting ready for bed. The hardest part was trying to figure out what I was going to wear to bed. I finally decided on my boxers and t-shirt. It was more than I usually wore, but she probably wouldn't be comfortable with less. I climbed into bed next to her and scooted closer to her.

"Why don't you lay on your side and I'll put this pillow in front of you to support your tummy and your legs. Then I'll lay behind you to support your back. I'm a lot harder than a pillow."

I practically groaned in embarrassment at my statement. That sounded so bad. "I mean, my body is harder, not...other areas of my body."

She started laughing at me. "I know what you meant, but it's cute hearing you try to explain yourself."

I pushed up behind her and helped her situate the pillow, then wrapped my arm around her belly, letting my hand rest on her belly button.

"Is this okay?"

"Yeah. It's kind of nice. It's been so long, I kind of forgot what it felt like to be held."

She was right. This whole thing was something I hadn't felt in a long time. Harper wasn't mine to lay with, so I rarely got the opportunity anymore. "I kind of forgot what it felt like to hold someone."

"Have you not...slept with a woman since your wife?"

"I haven't been with anyone since her. For a while, when I first moved here, I slept in bed with Harper. That only lasted until last year when she finally moved in with Jack. There was never anything between us, but it was comforting to lay next to someone again."

Silence stretched on until I heard her slow breathing signaling that she was asleep. I was just about to drift off to sleep when I felt the tiny kicks coming from her belly. They only lasted a minute before her tummy went still again.

THE SUN PEEKED through the windows the next morning, and for the first time in a long time, my body was reacting to the gorgeous woman lying beside me. Sure that she would not be okay with my erection poking her in the ass, I moved away from her and got up to use the bathroom. When I went to the kitchen, I saw it was still early, so I made some coffee and checked out the fridge for breakfast.

When I was just about to go call her for breakfast, she walked sleepily into the kitchen and plunked down at the table, rubbing her belly.

"Coffee. I need coffee."

"Did you not sleep well?" I asked as I grabbed a mug and filled it for her.

"No. That was the best I've slept in months."

"Ah. So, just not a morning person then."

"I don't think I moved all night. When I woke up, my arm was numb from sleeping on it."

"Well, breakfast is just about ready and then we can work on getting the babies' room set up."

I dished out the food and we sat in silence as we ate. Sarah kept moaning when she put a bite of food in her mouth and it was making me rather uncomfortable. I had to shift in my chair several times to find a more comfortable position. When she bit into her bacon, I had to leave the table before my cock took hold of my body. She looked at me strangely as my chair practically flipped backward in my haste to get away from her.

"Uh, I think I'm gonna run home for a while."

"I thought we were setting up the room?"

"Yeah...definitely, I'll just head...run! I'll run home and use the bathroom."

"You can use my bathroom."

"I have things that I have to take care of...there."

She looked confused and then smiled at me. "Oh, well, you know I have air freshener in the bathroom. It's nothing I haven't smelled before."

Shit. That was even worse than telling her I had to get away from her because I had a boner that was threatening to break the zipper on my jeans.

"No. I mean I have to take a shower. In my house. Alone."

"Oh. Okay." She was so cheery. She didn't even get that I was a mess right now, trying to figure out why my body suddenly decided after all these years to be attracted to the one woman I should probably stay away from. She was going through her own shit and about to have twins. She didn't need me acting like a horny teenager around her.

"Alright. I'll go. Home. To shower."

Goddamn, I couldn't even talk around her. I was so focused on keeping my erection from her line of sight that I couldn't form a sentence. The problem was, I was standing behind the counter in her kitchen and I had to walk around her to get to the front door. When she looked at me, expecting me to leave and showing no signs of getting up herself, I finally walked out from behind the counter. I saw the moment when she saw the rather large tent in my pants. Her face turned bright red and her eyes widened, then shot up to meet my gaze.

I cleared my throat and tried to move, but I was frozen as I stared at her. I didn't know what I expected to happen, but I wasn't prepared for what she said.

"You should go take care of that," she said, pointing at my cock. "It looks, uh, painful."

She blushed an even deeper red, and not knowing what to say in response, I walked around her and headed for the door. I made my way quickly to my house and went to my bedroom, stripping my clothes on the way. I hadn't gotten hard for a woman in years, not since my wife. Thoughts of her and the final months of her life had stripped all desire from my body. I had been to plenty of bars where women would try to drape themselves on me and get me to take them home, but not one had any effect on me.

I stepped into the shower and grabbed my cock, needing to find some release before this became my permanent state. I felt like I had taken Viagra and was one of the unlucky people whose erection lasted longer than four hours. I fisted my cock and jerked myself off, but the face that I saw was Sarah's. I saw her crawling into bed in those cute little things she called pajamas. I saw her sitting outside in her garden. I saw her moaning as she ate bacon. None of those things were something I would've ever classified as sexual before, but as I jerked myself faster and harder, the images of her continued to flow through my mind.

When I finally found my release, I leaned my head against the shower wall and guilt flooded me. I hadn't even considered thinking about Iris once while I was walking over here or when I was in the shower. Little by little, Iris was leaving me, and I wasn't sure how to feel about that. Part of me was relieved that I might finally be able to move on, if not with another woman, at least move on from feeling sad all the time. The other part of me knew that as soon as I started to let her go, she would slip faster and faster from my memory, and one day, she would hardly exist. I wasn't sure if I was okay with that.

As I got dressed, I realized for the first time in a long time, I had missed my night with Iris. I hadn't even thought about sitting out on the porch and waiting for her to wrap her warmth around me. Sarah had asked me to stay and I hadn't even thought twice about it. I sat down on my bed and stared at the floor, not knowing where to go from here. I had to make a decision. I could head over to Sarah's and talk to her about what was going on, or I could stay here and pine over my dead wife.

Going over to Sarah's wouldn't mean that I could have something with her, but it would definitely be a decision to move on from my wife. The problem was I felt something for Sarah. I wasn't sure what exactly, but I knew if I gave myself time it could turn into something more. But I didn't know if she felt the same. She may not be ready to move on with me. So, if I went over there and she didn't feel the same, would I be leaving Iris behind for no reason?

I needed to talk to someone about my issues. It was time to let someone in and not keep everything bottled up so much. I couldn't just leave Sarah, though. I wouldn't push her away just because I was becoming a head case. I picked up my phone and dialed her number.

"Hello?"

"Sarah, I need to reschedule putting the room together. I have something to take care of."

"Oh. Is everything okay?"

"I..." I blew out a breath. I didn't want to lie to her, but I wasn't sure what to say either. "I just need to figure some things out. How about I call you later?"

"Sure. That's fine. I have some other things to do anyway."

That was total bullshit. She wanted the room put together this weekend so she didn't have to worry about being unprepared.

"Give me a few hours and I'll be over there to work on the room." Silence greeted me on the other end. "I...give me some time."

"Okay, Drew. Anything you need."

I ended the call and then tried to decide who would be best to call. Going through my list of friends, I didn't recall anyone that would really understand my predicament, but two names came to mind that I should call. I sent a text to Harper and when I got a response, I headed out to her house.

∼

"Hey. You said you needed to talk?"

Harper stood at the front door, holding Ethan on her hip. She was smiling at me when Jack came up behind her, pulling his son off her hip.

"Hey, little man. You're supposed to be taking your nap. Come on. Let's head to your bedroom."

He walked away with his son in his arms as Harper gestured for me to come in. We headed to the kitchen where she brought out coffee mugs and the fresh coffee she'd made for my visit.

"So, what's this all about?"

"Um, I need to talk to you and Jack about something."

"Okay, well he should be out in a minute. Ethan never takes very long to fall asleep."

I sat uncomfortably for a minute as I tried to figure out what exactly I was going to say to them. Luckily, Jack didn't take too long and I didn't have to stew about it. They both sat and stared at me for a minute, waiting for me to say what I came to say. Deciding that just saying it would be best, I did.

"I'm attracted to Sarah."

Harper had a big grin on her face and Jack quirked an eyebrow at me.

"That's fantastic, Drew. I'm so happy for you!" Harper jumped up from her chair and hugged me.

"Whoa. Relax. It's not like we're getting married."

"So, what's the problem? Is it because she's pregnant?" Jack asked.

"She's not the problem. I am."

Harper was looking at me expectantly. All this time, she never asked what happened in my past. She had always respected my privacy and waited for me to confide in her.

"I was married about eight years ago. Her name was Iris. She was...everything to me. After we were married about a year, she found out she was pregnant and we were so excited, but then we found out not long after that she had cancer."

Understanding lit Jack's face. When Harper had been so sick when she was pregnant, he had mistakenly assumed that her nausea medicine was because she had cancer. He had read something on my face and knew that it had upset me for reasons other than Harper being my friend.

"She died before our two year anniversary and I lost my mind. Like, really lost my mind. I couldn't stand to live there without her, so I left a few weeks after she died. I left her parents behind and ran with a duffel of clothes and the money I had from selling everything we owned. I wandered around the country for five years before finding you. Up until I met you, Harper, I didn't think I would ever be happy again."

"Drew, I'm so sorry," Harper said. She was squeezing Jack's hand as he looked down at their linked hands.

"I didn't like Sarah when she first moved here because she reminded me in some ways of Iris. Maybe a version of Iris. I only thought of her as a friend until recently. Then last night after the party, after we unloaded all the gifts, she asked me if I would stay with her. She was a little wrung out from the party, so I stayed with her. When I woke up this morning, I was....attracted to her."

"Dude, that didn't happen when you slept with Harper, did it?"

Harper slapped Jack across the chest and gave him a scathing look.

"What? It's a valid question."

"No. It didn't. This is the first time since Iris that I've been attracted to any woman. She saw my...attraction."

"Dude, we're not in high school. She saw your erection. Just say it. She saw you had a boner." Jack muttered.

"Fine. She saw I had an erection and I left to go take care of it." Fuck, this was hard to talk about. "The problem is...the whole time I was taking care of it, I was thinking about Sarah."

"Well, yeah. Who else would you be thinking about? You better not ever think of Harper."

"God, you're such a neanderthal. He's upset because he was thinking about Sarah and not Iris."

We sat in silence for a moment as I waited for their reactions. I thought Harper would be the one to have the words of wisdom, but surprisingly, it was Jack that spoke up.

"Look, Drew, I don't know what kind of woman Iris was, but I'm assuming she wouldn't want you to be alone, right?"

"Yeah."

"So, it's been, what, six years? I think she would want you to move on and be happy."

"I know she would. That's not the problem. I can still feel Iris with me. It feels like the more I move on with my life, the less I can feel her. I don't know if I'm ready to lose her yet. The first time was hard enough, but I still have part of her with me. Last night, though, I stayed with Sarah and completely forgot about Iris, and then this morning...So if I make the decision to try to make something with Sarah, I have to give that up. Otherwise, it would be like I was always choosing Iris over Sarah." I stared at them, almost as if they didn't truly get it. "I would have to give up Iris. I would have to let her go." Repeating it just punctuated how sharp the pain was at the thought of losing that. Before I could stop it, tears started to leak down my face and I buried my face in my hands. I quickly got myself under control and wiped the moisture from my face. "So, if I decide to move on, I have to let go the little bit that I still have of my wife."

I looked up at both of them hoping that they had the answers, but neither of them said anything.

"What if I let her go and nothing happens between Sarah and me? I don't know if I could handle that."

Harper, who had been quiet the whole time, finally spoke up.

"Drew, I know you don't want to let Iris go, but what if you miss out on something great with Sarah because you can't let go of your wife? She's gone. I'm not trying to be cruel, but she's not here. She's not coming back, and the longer you live in the past, the more you're giving up on your own future. Whether it's Sarah or not, if you don't let go of Iris, you'll always be alone and Iris wouldn't want that."

"Does Sarah know about Iris?" Jack asked.

"Yeah. I told her a little about Iris."

Harper looked shocked and slightly hurt, probably because I had talked to Sarah about Iris before her, but I couldn't help that she was the first person I opened up to.

"How did she react when you told her about Iris?"

I looked from Harper back to Jack. "She was pretty understanding. She's dealing with something herself, so I think she gets it."

"Does Sarah feel the same toward you?"

"I have no idea. I think she's still wrapped up in the babies' father."

"She's talked to you about him?"

"All I know is that he's dead. She hasn't said anything other than that. I don't know if they were married or if he was a boyfriend."

"All you can do is talk to her. Maybe feel her out and see where she stands, but you have to give yourself the opportunity to move on. Would you really be happy with just your wife's memory for the rest of your life?"

CHAPTER 12

SARAH

I hadn't heard from Drew since he left in a hurry this morning. I'd been so stupid, not even realizing that asking him to stay with me last night could bring up...issues. I'd slept better than I had in a long time and I'd be lying if I said I wasn't attracted to Drew, but that wasn't what last night was about for me. I just didn't want to feel alone anymore. That might have been selfish, especially since I hadn't taken his feelings into consideration. He was still trying to get over the loss of his wife, and I had invited him into my bed in a purely platonic way.

Still, when I saw his tented pants this morning, it was like a slap in the face that he was a man and had needs. Hell, I was a woman, and this pregnancy had left me feeling more unfulfilled than I had in a long time. When he was making breakfast this morning, I couldn't help my eyes wandering over his body. He was a big man, and all his muscles bulged through the sleeves of his t-shirt. I had felt those muscles wrapped around me last night and the weight of his arm around my belly. When I pictured arms wrapped around my swollen belly, it had always been Todd's arms I thought of, but I couldn't say that Drew's arms felt wrong. That was the kicker of the whole thing. I was attracted to a man, and my husband had been gone less than a year. It felt wrong, but right at the same time.

After he stumbled out my door this morning, I tried my best to calm down before he came back over. When he called and said he wasn't coming back, part of me was relieved that I could forget about this morning for a little longer, but the other half was disappointed that I wouldn't see him again. He said he would come back later, but I wasn't so sure about that. He seemed pretty shaken up about what happened in the kitchen. I wondered if he was serious about not sleeping with any other women. He was quite the treat to look at, so I couldn't imagine women not crawling all over him.

I spent the rest of the morning sorting through clothes that people had gotten me. I hadn't gone over my list, but I was pretty sure that most of the items on my list were taken care of. I had never known such generous people. Honestly, even my friends back home wouldn't have given me such a wonderful baby shower. Most of them weren't even interested in having kids yet, so I probably would have been completely alone with my pregnancy.

After the clothes were rid of their tags and I had a laundry basket full to wash, I glanced around the babies' room, not sure where to go from there. I couldn't put stuff away until the furniture was set up. I looked at some of the lighter items and decided to start there. The first box I pulled out was some sort of baby garbage can called a Diaper Genie. I didn't know what the big deal was. Didn't you just throw away diapers in the garbage? Why would they need their own special garbage can?

I tore open the box and was just about to get it all set up when there was a knock at the door. Butterflies appeared in my tummy and my hands shook slightly. All this because of a little morning wood. Ridiculous. I straightened up as best I could and made my way to the front door. Drew had knocked several more times by the time I got there.

"Thank God you answered. I was about to break down the door. I thought something had happened to you."

"No. I was just putting together something and it took me a while to get up."

He stepped through the door and headed back to the babies' room. "I told you I would be back to help you with it. You didn't have to start without me."

"Well, I just opened the garbage can thing."

"The Diaper Genie?"

"Yeah. I'm not really sure why it's so important to have one in the room, but Harper insisted."

"Well, I'd trust her on this one if only because she's been through it."

Drew started ripping apart boxes as I tried to figure out how the liner for the Diaper Genie went in. Apparently, you had to push the liner back through the center hole. When I finally got it in the diaper genie and closed the lid, I looked up to see Drew had unpacked both pack n' plays and had them assembled already.

"Geez. You're really fast. It took me forever to do that." I pointed to the diaper pail that was sitting all alone in the corner of the room.

"Well, I have helped Harper do it once or twice, so I cheated a little."

Drew moved the pack n' plays where I directed and then moved the rocker in place.

"Are you gonna breastfeed the babies?"

"I plan to. Why?"

"How do you do it? Do you feed them both at the same time or one at a time? And what do you do if they're both hungry at the same time, but you only feed one at a time?"

"I have no idea. From what I've read, I should feed them at the same time to get more sleep, but I don't know how all that works. I guess I'll find out in the hospital."

"Doesn't it freak you out? You seem so calm about all of this."

My mood fell slightly. "The idea of doing this alone is daunting, but what choice do I have? I have to remain positive. It's the only way to keep from breaking down. I know it's going to be hard, and I haven't quite figured out yet how I'm going to handle it all. I figure I just need to take it a day at a time."

"Harper said something about getting a nanny so when you go back to work they would still have the same routine. Have you thought about that?"

"Yeah, but I don't have the space in the house for another person."

"What if we built on an addition?"

That made me laugh. "An addition? I doubt that I could afford that, and I don't think there's enough time before the babies are born."

"Well, that's not necessarily true. What if I could get Ryan and Logan to do it at cost for you?"

"Seriously? Drew, I'm not some charity case. They have a company to run. I can't even imagine asking you to do that for me. Besides, they would have to do it quickly and that requires more workers. There's no way they could do it at cost."

"Okay, so what if I paid for it?"

I stared at him for a minute. "Drew, you can't possibly be serious. It's one thing for you to come over here and help me out with stuff around the house. It's another thing to have you pay for the addition to my house. I'll just take them to daycare like other normal parents do."

"That's not going to be any cheaper. Daycare is expensive enough for one child, but you have two, and aren't infants more expensive? You'd be working just to put them in daycare."

"I don't know what I'll do, but I'm not having you pay for an addition for me."

Drew started pacing around the room as I fumed at the idea of him taking care of things for me. I didn't understand where this sudden need to take care of my life came from, but it had to stop. Drew suddenly stopped pacing and turned toward me.

"Let's go to the living room. We need to talk."

Confused by his sudden change in mood, I followed him into the living room and sat down on the couch while he paced for a few more minutes around the living room. Finally, he stopped and turned to me with an expression I couldn't read.

"I've told you about my wife. You know how hard these last six years have been for me, right?" I nodded. "Lately, I haven't been quite so…lonely."

Seriously? He was bringing me into the living room to tell me he was getting laid? I stood up and raised my hand to stop him. I didn't need to hear this, and frankly, it kind of hurt me to hear about it. I mean, I knew I wasn't the most desirable prospect, being pregnant and all, but still, I didn't need him to point it out to me.

"You don't need to tell me this. What you do when you aren't here is your own business and I really don't need to hear about it."

"I need to explain—"

"No, you don't, Drew. It's really not necessary. You're a man. I get it."

"You don't get it. This morning when I was here—"

"Drew, I don't need to hear about you having sex with other women!"

My voice had grown shrill in my attempt to block out what he was about to tell me. No doubt after he left this morning, he called some woman to hook up with so he could take care of his problem.

He stood stunned for a moment before grinning widely at me. "I'm not having sex with other women."

"Drew, I don't need to…wait. What?"

"Sarah, I'm not having sex with other women. I'm not lonely because of you."

"Because of me?" I asked, a little shocked by his admission.

"Being around you has helped take my mind off Iris. I don't think about her as often and I don't feel this giant pressure on my chest anymore. I mean, it's not gone, but most of the time it's not there."

I was glad that I could help him feel more at ease. In fact, over the past few months, he had been doing the same for me.

"Well, that's really good, Drew. I'm happy that you aren't so lonely."

"The thing is, I'm attracted to you, and I want to see where it goes."

I pulled back in confusion. I had never in a million years expected him to say that. I was so sure that he was going to tell me that he'd found someone else and he wouldn't be spending as much time with me anymore. Or that he didn't want me to rely on him when the babies were born. I stood there for a few minutes and stared at the ground. I didn't know what to say to him. Was I ready to move on? I mean, I knew that I couldn't stay alone forever, and Drew was a good man, but I had to be sure.

If I was honest with myself, I found Drew extremely attractive and more than once he had entered my dreams at night. More and more I felt a pull to him that was leaving me more and more confused. I never imagined that Drew could feel the same way, so I was a little thrown and unsure how to feel. Also, I had to consider that I was about to have babies, and I wasn't so sure that now was the time to start something with Drew. Was he really ready to have a ready made family in a couple months? What if I started treating him like a husband and getting upset when he didn't help enough with the twins? No doubt that would happen because this whole situation was going to be stressful enough without adding in a new boyfriend on top of it.

No matter how I spun it, I couldn't see how starting something now would work. Funny enough, Todd was actually not as much of a factor as the impending birth of my twins. I couldn't do it. If we wanted to have a chance at anything, it was going to have to wait a while. The twins had to be my first priority. After what had to be ten minutes of me staring at the floor, Drew stepped toward me.

"Sarah, talk to me."

I looked up at him, his face questioning mine. "I can't, Drew. It's not because of...him. This isn't the time for us. I'm going to have twins in a couple months, and I can't focus on a new thing between us knowing that I won't have time for us soon. It's not fair to you."

"Sarah, we have plenty of time to figure us out. I just want you to know that I want to see what happens with us. The question is, do you want that too?"

"I…" He stepped right in front of me, filling the space between us with his large frame. His hand came up behind my neck and caressed my skin. His breath fanned across my face as he leaned in closer. His lips brushed against mine, whisper soft. The room spun at his closeness and I found myself shifting until I was pressed against him as much as my belly would allow.

"Tell me you want to explore this, Sarah. I can wait. I just need to know you want it too."

"Yes," I whispered breathily.

The word barely left my mouth before his lips were crashing down against mine. His tongue explored my mouth and I greedily accepted all he gave me. For the first time in months I felt alive, felt my body come to life. I hadn't wanted anyone but Todd in so long, and as I kissed Drew and felt his hands on me, it suddenly felt wrong. It felt like Todd had just been buried and I was already kissing another man.

I pulled back from him as pain ripped through my chest. Tears streamed down my face, and I quickly tried to hide the tears from Drew. I liked Drew a lot and I couldn't deny my attraction to him, but Todd…he had been everything to me. He had died to protect me and our child. I hadn't even had our kids and I was moving on. It was wrong. Everything about this was wrong.

Drew pulled me into his arms and held me tight as I tried to pull myself together. This was wrong also. I couldn't keep accepting help from Drew but offer nothing in return. This had to stop.

"Drew, this can't happen. It's too soon. I can't do this."

"Sarah, nothing has to happen right now. We can wait. We can take things slow. I just need to know that you feel this connection too."

"It's not that simple."

"Then explain it to me. I've opened myself up to you. I've told you about Iris. Do you not trust me enough to do the same?"

His voice had taken on a harsh tone that I hadn't heard since the first couple of months that I had known him. The problem was that I completely trusted him, but I wasn't allowed to tell him anything. I didn't know what I could possibly say to him that would explain all that I was feeling without giving away who I truly was. I couldn't explain that Todd had died for me because it wasn't in my background. He would never understand the sacrifice that was given and how much that weighed on me.

"Well, I guess that's my answer."

Drew turned and walked out the door. I wanted to stop him. I wanted to yell for him to give me time, but there was nothing I could say that would appease him. I ran to the window and watched him stomp back over to his house.

Feeling completely depressed, I walked back to my bedroom and laid down on the bed. As my eyes drifted shut, Todd's voice wrapped around me.

"You'll know when you're ready, Sarah."

∽

I CALLED MY CASE AGENT, Sanders, Monday morning. There was one thing Drew brought up that I couldn't ignore. I was going to need someone to take care of the kids when I went to work and putting it off wouldn't be helpful. I needed my money from the sale of all of our belongings, and I needed to find out when that would be put in my account. I was going to need to either send my kids to daycare or hire someone to take care of them at the house. Either way wouldn't be cheap and my job wasn't going to be enough to support us for very long.

"Sarah, is everything okay?"

"Yes, I'm sorry for contacting you. I know it's supposed to be only in an emergency, but I need to know about the funds from the sale of my belongings. I'm going to have twins and I need that money."

"Sure. Hold on a minute while I check your account."

I waited patiently for five minutes while he clacked away on the keyboard on the other end. Finally he came back on, but what he said didn't reassure me.

"Sarah, I'm gonna have to look into this and call you back. It says that the funds were already transferred, so I'm guessing they ended up in the wrong account. Give me the morning to try to sort this out. I'll call you back as soon as I know something."

"Okay. Thank you."

I hung up and got ready for work. My gut was churning, but there was nothing I could do until he called me back, so I went to work. Hank had been teaching me all about the bar and everything that went into managing during the daytime. After the babies were born, I would be taking maternity leave and then coming back as the daytime manager. I was planning to take six weeks off, but I wasn't sure if I could afford that. Everything depended on what Sanders said when he called me back. Plus, there would be hospital bills that I had to consider.

One thing was for sure, the long days at The Pub were starting to wear on me. The Braxton Hicks contractions were coming more frequently, and I was pretty sure that was because I was overdoing it at work. It wasn't like I was lifting heavy things or anything, but I spent a lot of time on my feet, which was evident when I went home with feet that were so swollen they looked like two feet in one.

I had just walked in the door when my phone rang. I was relieved to see that it was Sanders calling me back, hopefully with good news.

"Hello?"

"Hi, Sarah. It's Sanders. I've found out where your money was sent and it's being transferred to your account as we speak. The funds should be available in a few days."

I blew out a breath, relieved that I would be able to provide for my children. "That's fantastic. How much will I be receiving?"

"It's close to 1.5 million."

"Wha—what? That can't be right. We didn't own anything worth that much."

My heart was pounding wildly in my chest at the thought of what that money could do for me.

"Your estate totaled about three hundred thousand, but your husband had two separate life insurance policies. One was through the security firm he worked for and the other was a personal policy."

"But wouldn't the policy through his job only go through if he died on the job?"

"That policy didn't go through, but his boss wanted to be sure that you were provided for. I don't know if you're aware, but one of his bosses was a man he served with. They were very close and he gave the money to you."

I was completely shocked. I hadn't known any of that. I'd never met anyone that Todd worked with, and he had never told me much about his job. Frankly, I hadn't wanted to know because it was like the military all over again, except now the danger was closer to home.

"Is there any way I can get a message to him?"

"I'm afraid not. He's aware of your situation. Not the particulars, but he's a smart man. I'm sure he's figured out what happened after your husband passed away."

"Wow. I don't know what to say. Thank you for taking care of all that for me."

"It's just part of the job, Sarah. How is everything else going? Are you adapting okay?"

"Yeah. That's all fine. I've got a job that will provide for the kids and me, so I guess that's something."

"Are you making friends?"

"Yeah, I've got a few friends. They've been really good to me."

"Are any of them suspicious of anything?"

I thought of Sebastian and hesitated for a moment. I couldn't say anything. It wouldn't matter how trustworthy Sebastian was or if he was in security. They would yank me out of here so fast and change my name. I would lose everything I had gained by coming here, and I couldn't allow that to happen.

"No. I'm sure people wonder about some things, but no one suspects."

"Are you sure? I sense some hesitation."

"I'm sure. I'll let you know if that changes."

"You know we can only keep you safe if no one knows who you are. I don't care how much you trust them. We can't take the chance. I'm not trying to scare you, but Cordano has a hit out on you. Five million dollars. There aren't a lot of people that would pass up that opportunity."

Wasn't trying to scare me, my ass. I knew he was trying to pry something out of me, but I had full faith in Sebastian and I was going with my instincts. "I'm aware of the rules. I promise, I haven't let it slip to anyone."

That was mostly the truth. After all, Sebastian had approached me. I hadn't said a thing to him. I wasn't sure that I had convinced Sanders, but he didn't press any further. He reassured me a few more times that they would keep in contact with any new information, then wished me the best and hung up.

All of that had been a lot to process and I wished more than anything that I could talk to Drew about it, but the way he stormed out of here, I knew he wasn't ready to see me. Besides, I couldn't really tell him anything. There was one person I could talk to, so I pulled out my phone and dialed his number.

CHAPTER 13

SARAH

"Is everything okay? You sounded a little upset on the phone?" Sebastian had agreed to come talk with me and decided that my house would be the best place. He didn't want to meet in the office because everyone would wonder why I was there and start asking questions. He didn't think anyone would recognize me, but he didn't want to take the chance.

"Please, come in." He stepped in and I walked over to the couch where he joined me. "I talked to my case agent today. Todd had a rather large life insurance policy. Actually, two. He had his own and then one through work. His boss knew what happened, and since it wasn't a work-related death, the insurance company didn't pay out, but his boss paid anyway."

I swallowed, now feeling a little ridiculous for calling him over. I wasn't sure what more to say.

"That's good. You'll be able to take care of the kids now without worrying, right?"

"Yeah." It didn't sound convincing coming from my mouth. He was looking at me with a mixture of concern and confusion.

"So, what's the problem? I can tell something is bothering you."

"I don't know. I just...I guess I'm feeling guilty."

He glanced at me questioningly. "What would you have to feel guilty about? Were you cheating on him?"

"No! Never." I blew out a breath and tried to sort through my thoughts. "I don't know how to explain it."

"Why don't you just start talking and we'll see if we can sort it out."

"I guess I'm feeling guilty because Drew and I have become close. He said he wanted to see where things could go between us and I just couldn't. It hasn't been long enough, and I don't think I'm ready to move on."

"Okay. Well, there's nothing wrong with that. Drew will understand."

"He wants to know what's holding me back and I can't explain it to him. There's nothing I can tell him because it isn't in my WitSec profile. He told me all about his wife, and now he thinks that I don't trust him enough to tell him about Todd."

"His wife?"

"Shit. I shouldn't have said that."

"It's fine. Don't worry about it."

"It's just that Todd gave up his life to protect me and our children. I'm just not ready to move on yet. He's only been gone about six months. Even though I'm attracted to Drew, I just can't. I have the twins coming, and that's going to be hard enough without trying to figure out a new relationship. Then I found out that Todd had this huge back up plan in case anything happened to him. He wanted me taken care of, and now I can provide for my kids the way I want to." Emotion clogged my throat and I knew I was on the verge of a breakdown, but I couldn't stop it. "I almost moved on without Todd. I kissed Drew and I liked it. My husband gave everything, and I kissed another man."

The tears were coming fast now and Sebastian rubbed my back, trying to calm me down. When that didn't work, he pulled me into his arms and held me tight.

"Shh. Come on, Sarah. You're putting too much on yourself. Todd wouldn't want you to feel guilty about moving on. Drew's a good guy, and I'm sure Todd would have liked him because he would know that Drew would do everything to take care of you. You can't beat yourself up over this."

"What do I do about Drew now? It's not just that I'm attracted to him. We've become friends and now he's pissed at me. I've ruined everything because I can't tell him what's really going on."

Sebastian looked at me for a moment, studying my face. "I can't tell you what to do about Drew. You know the rules of WitSec. Drew would never give you up to the mafia, I can promise you that, but those rules are in place for your safety and you have to consider your children. I'm not saying that you should never tell him, because that would be a little hypocritical considering that I practically forced you to admit it to me, but you need to be in a good place with him. I will tell you this. Unless you know that you're going to be spending your life with Drew, you can't even consider telling him. If WitSec ever found out, they would force you to choose, stay in the program and relocate, or leave the program and take your chances. The one thing you have going for you right now is that you didn't tell me, I found out on my own. If WitSec ever found out, you could deny one hundred percent that you told me. They would still relocate you, but you wouldn't have broken the rules."

I nodded, wringing my hands together. "I know I can't tell him, I just don't know how I would ever have any kind of relationship with him if I didn't tell him. He's not stupid. He knows that I'm hiding something, and he'll always think that I'm not telling him because I can't trust him. That isn't true, but..." I shrugged. We both knew the predicament I was in.

"For now, focus on your babies. Don't worry about what Todd would think, because I'm pretty sure he would just be happy that you're alive and have a life to live. As for Drew, I think the most you can do is ask him to trust you. Tell him that you can't tell him any more about your past and ask him if that's enough. If not, I guess you have your answer. I wish this could be different for you."

Sebastian pulled me in for a hug and I willingly went into his arms. He was the one person that I could be completely myself with, and this was the first time I had truly opened up to him. I closed my eyes and relaxed against him, relishing in the fact that for once, I could openly talk to someone and share all my feelings.

"Shit."

I looked up at Sebastian to see him staring at the window. I glanced over and saw Drew looking in at us. His face was enraged because I was in another man's arms hours after he asked me to take a chance on him. I stood and ran to the door, flinging it open as he started to walk down the porch steps.

"Drew. Wait!"

He spun around so fast that I took a step back in surprise. He stalked toward me, his eyes menacing as he glared at me. "What? Now you have something to say?"

"Drew, it's not what it looks like."

"Really? Because it looks like hours after I asked you to trust me, you turned around and ran into the arms of my friend."

"There is nothing between Sebastian and me. We're just friends, and we were just talking."

"And when he was over here the day of the barbecue, you were just talking for forty-five minutes?"

"Yes!"

"So, tell me, what is it you can talk to him about, but not me?"

I looked at Sebastian for help, but he did nothing. It was up to me to decide what to do here, and I didn't have a clue. What could I possibly say?

"We were talking about the babies. That's all."

He nodded. "Right. He came over to talk about the babies and you ended up in his arms."

He took another step toward me and I took a step back. I wasn't scared of Drew usually, but right now he looked like he could rip my throat out. His tall, bulky frame was practically looming over me as he spewed his anger at me.

"Tell me. How many of my friends come over here to comfort you, besides me? Is this some kind of sick game where you see how many guys you can use? See how much sympathy you can collect? See how much people will do for you?" I shook my head vigorously as my eyes welled with tears. His voice got quieter and sharper with every word he said. "Because I've been over here helping you. My friends came to help fix up your house for the babies. We had a baby shower to ease the burden. We've welcomed you into our group and tried to support you. I let you into my life," he hissed at me.

"Drew." Sebastian stepped forward, at last intervening. His tone was sharp and cutting. He left no room for argument. I didn't know how much more of this I could take from Drew, and at this point, I wanted it all to end. I had never felt so horrible in all my life. I knew there was nothing I could do about it, but I hated that Drew felt so betrayed. He was right. He had let me into his life and I hadn't given anything in return.

Drew scoffed at Sebastian. "What? You have something to say? Save it. What's the saying? With friends like that, who needs enemies?" He glared at Sebastian before turning and taking off across the lawn to his house for the second time that week.

Sebastian guided me back into the house and over to the couch. "I'll go talk to him. Just stay here and...well, just stay here. I'll see if I can fix this."

I nodded, not knowing what else to say. I dropped my head down into my hands and prayed that Sebastian would be able to fix this.

CHAPTER 14

DREW

I should have known better. I should have fucking known that I couldn't trust her. Everything about her screamed that she was hiding shit. I had gone over there to apologize for not giving her the time she needed. After all, it took me six years to tell anyone about Iris. I hadn't expected to see a truck on her side of the driveway, and I was even more shocked to see Sebastian inside with her, holding her.

It's not like Sebastian and I were close friends. In fact, I only saw him when he was hanging out with everyone else. I hadn't exactly been the most friendly person since I moved to town, and I doubted we would be friends if it weren't for Harper and Jack. I liked everyone well enough. They were a great group of friends, but that had been the furthest thing on my mind when I moved here. Now I could see that I had been stupid. Refusing to talk about Iris and keeping her all to myself hadn't helped me hold on to her. It had only kept me from getting attached to this place. Maybe subconsciously that's what I had been doing. I knew it would be hard to leave Harper, but everyone else would have just been people I met along the way.

A loud banging at the door interrupted my thoughts and I had a pretty good idea of who was on the other side. I flung the door open and glared at Sebastian.

"Calm the fuck down." His tone was icy as he pushed past me into my house. "You were out of line back there. You had no right speaking to her like that."

"What the fuck do you know about it?"

He fisted the front of my shirt and slammed me up against the wall. He was a big fucker. He was easily the same size as me, if not slightly larger. I took a swing at him, but he dodged my fist and took a few shots of his own. I tried to fight back against him, but I only got one hit in before he had me down on the ground on my stomach with my arm torqued behind my back. I was generally a good fighter, but even I knew I was no match for Sebastian. He had been in the military, and though I didn't know a lot about his service, I knew he was a badass. I had heard stories from some of the guys he worked with and the man they described was nothing short of lethal.

"Are you done, shithead?"

I gave up on my struggle and relaxed. He finally released me somewhat hesitantly and stood. I wouldn't have been surprised if he kicked me, but Sebastian let his shear size and death glare intimidate people into thinking twice before taking him on.

I rolled over and stood up, facing the beast that was currently shooting daggers at me. "You've done enough. Leave."

"You don't know what you saw. Just shut up and listen for a minute."

I didn't really want to hear what he had to say, but if letting him spew his garbage expedited his departure, I could deal with it.

"Fine. Talk."

"Sarah was upset and needed someone to talk to. There are things I know that I'm not supposed to know. I told her to call me if she ever needed me. That's all that was. There's nothing going on between us."

"So she trusts you and opens up to you, but won't trust me." I huffed in exasperation. It didn't matter what he said. It came down to trust and she didn't trust me.

"You want to talk about trust? How about we talk about your wife?"

My head snapped to his. "What did you say to me?"

"How long have you lived here, Drew? All of us have given you time to talk to us about what's going on with you, and you don't say a damn thing. You've been here for a year and a half and you hang out with us every week, but you don't say shit to any of us. Ryan and Logan gave you a job when you moved to town, based solely on Harper's word. Jack trusts you with her more than anyone else, and yet you still don't say jack shit."

"How did you find out about my wife?" I roared. He stepped right up to my face and jabbed his finger into my chest accusingly.

"It doesn't matter. I didn't find out from you, so stop your self-righteous bullshit and man up."

I stepped back from him, knowing he was right. It didn't matter what was going on with Sarah. I hadn't been honest with the rest of my friends, yet I was accusing Sarah of being untrustworthy. I had done nothing to earn their trust, yet they treated me as one of them. When I came here, the only thing I said was that I had to leave where I was living and I had been traveling around the country for five years. That could have meant anything. I could have been a murderer and they wouldn't have known. God, I was a jackass.

Not willing to totally bare myself to Sebastian just yet, I gave him what I could at the moment.

"I was married for close to two years when my wife died of cancer. I couldn't deal with it, so I sold everything and left. That's the gist of it."

"But not all there is to it."

"That's all I'm willing to share at the moment."

He nodded, but looked like he wanted to ask more. "What was her name?"

That wasn't at all what I had expected, and I looked at him suspiciously for a second. "Iris."

"Beautiful name." I nodded. He gripped my shoulder and gave a squeeze. "When you're ready, you'll tell us the rest."

We stood there in silence as I tried to decide where to go from here. I was uncomfortable with sharing even that little bit of myself with someone. It had been different with Sarah because I knew she was suffering the same as I was. I didn't know the specifics, but she lost something and it was killing her. It might've had something to do with the fact that she was a girl and I didn't feel like such a pussy for telling her.

"I told Sarah about her, more than I ever told anyone."

He was silent for a moment, and I knew he was trying to figure out what to say without breaking her trust. "There are things she can't tell you."

"What do you mean she can't tell me? If she wanted to, she would."

"She *can't* tell you."

"What the fuck does that mean?"

"Drew, listen to me. I mean really listen to what I'm saying. She. Can't. Tell. You."

I looked at him, trying to decipher what he was saying, but I couldn't think of a single reason that she was not able to tell me about herself. Unless...

"Is she in danger?"

Sebastian weighed the question for a minute, no doubt trying to figure out how to answer the question. "Not at the moment."

"Not at the moment? What the hell does that mean?"

"Like I said, she can't tell you. You're gonna have to either trust her, knowing that you'll probably never know her secrets, or you walk away from her. I'm telling you though, she's a good person that deserves your faith in her."

"How do you know her secrets?"

"Let's just say I came across them unintentionally, and I let her know I knew."

"The day of the barbecue," I surmised.

"Yeah. I wanted her to know that she could talk to me if she needed to."

"So, are you protecting her?"

"No. She doesn't need it, but if a situation comes up, she has my number."

"Can you let me know if she is in trouble?"

"I can't promise that."

I nodded. I figured that was about all I was going to get out of him, so I let it drop. I held out my hand to him and he gripped it with a firm squeeze. "Don't fuck this up."

He walked out the door and back to his truck. When he left, I made my way back over to Sarah's to apologize for being the ass I was.

CHAPTER 15

SARAH

I watched as Sebastian pulled away a half hour later and then heard Drew's footsteps on my porch. I wasn't sure if he was coming in a friendly capacity or to tear into me some more now that Sebastian was gone. The knock on my door seemed to echo all around me. Dread rippled through me, but not because I was physically scared of Drew. I just didn't have any fight left in me. There was nothing more to say to defend myself to him. I wished I had asked Sebastian to stay, but logically I knew he wouldn't have left if he hadn't gotten Drew under control.

The knock came again and I willed my feet to take me closer to the door, but I didn't open it.

"Hello?"

"Sarah," his rough voice came through the door, "can I talk to you for a minute?"

"I don't think that's a good idea. Go away." Damn, I hated that my voice was shaking.

"I just want to apologize. Can I please come in?"

Against my better judgement, I opened the door and stepped back when he started toward me. My whole body was shaking. I wasn't sure why exactly, but I couldn't help my response to him. He was mean to me like he had been in the beginning. But then he was nice. I was terrified of him staying mad at me, but even more terrified that I would lose him completely.

He swore under his breath when he took in my state of distress. Then, he walked forward and placed his hands up in a placating gesture. "I won't hurt you, Sarah. I'm so sorry I scared you."

I nodded several times, trying to make myself believe him. Deep down I knew the kind of man that Drew was, and while his anger scared me, I knew he didn't have it in him to ever lay a hand on me. I walked further into the room and sat down in an armchair after he sat on the couch. When he saw that I was still hesitant to be near him, shame washed over his face.

"I'm so sorry I scared you. That was never my intention. I let my anger get the best of me and said some really shitty things."

"I know. I wish it was different, Drew, but there are things that I can't tell you, not because I don't want to, but because I can't. I need you to accept that and know that if I can share something with you, I will."

He nodded, his head still hanging in shame. "I understand. I don't know what you're running from or why you can't tell me, but I'm here for you regardless."

I wanted so badly to believe that. Drew had become someone I felt I couldn't live without. He wasn't my husband or my lover, but he was my friend, someone that seemed to understand me when I was at my lowest. If I lost him, it would be like losing everything all over again.

"You said you wanted to make something with me. I'm not ready for that. That doesn't mean that I don't want to try eventually, but I'm just not there yet. I need to focus on my babies. The next few months are going to be challenging and I don't want to be worrying about a new relationship. It wouldn't be fair to either of us."

He got up and walked to the window for a few minutes. "I used to be good at this stuff, with Iris, I mean. I never used to be this irritable. I think because she was so full of life, there was never any mystery to her. I never had to figure her out. She always told me what she was thinking." He turned and looked at me and the sadness that was in his eyes the night he told me about Iris was back. "You're the complete opposite of Iris, and I'm not trying to compare you, it's just you're so different and I need to remember that. I know you aren't ready for anything, and you may never want anything with me, especially after the things I said to you. But I can still be your friend. If something more comes eventually, that's great, but if not, I'd be happy to have you as a friend. That is, if you'll accept my apology."

I got up and walked over to him, my nerves having finally settled. I put my hand on his strong forearm and looked up into his handsome face.

"Can we forget about this and move on? I just want to forget this day ever happened. Well, all but this morning."

I blushed as I remembered the steamy kiss he gave me. I hoped I wasn't leading him on. The kiss was great, even if I wasn't ready for more. He leaned down and gave me a sweet kiss on the lips.

"Now that that's settled, I have some things to run past you."

CHAPTER 16

DREW

"Okay. What is it you need help with?"

I would do anything for her right now. After I royally fucked up today, she could ask me to trade houses with her and I would do it in a heartbeat. There wasn't anything I wouldn't give to make her happy right now.

"I thought about what you were saying about me needing to have a plan for when I go back to work. I think you're right. The best thing to do would be to hire a nanny to come stay with me."

"Will you have the money for that?"

"I made some calls and it turns out that I'll have plenty of money to take care of the twins and myself. I could actually take time off if I wanted and stay home with them, but Hank has been training me for this manager's position, and I don't want to lose that. I don't know if another position like that would come around."

"I know you won't accept, but you're welcome to stay with me. I could help you with the babies."

She smiled at me, her face beaming like I had just lit up her world. "You're right. I can't accept. I appreciate the offer, but I need to do this on my own."

"Okay, so what can I do to help?"

"Well, I need to put an addition on the house in case I find a nanny. I can't hold off until I find someone because then there won't be time."

"There's not a lot of time now."

"I know."

"What do you have in mind for the addition?"

"I guess a bedroom and bathroom. I want it spacious enough that whoever takes the position would feel comfortable here."

"Okay, well how about tomorrow you come by and talk to Ryan and Logan. We'll see how fast we can get this going."

"Can it be done before the babies come?"

"It'll be cutting it close, but I think we could do it."

There was an awkward silence because I no longer knew what to say to her. I figured leaving would be the best thing to do. I'd done enough for one day.

"Well, I'll let you get some rest. I'll see you tomorrow."

I hesitated, wanting to kiss her again, but I couldn't mess with the fragile state of our relationship. No matter what we said about moving past today, I couldn't risk doing anything to lose her. She was quickly becoming a part of my life that I couldn't live without. Giving her a smile, I walked out her door.

I headed back to my place feeling a little lighter, but generally still pretty shitty over everything that happened. I couldn't get the words that I spoke to her out of my head. I had never spoken to any woman like that before, especially Iris. If she were here, she would be so disappointed in me. She'd probably kick my ass. I thought back to the most intense fight I ever had with Iris, if you could call it that.

I HAD JUST WALKED in the door after a long day of work, and I immediately took off my dirty clothes and tossed them into the hamper in the laundry room. Well, sort of. They were almost in the hamper, but after the day I'd had, I didn't give a shit if they ended up outside. I took a quick shower, letting the grime of the day pour off me. The bottom of the tub was filled with dirt. I had been on a job when I had to tackle a fellow employee into a mud puddle after some idiot driving a forklift didn't look where he was going. After getting out of the mud, I realized the guy I tackled was the newbie who thought he knew everything. Obviously paying attention to his surroundings wasn't something he thought was necessary.

After my shower, I headed to the kitchen and grabbed a beer from the fridge, tossing the cap on the counter. I drank down the beer and then grabbed another. My feet were killing me, so I went to relax in the recliner with the second beer. I heard Iris come in and called over my shoulder to her.

"Hey, baby. What's for dinner tonight?"

She didn't respond right away, but I didn't really notice because I was watching some show about fishing, something I rarely got a chance to do anymore. After about a half hour, I got up and went in search of Iris. I found her lying down in bed.

"Baby, what's going on?"

"Excuse me?"

"Why are you in bed?"

"Because I'm tired."

"Sooo, are you gonna make dinner or should I order in?"

"Am I gonna make dinner? Seriously, Drew? I just told you that I'm tired and the first thing you ask is if I'm gonna make dinner?"

"Baby, I'm sorry, I—"

"Don't you 'baby' me. Tell me, do I have maid stamped on my forehead?"

Although I should have just said no, instead I walked closer and examined her forehead. "Well, I don't see it, but should we put it there?"

"I am not your fucking maid, Drew. I work too, and my hours are longer than yours. It would be nice if for once I didn't have to clean up your shit and cook all your meals. I swear, sometimes you are completely helpless."

"Hey now, let's not be too harsh. There are other things I'm good for."

I grinned at her, but she just scowled harder. I was still learning this whole marriage thing, and so far I was fucking it up. She grabbed my hand and dragged me through the house. She picked up the towel I left on the ground and stomped over to the bathroom.

"You see this hook here? It's for hanging your towel. Use it." Pulling the shower curtain open, she pointed to the bottom of the tub. "Do you see all that dirt in the bottom? If you would rinse it down the drain, I wouldn't have to scrub it out later when I want to take a shower."

Then she pulled me into the kitchen and grabbed the two bottle caps off the counter. "We also have this handy container called a garbage can where you can throw shit away so that we don't look like we live in a dump."

She threw the caps away and then pulled me over to the sink. "Please tell me why you stack dishes in the sink with food still on them? You can scrape the food into the garbage and then rinse the dishes and put them in the dishwasher. It takes one minute. Instead, I end up having to stick my hands in the dirty sink and scrape out food with my hands. With my hands! It's disgusting. So, you first scrape the food into the garbage and then you rinse the dishes and place them in the dishwasher, that will magically give you clean dishes in the morning."

I rolled my eyes as she dragged me to the back hall where my laundry was laying half in the basket and half on the floor. "Do you see this basket? It's called a laundry basket. The laundry goes IN the basket. Not half in." She picked up the laundry and put it in the basket. "Do you see all the dirt that's all over the floor now? Guess who has to clean that up? Me. That's right. I do it. Almost every day I come home and clean up messes that you've left behind. Then I cook dinner and clean up the kitchen. For once, I would like to come home and not have to clean up after you."

She stomped off to the bedroom and I stood there feeling like a *scolded child. I shaped up after that and tried to always think of ways to make her life easier. I still messed up from time to time, but it was amazing how much better we worked when I thought of the little things that would help her out.*

It's funny because in all the time I was with Iris, I never thought of yelling at her or picking a fight with her. She always told me what she needed from me, and I patiently listened and tried to do what I could for her. I was a patient man back then. Somewhere along the line after she died, I changed. I lost all the good that she saw and brought out of me. I became a grouchy bastard that didn't have tolerance for anyone, except Harper. I still wasn't sure why I had immediately accepted her, but I had.

I wasn't sure if I could ever get back to the man I once was, but I wanted to at least try. I was going to have to or I would never have a chance at winning Sarah's heart.

∽

Sarah stopped by on her lunch hour to talk with Ryan and Logan. I was out at the job site working, so I wasn't part of the meeting, which was fine. I had put my two cents in enough when it came to her life. It was time I stepped back and helped in a different way.

I was just about to leave the job site when Ryan called and asked me to come back to the office when I was done. I was tired and didn't particularly want to, but when the boss asked, you did.

I knocked on his door and walked in when he waved me inside.

"Hey, Drew. Thanks for coming by. I know you're probably tired, so I won't take up too much of your time. Sarah stopped by to go over plans for an addition to her house."

"Yeah, she talked to me about it yesterday."

"Here's the thing, we don't have a crew to work on her addition at this time. We have too many other projects going on. We won't have any crews available until the new year."

Well that sucked, but I wasn't sure why he called me in here. I leaned back against the wall and waited for whatever he was going to say.

"I don't know how close you are with Sarah. I'm not gonna get involved with all that. I have an option for you if you're willing."

"What does this have to do with how close I am with Sarah?"

"We could have some guys do weekends at her house. I know a few guys would love the overtime. It would take a long time to complete, though. There would be issues we would have to work out with making sure supplies are there when needed, but it's doable."

"It sounds like a good option for her."

"The problem is when we get down to the dirtiest part of the job, she'll already have the twins or they won't be far off. I don't want them there when we're doing construction. It's just not safe."

"So, what's your suggestion?"

"How would you feel about her living with you while we do construction?"

"I don't have a problem with it, but I'm not sure how she's gonna feel about it. We had a little bit of a falling out yesterday. Things are fine now, but I have a real good feel for what she's okay with, and I'm not so sure that's going to be one of them."

"Okay, well, talk to her about it and let me know as soon as possible. She mentioned other options, but I told her I would look into this. That's all I have to offer her right now. If she agrees, we'll draw up some plans and start construction within a few weeks."

"Alright. I'll let you know."

I headed home and went straight to Sarah's door. We were going to have to figure this out sooner rather than later if she wanted her house finished this year. I knocked on her door, hoping I wasn't interrupting her evening.

"Hi," she beamed up at me. "What's going on?"

"Can I come in for a minute? I talked to Ryan and we have some things to discuss."

"Okay."

She opened the door further and I followed her back to the kitchen table where she was sitting down to dinner.

"Would you like some? I have extra."

She had made lasagna. It smelled delicious, and if I wasn't mistaken, she also had homemade bread.

"Please. That would be great."

After she made a plate for me, she sat down and we tucked into our dinners. I knew better than to get in the way of her and her food, so I waited until I was finished before bringing up the addition.

"This is delicious. Did you make this from scratch?"

"Yep. I'm pretty proud of myself."

"You've come a long way from when you first moved here."

"Well, when I found out I was going to have a baby, I decided that I was going to have to learn to cook. We...I ate a lot of take out before, and I knew that I couldn't do that when the baby was born. Then I found out I was having twins and I thought, if I don't learn to cook, I'm going to go broke. So I've been practicing a lot, but this is my first attempt at lasagna."

"It's fantastic."

I let her little slip go. She had said *we*, which meant there was someone else she used to live with. Perhaps it was the babies' father. Either way, I had promised I wouldn't push, but that reminded me of something Sean had said to me when she first moved here. I reminded myself to call him later.

"Okay, so what did Ryan say?"

"Well, basically, he won't have any crews to build an addition until the new year."

"Yeah, he told me that."

"There's another option if you're really interested. He can form a crew to work on the weekends. The addition will take longer, but they could have it done in a few months if they got started right away."

"What's the catch?"

"It's not safe for you and the babies to be there during construction. I mean, part of it would be fine, but that's all the initial stuff before the babies are born. Then when they get into tearing down walls and electrical work, that's not a good environment for newborns to be around."

"So I would have to move out for a few months?"

"His suggestion is that you stay with me until construction is done."

"And you're okay with that?"

"Sarah, you know I'm okay with that. I would even switch houses with you for a few months if you didn't feel comfortable staying in the same house with me."

"No. I could never kick you out of your house. That's ridiculous."

"My house has three bedrooms upstairs and a den downstairs. It could be converted into a temporary bedroom while you're staying with me. If you found a nanny, she could stay at the house also so you wouldn't have to wait until construction is over."

"Well, it would be nice to have someone from the early days to get comfortable with the babies while I'm around."

"It's totally up to you. If you aren't comfortable with it, Ryan said he could put you on the books for January or February."

Sarah blew out a breath and her hair flew around her face for a moment. "Let me think about it. I'm supposed to meet with Harper tomorrow to talk about someone she knows that might be looking for a job and a place to stay. After I talk to her, I should have a better idea of what I want to do."

"Alright. I'll let Ryan know." I got up and took my dishes to the sink and rinsed them before putting them in the dishwasher. Old habits and all. "I'm gonna head home. Thanks for dinner."

I was about half way to my house when I pulled out my phone and dialed Sean's number.

"Hello."

"Sean, this is Drew."

"I know. I have caller ID."

I ignored the jab and got to the point. "Remember you told me when Sarah moved here that you had a lead on who she might be?"

There was a pause and I looked at the screen to see if I had lost him. "Yeah. I remember."

"Did you ever find anything out?"

"I did."

"What did you find out?"

"I can't tell you."

"Figures," I huffed. "No one can tell me anything."

"Who exactly are you referring to?"

"Sebastian. He told me the same thing. Is there anyone else that knows about Sarah, but can't tell me anything?"

"I didn't know that Sebastian knew anything about her, but I'm sure he has the same reasons I do."

"Fine. Are you keeping an eye out for whatever it is that you can't tell me?"

"You know I am. Don't worry. If anything comes up and I can tell you, I will. I really don't think it will, though."

"Alright. Later, man."

I was just about to walk in the door when the phone rang. I answered without looking, thinking it was Sean calling me back.

"What'd you forget?"

"Drew! You have to come back here. Now!"

Sarah's voice was panicked and my heart did a stutter step at the fear I heard. I turned and sprinted back to her house, pushing the door open before I could even consider knocking.

"Sarah! Sarah!"

"I'm in the kitchen."

I ran back to her and saw her sitting on her knees on the kitchen chair with a frying pan in her hand.

"What's going on?" I looked around the room, thinking there must be an intruder if she was wielding a frying pan. "Where is he?"

"Under the fridge!"

I started for the fridge and then stopped suddenly. "What?" I looked back at her in confusion. "Sarah, who's under the fridge?"

"The mouse! There was a mouse, and he ran over my foot with his little, tiny feet. It touched me!"

I tried. I really did, but nothing could keep the laughter from breaking free from my throat. Sarah glared at me as I laughed for a good five minutes. I had tears streaming down my face and I was doubled over with stomach pains. I couldn't remember the last time I had laughed like that. It had been years.

"I'm sorry, sweetheart, but I thought something was wrong, and I ran in here expecting you to be on the ground or having to fight off an intruder."

"Something *is* seriously wrong. There's a mouse in my house!"

I laughed again and walked over to her, giving her a big hug.

"Thanks, sweetheart. I needed that."

I picked her up and started toward the living room.

"Drew! Put me down. What are you doing?"

"Well, you didn't look very comfortable on that chair, so I'm taking you to the living room. I'll go back to my place and grab some traps."

She looked at me with a horrified expression. "You're leaving me here? Alone? With that mouse?"

"I'll be gone five minutes."

"I am *not* staying here with that mouse!"

"Well, the traps won't catch him right away. I'm sure he's not going to come out again until you've gone to bed."

"You mean that mouse will be with me all night long?"

"Yeah, but you don't have to worry. He'll probably hang out in dark corners. It's not like he's gonna crawl into bed with you and take a nap."

She shivered, making me think that was not as reassuring as it sounded in my head.

"Do you want to stay at my house tonight?"

"Yes!" She said, stepping off the couch. I had expected some snarky comment, so that was wholly unexpected.

As if she had just remembered that she had a mouse in her house, she got back onto the couch and furrowed her brow.

"I'll grab a bag for you. What do you wear to work?"

"Um...I should have some black pants on my bed and shirt in the closet. Just grab something that matches."

I saluted and started down the hall. "Oh, and some underwear, and you better not laugh at the size. Remember I'm carrying twins."

"I'm well aware, and don't worry. I think your ass is the perfect size."

She narrowed her eyes, but a blush worked its way across her face. "I'll also need my makeup bag. Oh, and face wash. And lotion. It's on the counter by my makeup bag. And..."

"Don't worry. I won't miss a thing."

I turned and headed back for her bedroom, grabbing several clothing options and everything that was in her bathroom. There was no way I was coming back because something wasn't packed. I came out of her bedroom five minutes later with a duffel bag that could have packed a week's worth of clothes for a guy, but only an overnight stay for her. She rolled her eyes at me, but smiled.

"I'll come back and set the traps, and I'll even call an exterminator in the morning to see if they can plug up any holes."

"You're the best, Drew."

She linked her arm with mine as we walked home, then headed straight up to my bedroom where she proceeded to take over my bathroom. I was about to get a good look at what it would be like to live with her if she chose to stay with me while her addition was being built.

CHAPTER 17

SARAH

I thought a lot about Ryan and Drew's suggestions last night. I wasn't any closer to making a decision, but I couldn't deny that it wasn't a bad idea. I didn't want to wait until January to start construction because I wanted someone with the kids right away, to learn what my expectations were and help out from the start. It was going to be hard enough having a new baby on my own, but two was bordering on impossible. Harper and I were getting together today to talk about a potential candidate she had in mind. All she told me was to keep an open mind.

Drew and I had stayed in the same room since his other rooms weren't set up yet. I had to admit, it was nice to stay in his bed. Not only was it extremely comfortable, but having him close was comforting. Nothing happened between us, but I woke up with his erection poking me in the ass. I let him believe I was still asleep because I knew he wouldn't want me to be uncomfortable. Honestly, it was nice to know that he was attracted to me and helped me to reconcile the idea of being with him and my hesitancy because of Todd. There was no doubt that I was attracted to Drew. The wetness between my legs this morning proved that. When my heart and my brain finally caught up with the rest of my body, I knew I would be ready.

Drew had packed a whole array of clothes and bathroom products for me, and I smiled to myself when I saw how neatly he had organized everything. I quickly got ready and headed downstairs for some coffee. I really liked tea, but I doubted Drew was the type of guy to have tea on hand. The smell of bacon and eggs hit me about halfway down the stairs and my nose started twitching at the smell. I practically ran to the kitchen and found a large plate of food waiting for me at the table. I licked my lips as I walked over to the table and sat down.

"So, if I move in here for a few months, can I expect this every morning?" I teased.

"Sure. I'd make you breakfast every morning."

I looked at him expecting to see a lighthearted smile, but he looked totally serious. Okay. That was one point in his favor. I doubted I would be up for cooking too much right after the twins came, and staying here with someone that would willingly cook for me? Major points in his favor. It suddenly hit me that I was way more relaxed about him giving his help this time. For some reason, I had easily accepted his invitation last night when at another time I would have done the whole brave woman that can do it on her own thing. I didn't examine the reasons behind this sudden change too closely.

"Rise and shine, beautiful. I made you breakfast in bed."

"Wow. You're really going all out here, aren't you?"

"Well, I'm trying to impress this woman I'm seeing, so I thought I'd test out some things on you."

I grabbed my pillow and threw it at him. "You ass."

He laughed at me, then pulled me in for a kiss. "You better eat before your food gets cold. Eggs and bacon aren't very appetizing when they're cold."

"I could have gotten up and made my own breakfast. You didn't have to go to all the trouble."

"Usually when someone does something nice for you, you just say thank you."

I grinned at him, blushing slightly. "Thank you, Todd. I appreciate the effort."

"You're welcome. You know, you are so damn stubborn. I'm not sure what I'm going to do with you."

"Well, I guess you'll just have to keep me around for a while and see what happens."

"Yeah, about that. I wanted to ask you something."

He looked nervous as he ran his hand over the back of his neck. Surely, he wasn't breaking up with me. He just made me breakfast in bed.

"I want you to move in with me."

Okay. I was not expecting that. "Todd, I don't think so. You leave for another six months in two weeks. That's not a good idea. What would I do in your space for six months?"

"Well, it wouldn't be my space, it would be ours. Besides, I want you here when I get back. I like knowing that you're here with my stuff. It makes me feel like you're with me."

"And what happens when you don't come home?"

It was one thing to date a military man. It was another to become fully ingrained in his life. Moving here would take me too close to the reality of his world.

"Sarah, I will always do everything I can to come home to you. Please tell me you'll give me this."

After a few days of considering all my options, I gave in and moved to his apartment. It was horribly lonely when he left and I was surrounded by all his stuff. The upside was that I had his shirts to wear to bed. They all smelled like him, and it brought me comfort when I didn't hear from him for weeks at a time.

. . .

"I PUT in a call to an exterminator and they should be out sometime this afternoon."

Drew's voice snapped me out of my thoughts and brought me back to the conversation and my breakfast. I cleared my throat and did my best to cover up the fact that I had just been off in a different world.

"How long do you think it will take before all the mice are gone?"

"I really don't know."

"Well, I'm not going back there until they're gone. There is no way I'm living with mice."

"You do know they're more afraid of you than you are of them, right?"

"I beg to differ. They can hide and never be seen, but they always know where I am. Who do you think has the bigger scare factor?"

"Touché."

"Alright. I have to get to work. Thank you for breakfast."

"Any time."

I got up to take my dishes over to the sink, but Drew stopped me with a hand on my arm.

"I'll take care of it."

"Thanks. I'm meeting with Harper at lunch today, so I may have an answer about the addition by tonight."

"Sounds good. I'll see you tonight."

I ran upstairs really quick and brushed my teeth, then headed out the door. The whole way to work, I couldn't get over how domestic and natural that all felt. I wondered if that's what it would be like to live with Drew all the time, or would we fall into different routines after a while?

Work was hectic as usual, but Hank always made sure I took breaks nowadays.

"Sarah, you have to slow down. The work will get done. That's what delegating is all about."

"I'm not about to slack off and have someone else do my job just because I'm pregnant. I'm perfectly capable of doing things myself."

"Yeah, until the babies come early, and then I'm down a daytime manager sooner than I thought."

It came out all surly and angry, but I knew it was based on concern for me and not whether or not he would be down a manager. He had already told me to take at least three months off after the twins were born.

"First of all, I'm just doing my job. Second, if I felt like it was too much, I would stop."

He grumbled as he walked away about the damn woman needing to know when to slow down. I smiled at his retreating form and went back to work. At noon, I let Hank know I was going out and met Harper at Maggie's down the street. It was a cute little diner that had great food, and Harper's friend, Cece, worked there. Harper was already seated at a table when I got there, so I headed for her booth. There was a woman sitting next to her in the booth and I recognized her as Sean's sister, Cara.

"Hey, Harper. Cara. It's good to see you again."

She looked uncomfortable to say the least, and it didn't go unnoticed that Cara seemed to be shrinking into the wall while Harper appeared to be guarding her from the rest of the restaurant. I had no idea why, but I figured bringing it up would be tacky.

"Sarah, you look really good. I hope Hank's not working you too hard."

I rolled my eyes. "He keeps telling me to sit down and take a break. You would think I was the first woman to have a baby."

"Well, no, but you aren't having one baby. You're having two."

"True, but I wouldn't overdo it. Not when I'm the only one to take care of them."

"Well, that's what I wanted to talk to you about. Cara has been looking to move out of Sean's place and is looking for someplace to stay. Are you still looking for someone to help you out?"

She knew damn well I was and this was the most awkward way of talking about a potential candidate. I didn't think she would bring her with! I nervously glanced between the two, trying to figure out how to proceed.

"Um, well, Cara, do you have experience taking care of babies?"

Her cheeks flushed and she looked down. "This was a bad idea, Harper. You shouldn't have bothered."

She tried to push her way out of the booth. Something more was going on than I knew about.

"Hold on. Why don't you tell me the whole story, because I get the feeling you aren't telling me everything."

Cara leaned back with a sigh and Harper started to fill me in.

"Cara has been living with Sean for about four years now. She was attacked by a serial killer and escaped out of sheer luck. You remember Cole talking about his girlfriend, Alex?" I nodded. "The same man attacked her also. They caught him about nine months ago and Cara wants to take the steps to move out of Sean's place. Sean doesn't want her to go yet because he doesn't think she's ready."

"Are you?" I couldn't help but ask.

"I want to be," she said firmly. "I don't think I'm ready to live on my own, but I could handle living with someone else. I just don't want to live with Sean anymore. I'll never get better if I'm always being babied by my brother."

"Do you think you could handle taking care of twins? I mean, what if you get scared? How would you handle it?"

"Honestly, I don't know. I wish I could tell you that everything would be fine, but I won't know until I try. I love kids, so that's not a problem. I haven't had any issues with being alone at my brother's house, but I'm sure he would insist on installing an alarm system at your house. I mean, he wouldn't expect you to pay for it."

I nodded and thought about it for a minute. I didn't really know anyone else that could help, and I really didn't want to take the babies to daycare. It would be better for them to be in their own home, if possible.

"Well, I'm planning on starting construction on my house as soon as possible. In the meantime, I would be living with Drew. Ryan thinks my house could be completed before Christmas. Would you be comfortable living with Drew and me until the house is ready?"

"Yes."

I looked at Harper, but I couldn't tell what she was thinking. She obviously wanted me to hire Cara, but wasn't going to push.

"Have you thought about a salary?"

"I would do it for free if it meant I could get away from Sean."

I laughed at her honesty. "Well, I would still have to pay you. You won't be a nanny forever and you would want money saved up for when you're ready for something new. Let me think it over and I'll get back to you tomorrow."

Harper and Cara both seemed satisfied with that answer. Cece came up to the table looking quite worn out, her belly protruding just enough to let on that she was pregnant.

"Sorry it took so long. We're slammed today."

Harper looked up at her with a smile. "No problem. We were just chatting anyway."

"So, what can I get for you?"

We all placed our orders before the conversation turned back to pregnancy and the impending birth of children. It seemed babies were in the air right now. I was due in a couple of months, Cece was due in roughly five months, and Harper was just about a month along. I thought about all of us raising our kids together, and for the first time in a long time, I actually let myself consider what it would be like to have a family of friends that my kids would grow up with.

"So, Harper, based on Jack's reaction to your news, I'm guessing this wasn't a planned pregnancy?"

"Definitely not. I wanted Ethan to be at least two before we even thought about having another, but we haven't been the most careful since he was born. I suppose it's all my fault, but if he wasn't mounting me every five minutes, this probably wouldn't have happened."

"Well, all your kids can grow up together now." Cara, who had been quiet, finally joined in the conversation. She looked uncomfortable talking, but I smiled to help put her at ease. I wondered when the last time was she even considered a relationship with a man.

"So, what are your plans for the rest of the day?" I asked them.

"We're going to see Alex. She's still recovering from the attack, but she's doing much better. She and Cole are talking about finally getting married, so Cara and I thought we would bring over some bridal magazines to perk her up."

"How was she injured?"

"We were in the bar at New Year's and she was attacked and beaten with alcohol bottles. She suffered a traumatic brain injury and it's taken all this time for her to recover," Harper said.

"Oh my gosh. That's terrible." I looked over at Cara who had tears in her eyes. "Was this the same guy that attacked you?"

"No. He was killed a few months before that. This guy was a fan of his. He was upset with Alex for taking away his mentor."

I put a hand over my mouth as I digested all that was said. As horrible as it was to run from the mafia, I couldn't imagine a serial killer being after me either. Cece arrived with our orders, breaking the tension in the room. She had four plates with her and waved me over so she could sit with us. I slid over and she tiredly sat down.

"My feet are killing me. This is my first break since this morning. We've been slammed all day."

"Why's that?" Harper asked as she took a bite of her sandwich.

"Some convention in town."

"You know, Logan would be fine with you quitting your job," Harper said pointedly, but Cece just waved her off.

"There's no way I could sit at home right now. What would I do all day? When this little one comes, I'll gladly stay home."

"How did you meet Logan?" I asked.

She smiled, but her smile dimmed some. "I knew him from a long time ago. Long story short, he broke my heart ten years ago and when I saw him again, I took my revenge on him and almost destroyed his business. I lost my career and my reputation trying to fix it, but he forgave me. Now the only place I can get a job is as a waitress in a diner."

I started laughing, thinking this was some crazy joke, but when she didn't laugh along I stared in shock. "You're serious?" She nodded. "That's...the craziest and probably the most romantic story I've ever heard."

"It's romantic that I almost ruined his life?"

"It's romantic because you were reunited after all those years and despite some unwise decisions, you still found your way back to one another."

She considered that for a moment. "I guess I never thought of it that way. I guess it is kind of romantic. Crazy, but yes, it is kind of romantic." A smile lit her face as she rubbed her belly.

I finished up my food and headed back to The Pub. I still had a long day ahead of me, and I had one more call that I needed to make before I headed home for the night. When Sean stopped by, I took my afternoon break and took him back to my office.

"Thanks for coming, Sean."

"No problem. What can I do for you?"

"I met with your sister and Harper today for lunch."

A shocked look crossed his face. "Wow. She hasn't gone anywhere in a long time. How did she do?"

"I could tell she was uncomfortable, but she didn't break down or anything, if that's what you're asking."

"I noticed at your party that she seemed pretty okay with you. I was shocked because she hasn't really connected with anyone since she..."

"Since she escaped?"

"Yeah."

"Did you know she's considering moving out of your house?"

"What? Where would she go? How would she provide for herself?"

"Harper seemed to think that moving in with me would be a good idea."

"With you? Why's that?"

"I need someone to watch my kids when I go back to work. They seem to think this would be a good solution for her. It would give her some independence, but she would still be with someone. The reason I called you is because I need to put my kids first. I need to know if she's had any episodes or anything that would put my kids at risk."

He leaned back in his chair with a heavy sigh, running his hand across his face. "I don't know if it would be a good idea or not. Honestly, I'm not with her very often. She's pushed everyone away, including me. Mostly, we fight when we're around each other. She's never had any violent reactions toward anyone, just anger in general at what happened. She used to have nightmares a lot, but those pretty much went away when the guy was caught. It probably would be good for her, but I'm not going to ask you to take that chance with your kids."

"We would be living with Drew for a few months while an addition is being built onto my house. Do you think she would be okay with that?"

"She doesn't really know Drew. He's been around us for a while, but she doesn't exactly let people come over to visit her. I guess the only thing I could suggest is do a trial run with her. Maybe ask her to move in with you and Drew before the babies are born. She could do the cooking and cleaning and see how she handles it."

"That's a good idea. From the time I've spent with her, I like her."

"Two lost souls."

My back stiffened. "Excuse me?"

"I'm pretty sure I know your secret, but given the circumstances, I'm not going to ask you about it. I just want to know that if those demons come hunting you, you call me for help."

That shocked me. I thought for sure he was going to tell me to get the hell away from his sister. I was speechless, so I nodded. There were now two people in this town that knew who I was, or were at least pretty sure. That didn't bode well for me staying under the radar. The itch to run gnawed at me now. I didn't know how much more I could do to keep my identity a secret. Staying here was becoming dangerous.

"I see those wheels turning in your head. Don't run. I promise you, you're safe here. I only know because I happened to be following the story. I ran your picture through a facial recognition program and changed a few details. Don't worry. I did it on my home computer and then erased the file."

I nodded jerkily, but couldn't stop the anxiety creeping over my body. After blowing out a deep breath, I stood and walked around my desk.

"Thank you for stopping by, Sean. I need to get back to work."

"Sarah, you've made a life here. Don't run."

It was nothing but a platitude. It was easy enough for him to tell me not to run, but it wasn't his life at risk. It wasn't his kids.

"If you recognized me that easily, so could anyone else."

"True, but not everyone is a suspicious bastard like I am."

"Sebastian is too. That's two people that know. How can you tell me that's safe?"

"If Sebastian knows, you can bet he's keeping an eye on all movements from New York. I've been keeping an eye out also. If someone heads this way, you'll be the first to know, and there is no way we would let anyone hurt you."

Two men now knew who I was. Two men that vowed to look after me and my kids to make sure we were safe. Neither was the man that I wished more than anything knew about me. Still, these were good men and I trusted them with my life. I'm not sure why, but they just gave me a sense of peace and hope.

"I'll stay for now, but if anyone else finds out, I'll have to leave. You have to understand, it's not just me I have to consider."

"Alright, darlin'. I'll see you later. Let me know what you decide about Cara."

"I will."

WALKING into Drew's house that night, I was greeted by the aroma of pizza. Not just any pizza either. This was the pizza from the local pizza joint, Tony's Pizza. It was by far the best pizza I had ever tried, and even though I was exhausted and wanted to lie down, nothing could keep me from the mouthwatering goodness that awaited me in the kitchen.

Drew was getting plates and napkins out when I walked into the kitchen and sat down at the table. He smiled at me and shoved the pizza box toward me.

"Dig in. I figured tonight was a good pizza night. I had a long day and didn't feel like cooking."

"Ugh, I'm so glad because we would have ended up eating cereal."

"The exterminator said you should be good in a day or two."

"About that. I met with Harper today. She cornered me at Maggie's with Cara."

"What do you mean?"

"I mean, she showed up to our little get together with Cara and then suggested that Cara move in with me and take care of the twins," I said around a bite of pizza.

"What do you think?"

"Well, I talked to Sean and he said that he thought it would be good for her. He doesn't think that she would have any issues, but he didn't want to say she would be fine either. He suggested she move in here with us while the addition is being put on my house. I mean... not move in with us...this is your house. I just meant—"

"Relax. I know what you meant, but you're right. She would be living with us. It's fine with me. If you want to give her a chance and see how she does, then go ahead and tell her to move in. I don't have a room set up, so she would have to get a bedroom set, but she can take any room she wants."

"I think that would probably be best. I need someone, and I can't put it off too much longer. Besides, if I can help her out, then I want to."

"What about you? Where would you sleep?"

He didn't look at me as he spoke, and I got the feeling he wanted me to stay with him, but I didn't think that would be a good idea.

"I think it would be best for me to stay in one of the guest rooms. I could probably get a blow up mattress or something. There's no point in buying a bed for a few months."

"Are you kidding me? How would you get off the floor?"

"Are you saying I'm fat?"

"No. I'm saying that it would be low to the ground and difficult for a pregnant woman to get up from there. Besides, that wouldn't be comfortable, and it doesn't make sense to lose sleep so close to having the babies."

"I guess you're right."

"Besides, we can just move your bed over. It's not big deal."

"Okay."

"So, does that mean you're moving in here temporarily?"

"Yeah. I guess so. I need to call Ryan and set up a time to go over plans."

"Let me know what you need from me and I'll make sure it happens."

Two weeks later, Cara and I both moved into Drew's house and construction started on my house. Now I just had to see if I could live with Drew and not give in to temptation.

CHAPTER 18

DREW

One month until the twins' birth...

"SARAH, you need to slow down. If you keep going like this, you're going to have the twins early. The doctor already told you this."

"Drew, I'm fine. It's just Braxton Hicks contractions. I've been having them for months."

I turned to Cara, hoping she could get through to her. "Cara, talk some sense into her."

I walked away from Sarah as she laid on the couch with feet the size of melons propped up on pillows. Her feet were constantly swollen nowadays and her back was always hurting. I got her a bunch of pillows to put on her bed to help her sleep at night because she wouldn't take me up on my offer to stay in my room. When I moved her mattress into my house, I realized how bad it really was. Maybe it was fine for a regular person, but a pregnant person needed to be sleeping on something really comfortable. That's why I went behind her back and ordered her a new mattress. By the time it was delivered, it was too late to do anything about it.

Cara had been going with Sarah to her appointments because she thought it would help her prepare for the twins' arrival. I wanted to be there, but I wasn't the father, so I couldn't in good conscience ask for the time off. I did, however, ask Ryan for two weeks off when the babies were born.

"The doctor has told her every week that she's doing too much, but if she won't listen to the doctor, what makes you think she'll listen to me?"

"All the doctor said was that I should slow down, not that I needed to quit working. She hasn't restricted anything so far, so I'm not sure what you guys are complaining about."

I walked back over to her, trying really hard not to yell at her. The damn woman had always been stubborn, but right now was the absolute worst she had ever been.

"When you come home and look like your feet need to be drained of about a gallon of water, it's time to listen to your doctor."

"Drew, this is not in any way your decision. You are not the babies' father, so stay out of it."

I knew that she was tired and stressed. I knew that's why she said that, but I couldn't help how much that hurt. I had come to care about Sarah so much over the past few months and it seemed like after she moved in, she pushed me farther away. Where it was difficult to help before, now it was near impossible. If I made dinner, she scowled at me. If I offered to help her with laundry, she told me she could handle it on her own. I wasn't sure what had caused her to need such a high level of independence, but the tension between us was growing every day and something needed to give.

It was getting on the end of September and the sun was setting sooner every day. The days were chillier and I couldn't spend as much time outside when Sarah was in a mood. It wasn't that I didn't want to be by her, but it seemed to diffuse the tension if I just stepped outside.

I sat down in my lounger and watched the sunset like I did most nights. However, as the days passed, I felt Iris less and less. Sarah was helping me to move on even though she wasn't yet ready to do that herself. I couldn't help but feel a little sad that Iris wasn't around as much. I knew it would happen when I decided to move forward with my life, but accepting that it would happen and having it actually happen were two different things.

I closed my eyes and thought back to a month before my sweet Iris passed away.

"D<small>REW</small>, *we need to talk about what's going to happen from here on out.*"

"*No, we don't because you are going to continue to fight and you're going to beat this.*"

"*Babe, please. You heard what the doctor said. They don't think there's anything more they can do for me. They caught it too late. We need to prepare.*"

"*No. I will never prepare to let you go. It's not happening.*"

"*Drew.*" *It was a quiet plea that I barely heard from her beautiful lips.* "*I need to prepare. There are things I need to say to you.*"

Tears filled my eyes as I looked away. I didn't want to do this, no matter how much she said she needed it. "*Please, don't do this. I can't handle it. Not now.*"

"*If not now, then when?*"

I sat down on the bed beside her. She had taken to spending most of her days in bed. There were times that she could still get up and move around, but it was difficult for her because she was losing her motor function. The tumor in her brain was taking over and making life hell for her. I took her frail hand in mine and tried my best to be strong for my girl.

"*I'm listening.*"

"*I love you more than anything, and I want you to know that even though our time together was short, it was the best time of my life. I* wouldn't trade one minute with you for a long life without you. You've brought me so much happiness and made my life so full."

There was no keeping back my tears when she poured her heart out to me. I wanted so badly to be strong for her, but I couldn't. This woman always had the power to break me. I just hadn't expected it to happen this way. I thought I would screw up and she would leave. I never thought she would leave and no longer exist in this world.

"I want you to promise me that when you're ready, you'll find happiness again and hold onto it. Life is a gift, and I don't want you to waste it being sad over me. We had our time together, but soon you'll need to move on from me and find someone new to share your life with. Promise me you'll do that."

"I can't do that. I can't promise to forget you."

"You don't have to forget me, Drew. I'll always be with you, and when you're ready to move on, I'll still be with you in whatever way you need me. Someday, you'll want to live again. We haven't been doing that lately, and I want that for you so much. One day it won't hurt so much, you won't think of me so much, and you'll be ready."

I wiped the tears from my eyes as the bravest woman I knew asked me to move on without her, to find someone else to love. I promised her that day that I would move on, but I knew in my heart that it would be nearly impossible to live without her. How did you live without your other half? How did you make the decision to keep moving when it seemed impossible?

Another month passed and I knew the days were drawing to a close when she could no longer talk to me. She was basically in a vegetative state. A few days before, her vision had gone and I think that was the point that her body finally started to really give out. Today, I sat by her side and begged to hear her sweet voice one more time.

"Please, baby. I need to hear your voice. Don't leave me like this. Please fight."

I could barely hold my head up as I sat by her side and prayed night and day for God to let me keep her just a little while longer. It shocked the hell out of me when my wish was granted. My head snapped up and energy that I didn't think I had bloomed from within. She was back.

"I'm forever yours, Drew. Nothing can take me from you."

That was the moment I broke. Her voice had been so crystal clear, but that was all she said before she slipped into a coma. Though I hoped it was a sign she was coming back, I knew deep in my heart that she was gone. I laid down on the bed beside her and held her in my arms, needing to have her scent surrounding me one last time.

THE DOOR to the porch slid open and I quickly wiped away the tears, grateful that it was dark outside. I knew it was Cara by the way she walked. Sarah walked with a sort of hobble now that she was so big.

"You have to give her some space. You'll only push her away if you keep treating her like a child."

"I'm not treating her like a child. I'm trying to take care of her."

"Take it from someone whose older brother perfected the art of overprotection. If you keep trying to tell her what to do, she's only going to resent you. Right now, she needs to feel like she's in control. I don't know what happened to the father, but with all this responsibility bearing down on her, she has to do things her way."

"And who's going to tell her when she's overdoing it? She's so stubborn, she doesn't even realize that she's wearing herself out unnecessarily."

Cara came to sit down beside me on one of the loungers. She stared off into the distance as she spoke softly.

"I used to work as a nurse at the hospital. I always worked the night shift because I was the low man on the totem pole. My shift ended early that night because we were slow and I was going to end up with overtime. I stopped at the gas station because I was almost on empty, and I didn't want to forget before my next shift. I was always running late and I knew that I couldn't put it off."

I listened to Cara with rapt attention. Part of me wanted to know what happened to her. It would help me understand her and what might upset her, but the other part of me didn't know if I could stomach her story.

"I don't remember much from being at the gas station. I just remember starting the pump and the next thing I remember is waking up in a cellar or something. He came to see me every day for ten days. The first day was probably the worst in terms of fear factor. He had a large knife and..."

She swallowed thickly as she tried to finish her story. I closed my eyes as dread spread through my body. I didn't think I wanted to hear anymore, but I had to let her talk about it if it would help.

"He cut my clothes from my body and slid the knife all over me. Sometimes he cut me, but other times, he just wanted me to think he would. He taunted me, telling me he was going to send pictures to my family."

"Did he...did he rape you?"

"No. Thank God. I don't think I would have made it out of there if he had. He didn't do it for sexual reasons. He got off on the torture. After I had been there for a few days, he started to leave his mark on me. He carved the word whore across my breasts. It's still there. It's faint, but I still see it. I'll always have that reminder."

She turned and looked at me with a blank expression. It was as if she wasn't even there as she told me about her ordeal. "He did other things too, but luckily, on the tenth day after he left, I screamed and screamed, and someone heard me. A farmer was checking his field by the house I was in. He heard me and came searching for me. I was so relieved that I wasn't even ashamed of the fact that I didn't have clothes on.

"I was in the hospital for a few days and then I stayed at Sean's house. He took care of me and was wonderful with me, but after a while I needed space. Not my own space, but space to deal with what happened. There were so many days that I just sat there and stared at the wall, trying to process what had happened.

"People started coming over to check on me, and I got so annoyed because they all thought that their words of wisdom would somehow help me. *Try not to think about it, Give it some time, Don't let that man steal another minute of your life.*" She laughed wryly as she continued. "They all had the best of intentions, but what I needed was to be left alone. Sean's friends tried to get me out of the house, and my girlfriends all wanted to come over to paint our nails and gossip about the men at the hospital. None of that mattered anymore, and it angered me that pretending it didn't happen would help me. No one ever asked if I needed to talk about it. If I tried, I was told that I didn't need to relive it. Eventually, I just started getting angry when people came over. The more they tried, the more I pushed them away. Soon, no one came to see me, and I found that I resented that even more. It was like people gave up on me."

She turned to me with sad eyes. "The thing is, as much as I didn't want people there trying to make it all better for me, it hurt even more that they gave up on me. I didn't know what I needed, and that was part of the problem. I just needed someone to be there no matter what and be okay with it. I think that's what Sarah needs. She has to work through this on her own, but that doesn't mean that she doesn't want you around. Just give her space to figure it all out."

That was the problem. I didn't know if I could back off. I hadn't been able to control what happened with Iris and keep her safe, but I could help Sarah. I could keep her from pushing herself to the point of exhaustion. I could protect her, but I took Cara's advice.

"I'll do my best."

Two weeks until the twins' birth

I kept my promise to Cara and backed off. I watched Sarah closely and did everything I could to help her out without her realizing it. I talked to Hank and told him that she was pushing herself too hard. He knew she was also and gave her a job going over records and doing an analysis of the business over the years. It ensured that she had to delegate more at the bar and do less herself.

Cara had been doing a lot of the housework, laundry, and cooking, so that took some of the weight off my shoulders. I had to admit, I thought Cara would do an excellent job helping Sarah out. I didn't know how she was around kids, but so far, she was great around the house. Besides, she would have three months with the twins before she was on her own during the day.

Sarah's bag had been packed for a week now and was sitting by the front door. Every time she came downstairs, I had the sudden urge to ask if it was time. I knew that was silly, but it was so close to her due date, and I was one of those typical guys that freaked out because I wasn't sure what to expect. Unlike fathers, I was just the roommate. I didn't go along to the appointments, so I wasn't able to ask questions. I had googled some information, but everyone knows the more you google, the more you freak yourself out, which was exactly what happened.

After hounding Sarah and Cara with things I had seen on the internet, Cara calmly told me to chill out before she punched me in the nuts. Yeah, there was something about this group of women. Sarah just rolled her eyes and walked away.

I'd just gotten home from work and it was the weekend. Work had been a killer lately as we worked longer hours to complete some projects that were running behind schedule. I usually didn't mind the extra hours, but I was anxious for the babies' arrival. Then again, Ryan had already promised me some time off when the babies were born, so I wouldn't complain about a little overtime.

After shucking my dirty work clothes and taking a shower, I headed downstairs for some food. When I got to the kitchen, Sarah was already devouring her meal. Cara was watching her inhale her food as she slowly ate her own.

"Long day?" Cara was watching me watch Sarah with a twinkle in her eye. She had seen over the past weeks how my attentions were always trained on Sarah. It had become one of her favorite things to tease me about when Sarah wasn't around. I stepped into the kitchen and walked over to the stove.

"Yeah. We're trying to finish up a project and we're a little behind schedule. There were some problems with the materials, so now we're playing catch up."

I scooped the stir fry onto my plate and sat down at the table with the girls. "How's work going, Sarah?"

"Good. I think I might have to stop at the end of the week."

She said it so matter of fact, like we hadn't all been ragging on her to slow down for the past two weeks.

"Oh yeah? Why's that?" I tried to seem indifferent, but knew I didn't succeed when she stopped eating and glared at me.

"You've been trying to get me to stop working for weeks now, so don't pretend like you don't know that I'm worn out."

Geez, it was like a landmine around here. Be nice, boom! Show concern, boom! Avoid pissing her off, boom! There was no winning, so I kept my mouth shut. I was pretty used to doing that nowadays. Crap. I never had to deal with this emotional rollercoaster with Iris. She was always in such a good mood and rarely...

"Fuck."

I stood so fast that my chair tipped over in my haste to get away from the table. I ignored the girls' strange looks as I stalked over to the patio and slid the door open. I slammed the door closed and walked over to the railing, trying to rein in my temper. I clenched my fists and gnashed my teeth together as the fury bubbled up in my gut.

How could I have let this happen? How could I forget? The tears started coming, but it was for a different reason this time. It wasn't that I missed Iris so much that I couldn't pull myself together, it was because I had forgotten her. I was so wrapped up in my new life that I actually forgot the one person that I hoped to never be apart from.

Letting my anger get the best of me, I grabbed the patio table and flipped it over as I let out a roar. I didn't stop there. I picked up the chairs and flung them across the deck. Every chair that bounced off the deck was proof of the man I was turning into, a man that Iris would never have recognized or wanted. I bent over and grabbed fistfuls of my hair, letting out an agonized moan. In that moment, it was like she had just died and I had let her down again. I hadn't been able to save her, and now I had forgotten her. I slumped to my knees as the pain and anger took over.

"Drew? Are you okay?"

It was three days ago. Three fucking days was how long it took me to remember. What kind of asshole husband did that make me?

"I'm sorry that I've been so...prickly lately. I swear, I'm not trying to push you away, but I feel like I need to do this alone, and the more help I get, the more it feels like I need to rely on others."

The words were flying out of her mouth so fast that I could barely understand her. She continued to blather on about her issues and how she was feeling. All the while I wanted to scream at her that for once, something wasn't about her. That wasn't fair to her, but at the moment, I could barely contain my rage. When five minutes passed of her ranting and raving, I finally lost my shit and yelled at her.

"This isn't fucking about you!"

Shock crossed her face, and I expected her to turn around and run back inside. I had promised to never speak to her like that again and shame instantly welled up inside me. I was an asshole. Instead, she walked toward me and knelt down, wrapping her arms around me and holding me tight. Well, as tight as a woman who was pregnant with twins could. Her belly took up so much space between us that I had a hard time holding her the way I wanted to.

Her touch soothed me and calmed the fire raging inside me. I hadn't realized how much I needed this from her until right this minute. I didn't care if she wasn't ready or wanted me to wait another ten years. Right now, I just needed someone to tell me that it was okay that I forgot, that I wasn't a total asshole.

I wrapped my arms around her, pulling her in close to steal all the comfort I could from her. My chest ached so badly from everything going on in my life. I couldn't keep up anymore, and I'd left behind a piece of me that I could never get back. Tears slipped down my cheeks as Sarah silently held me and rubbed my back.

"I forgot about Iris. The anniversary of her death was three days ago and I forgot. For three days I forgot and hadn't even thought about her. I hadn't remembered the worst day of my life. I can't even feel her anymore."

She didn't say anything. She didn't try to make me feel better or tell me I was a jerk. She just held me tightly to her. After what seemed like forever, she finally spoke.

"I worry about that, too. I think that's why it's so hard for me to move on. I worry that I'll forget him. He was a great man and he deserves to be talked about all the time, and I can't. I won't even be able to tell his kids what a great man he was. They can never know."

I didn't know what she was saying exactly, but I imagined it had something to do with not being able to tell me things. What could she have possibly gotten herself into that she couldn't even talk about the father of her kids? I couldn't ask her. I promised her that I wouldn't ask questions that she couldn't answer.

"How long has Iris been gone?"

"Seven years."

It seemed like a lifetime now. She pulled back and looked up at me.

"I think that's why you've always felt her. She knew that you would need her, but now that you're settling down, she knows that you're ready to move on. She wouldn't want you to mourn her all the time or even feel depressed on the anniversary of her death. She would want you to feel happy that you had the time you did with her. She would want you to celebrate her life." She bowed her head and stood up. "At least, that's what I would want. I'm sorry. It wasn't my place to say anything."

"Thank you," I said, quickly snatching her hand. "That helps."

"Really?"

"I think you're right. I should be celebrating my time with her instead of getting drunk every year on the day she died. She would be so ashamed of me if she saw me today. I used to be a different man. I was happy and I wasn't such an asshole."

"You're still a good man, but life has changed you, and that's okay. It would probably be more depressing if you went on as if she never existed."

I stared out at the dark sky, hating that I missed my night with her. She was slipping away so fast now, and I had nothing to remember her by. "I don't have anything left of her. I gave everything to her parents, and the only thing I kept was her wedding ring. I don't even have a picture," I said quietly.

She squeezed my hand and sat with me for a few more minutes. Finally, I got up, hating that Sarah was on her knees in her condition. I helped her back inside where I excused myself for the rest of the night. I was going to have to put my ghosts to sleep and be the man that Iris knew me as.

CHAPTER 19

SARAH

Drew was a good man and there was so much that he had done for me that I wanted to do something special for him. It took a little work on my part, some begging for Sebastian's help, but I finally got what I needed— Iris's parents' phone number. Now I just had to work up the courage to make the call. I needed to make sure they knew I was only his friend. It wouldn't help them any to think he had moved on from their daughter. Finally, I pressed send and waited for someone to answer.

"Ward residence."

"Hello, my name is Sarah. I'm calling for Olivia Ward."

"This is she. How may I help you?"

"I'm a friend of Drew's."

There was a silence on the other end and when she didn't say anything, I pushed forward.

"I'm calling because I think Drew really needs you right now. He's struggling with guilt over moving on from your daughter, and I think he could use your help."

"Moving on with you?"

"No." Well, it was mostly true. We hadn't moved on together, even if he had suggested we do so. "He forgot this year."

"What do you mean he forgot?"

There was no judgement in her tone, just genuine curiosity.

"He forgot the day she died, and he's really beating himself up over it."

"Oh dear. I expected that he would have moved on years ago. It's been seven years."

"I know, and I'm very sorry for your loss."

"Dear, there is no need to be sorry. Iris was a shining star, and she would yell at anyone who mourned her seven years later. Is that what he's been doing all this time? He left so quickly after she died, we just assumed that he would start a new life somewhere else."

"It's my understanding that he moved around for about five years and only settled here about a year and a half ago. I've known him for just about six months. He told me he doesn't have any pictures of her. I thought...I thought that maybe you and your husband could call or even visit. I think it would help him."

"Of course. We never stopped thinking of Drew, but we assumed that he didn't want to see us. He loved Iris so much and her illness was very hard on him."

"When do you think you could come? I could have a room made up for you. I'm his next door neighbor, but I'm living with him while I'm having work done on my house."

"Oh. I see."

"No. I mean that I'm pregnant with twins, and I'm having work done so that I can have a nanny stay with the twins while I'm at work, but they're due any day now and Drew offered to let me stay with him so that the twins weren't exposed to all the construction. The nanny is currently living here too."

I was babbling and I wished I could get myself to shut up.

"Dear, it's fine. Even if you were with him, it would be fine. We didn't expect Drew to stay a widower forever."

"Okay. Well, anyway. Let me know when you can come and I'll

make all the arrangements. Why don't you give me your email address and I'll send you his address and my contact information."

We finished up a few minutes later and I hung up feeling better about the whole thing. Hopefully, Drew would be happy as well.

~

I WAS NERVOUS. No. Nervous didn't even describe what I was feeling right now. Gut churning, heart pounding, upset stomach, extreme sweating. I couldn't hide what I was feeling if I tried. Drew had already noticed and the concern was written all over his face. Today was the day. His in-laws would be here in less than an hour and I still hadn't told him they were coming. In my mind, it would go better if he didn't have time to think about it.

He was still beating himself up over forgetting about Iris, so I really hoped this visit put everything into perspective for him. I continued to pace around the house, finding little things I could do to make their stay more comfortable. I had set up my room for them to use, and I planned to stay with Drew over the next couple of nights. If he was upset and didn't want me to stay with him, Cara would let me sleep in her bed. She had a king bed, so it shouldn't be a problem. Then I thought of something else, what if Drew didn't want me staying with him because he didn't want his in-laws to get the wrong picture? Good Lord, I was an idiot.

I smacked myself in the head as I paced around the living room and grunted in frustration. Drew, who had been watching me pace from his perch on the couch, jumped up.

"Wha-what's wrong? Is it time?"

"No. Everything's fine. I promise. It's not time."

"Then what the hell is wrong? You look like you're on the verge of a panic attack."

Time to come clean. "Drew, I did something that you may not like. In hindsight, it may not have been the smartest thing, and I know I should have talked to you about it first, but I just couldn't stand to see you so upset last week and I wanted to do something to make it better. I'm so sorry—"

"Just tell me what you did."

"I—"

I didn't get to finish my thought because the doorbell rang, cutting through the air like a sharp knife. I closed my eyes and took a deep breath before heading to the front door. Drew beat me to it and flung open the door. I was behind him and couldn't tell what his reaction was to the couple standing before him. I could see Olivia standing there with tears in her eyes and Jonathan, her husband, holding her hand and looking kindly at Drew. I was so afraid that Drew was going to turn around and yell at me, but instead he stepped forward and took Olivia in his arms, giving her a big hug. When he stepped back, he held out his hand for Jonathan to take. Feeling like an intruder on this reunion, I backed out of the living room and headed for the kitchen, but was stopped by Drew.

His arms came around me from behind and wrapped around my large belly. He kissed the side of my head, then whispered in my ear.

"Thank you, Sarah."

Then he was gone. I didn't stick around for introductions. I assumed that Drew needed some time alone with them. I made myself some tea and grabbed my jacket off the hook by the back door. I sat outside on the porch for a long time, thinking about how nice it would be if I could see Todd's family again. They didn't get along, but I wondered what it would be like to see the family of the person I lost. Would I feel closure? Would I be more upset?

Nature called and I couldn't sit out in the cold any longer if I didn't want to pee my pants. I headed back inside to see Drew, Olivia, and Jonathan sitting at the kitchen table telling stories and laughing. I gave a quick wave before speeding off to the bathroom. I squeaked in surprise when Drew was waiting for me outside the bathroom door.

"Come with me. I want you to meet Iris's parents."

I took his hand and let him lead me to the kitchen. I was suddenly nervous again. Would they like me? Would I stack up against their daughter? Why did it even matter? I wasn't with Drew. I wasn't taking their daughter's place. I put a big smile on my face, reminding myself that I called them here for Drew, and that's what I needed to focus on.

"Olivia. Jonathan. This is Sarah. She's the woman who called you and asked you to come here."

They both stood and gave me hugs.

"It's so nice to meet you, dear. I can't tell you what this does for my heart to see Drew happy again."

I wanted to argue that Drew wasn't really happy, but I wouldn't ruin her moment.

"It's very nice to meet you, Sarah. Drew's been telling us that you're going to have twins. Congratulations."

"Thank you. I'm a little nervous, but excited too."

Drew wrapped his arm around my shoulder, pulling me close to him. "You'll do great."

We sat down at the table and the Wards filled me in on stories of Drew and Iris when they were dating. Apparently, Iris lived at home when they started dating and they snuck around quite a bit. Olivia told me how they knew from their first date that Drew and Iris were dating, but she and Jonathan decided to let them think they didn't know anything. The veil of secrecy ended when Drew was climbing the lattice on the side of the house to see Iris and it pulled free from the wall, causing Drew to fall into a rose bush. He spent the next few hours having thorns pulled from his body, all while her parents laughed at the ridiculousness of the situation.

Drew sat next to me laughing at his in-laws' stories. For the first time in a long time, Drew looked truly happy. This must have been the man they knew all those years ago. He no longer seemed to be carrying around the weight of the world.

At the end of the night, I showed Olivia and Jonathan to the room I had been using and left them for the night. Drew grabbed my hand and took me to his room without me having to ask if I could stay with him. I had already taken clothes into his room earlier just so that I was prepared when the Wards wanted to go to sleep. There was no question in Drew's eyes about where I would be staying tonight. After we both got ready for bed, I nestled into Drew's body, relishing in the comfort he provided.

As we laid there, Drew wrapped his arm around my belly, rubbing it lightly as the twins started kicking. "Thank you for today. I don't think I ever would have seen them again if it weren't for you."

"I thought you would be upset with me."

"If you had suggested it first, I probably wouldn't have even considered it. But when I saw them, I just knew I needed to talk to them again."

"I'm glad I called then."

"Do you still talk to anyone you used to know? I mean, the family of the father?"

"No. I don't talk to anyone."

It was more than I had ever really given him before, but since I wasn't actually giving out information about my past life, I figured it was okay.

"Goodnight, Sarah."

"Goodnight, Drew."

∼

When I woke up Sunday morning, I was alone in bed. My tummy was growling, so after quickly getting dressed, I headed for the stairs. I was just about to head down when I heard Drew talking with Olivia and Jonathan. It sounded like an important conversation and I didn't want to interrupt, so I hung out for a minute to see if I should head down or go back to the bedroom.

"You know we would have been there for you, Drew. We knew how badly you were hurting," Olivia said.

"I know. I just needed to get away. It was too difficult being there.

I probably shouldn't have stayed away so long, and I'm not even sure what I was hoping I would find, but it didn't really help either."

"Well, you found Sarah. She seems like a lovely woman. Maybe she's what you needed to find?" she asked.

"She's not...She's dealing with her own stuff right now. She's not ready."

"Son, my Iris was the best woman I've ever known. There's no replacing her." My heart sank at hearing his father-in-law's statement. "Sarah is different from Iris. Not in a bad way, just different. I can tell she's a good woman because she called us. Calling the widow's in-laws had to be a difficult thing for her to do."

"She did it to help me, but it's not a big deal to her because we aren't together."

"Sure. You keep telling yourself that, Drew. I see how you look at her. Any fool could see how much you love her," Jonathan said sternly.

"I don't love her. I can't. Iris is—"

"Iris would want you to be happy, and I'm guessing that she planned this whole thing." Olivia's voice was strong and full of conviction. "You know how Iris was when she wanted her way. She schemed to get you, you know."

"What?"

"Dear, you really didn't know, did you? Iris had her sights set on you since you were little kids. She had a crush on you all through high school. She planned for months how to get you. Of course, she didn't know that I knew, but I'm her mother and there wasn't much she could hide from me."

"Drew, it's time to stop running. Iris would have loved Sarah, and she would be glad to see you're happy again."

"But I forgot her."

"You didn't forget her. Just because you don't think about her and mourn her every single minute of the day doesn't mean that you forgot. Even if you only ever thought about her once a year, she would still be with you. If you died, would you have wanted Iris moping around seven years later?"

"It's time to let go, Drew. You have a great woman upstairs that needs you, and even if she's not ready yet, she wants you, too. Just give her time. That's how I got Olivia. I waited her out and when she was ready, I swooped in for the kill."

"Sure, Jonathan. You keep telling yourself that."

They chuckled and I felt like it was finally safe to come downstairs. I waited another minute, then made sure to make a little noise on the way down so they would know I was coming.

"Good morning, Sarah. You look like you're ready to have those babies any day now."

"Yeah, just another week and they'll be here."

Drew guided me to a chair and headed over to the fridge. "I'll make us all some breakfast."

I chatted with the Wards while Drew started making breakfast. They were only staying until tomorrow morning, so they decided they just wanted to visit at the house until they had to leave. After breakfast, Olivia brought a photo album from upstairs.

"I thought you might like to have this. You left everything behind."

I sat next to Drew on the couch and looked at photos of him and Iris. She was beautiful and you could see in their wedding photos how much they loved each other. I left Drew to look at the rest of the album and went to use the bathroom. That's when I felt it. It was different from the Braxton Hicks. The tightening around my belly was like nasty cramps and I leaned against the wall until it passed. I knew that I couldn't go to the hospital right away, but I didn't want to get Drew all wound up either.

Not wanting Drew to see me, I called to him that I was going to lie down for a little while. If he saw me, he would know. Drew was perceptive like that. I'd heard people say that it was best to nap before the labor got too intense. Whoever said that was possible was lying. Every time a contraction hit, it woke me up even more. After a while, lying down hurt and I decided that walking would be best. I got up and paced around the room, but all that seemed to do was make the contractions stronger and come faster.

I had been timing myself for the past two hours and I knew I didn't have much time before I had to leave for the hospital. The doctor had told me that since I was having twins, I shouldn't wait as long to go to the hospital. The contractions were about five minutes apart consistently. I was just about to head downstairs when Drew walked into the room.

"What's going on? I can hear you wearing a hole in the floor."

"It's time."

I swear his face went white. It was kind of comical, and I couldn't help but laugh. That is, until another contraction hit. I breathed through the pain, relieved when it finally passed. Drew finally snapped out of it and came over to grab my elbow, steering me toward the stairs. I had to roll my eyes at how he treated me like I would fall down the stairs if he let go. Olivia and Jonathan stood when they saw us coming down the stairs.

"Oh dear, you better get to the hospital. I know that look," Olivia said with a smile on her face. She walked over to me and gave me a hug. "You call me when the babies are born. I want to see them before we head back home."

I smiled at her and Drew promised that he would call as soon as there was news.

"Just make yourselves at home. There's plenty of food—"

"Drew, we've taken care of ourselves for the past how many years? I think we'll be just fine. Go. Get Sarah to the hospital."

Drew grabbed my bag, and in no time we were pulling up to the hospital. After getting checked in and getting changed, the nurses got me all set up with an IV and catheter. I would have an epidural whether I wanted one or not in case they had to do an emergency c-section. I was assured this was standard when having twins. Luckily, the babies were both head down, so that should make the delivery easier.

The nurse checked me and assured me I had a while to go before the babies would arrive. However, two hours later I was feeling pressure down south. I rang for the nurse and told her what I was feeling. After checking me again, she called the doctor.

"She's at nine centimeters. It's time." Then she turned back to me. "Are you ready to have some babies?" I nodded shakily and gripped Drew's hand tighter. "Okay, the OR is being prepped and when they're ready, we'll head over there. Dad, would you like to be in the room?"

"I'm not the dad."

"The father is no longer with us. Drew can be in the room. I mean, if he wants."

The nurse and I both looked at Drew who nodded once. The nurse came back a few minutes later with a suit for Drew to put over his clothes. When he pulled them on, I laughed at how ridiculous he looked. It was a good foot short for his bulky frame, but it would do.

Drew held my hand the whole time they were prepping me, but I told him he wasn't allowed to watch the babies being born. We hadn't even been intimate, and if there was any chance of that happening, this would not be how he saw me for the first time.

My baby girl was born first with no problems, and was a healthy six pounds. Three minutes later, my son was born at six pounds fourteen ounces. Both of them were absolutely beautiful. The nurse set them both on my chest, and Drew smiled down, brushing his hand over one of the babies' heads.

"Look at that, Mama. You did good."

I smiled up at him, almost like we were a family. It was this perfect moment. I had my children and a strong man at my side. I almost started crying. A million emotions raced through my body, but I didn't have time to process them. The babies were swept away to be cleaned up and tested, and then we were on our way back to the room.

A nurse came in to help me tandem nurse. I was glad she was there because not only was this my first time breastfeeding, but there were two of them. After much repositioning, we finally got the hang of it. Drew stood by and watched in fascination. Maybe it should have been weird, but it really wasn't. I guess since he had been in the room with me there was no point in holding back now.

When the babies were done, Drew held my daughter while I held my son. He looked at them with such adoration that it almost felt like he was their father. Just as those thoughts entered my head, I remembered there was one very important person that was missing out on all this.

Tears filled my eyes as I watched Drew stand in the place that Todd should be. It should be him holding his daughter and making silly faces at her. It should be him pressing soft kisses to her head. And no matter how grateful I was that Drew was with me, I couldn't help the pang in my chest because Todd never experienced this.

"Don't be sad. They're beautiful, Sarah. I'm still here with you."

I couldn't decide anymore if Todd was actually with me and I was hearing his voice, or if I was just hearing what I wanted to—like my brain had somehow tricked me into thinking that he was here as a way of coping. His voice was so strong though. He had been helping me through over the months, urging me to keep moving when I didn't want to. I had to believe he was here with me today. Otherwise, this was all just a little too depressing.

"So, what are you going to call this beautiful little girl?"

I looked over at her and decided that her name fit her quite well. Then I looked down at my son and started laughing.

"Well, she'll be Charlotte Leigh and he will be Henry Jones."

"Please tell me he's not a Jr."

"No, he's not," I said laughing.

"Someday, I would love to hear the story behind those names."

I smiled up at him. "Maybe someday."

CHAPTER 20

DREW

Jonathan and Olivia stopped by the hospital Monday morning on their way home and declared Charlotte and Henry the most adorable babies they had ever seen. When they were ready to leave, I desperately wanted to go with them and spend a few more hours with them, but I couldn't bring myself to leave Sarah. Iris's parents had insisted I was where I belonged, and Sarah insisted I should spend some more time with Iris's parents. In the end, I stayed with Sarah and the babies. As much as I wanted a little more time with my wife's parents, they were right. I had a new place now, and it was next to Sarah.

Sarah and the babies were released the next day, and to say I was nervous was an understatement. I had installed the car seats in my truck since Sarah's car was a death trap. She kept telling me she was going to get a new car, but had yet to do it because she was so busy at work. Until then, I would be taking them wherever they needed to go.

As we pulled out of the hospital parking lot, I drove extra carefully and probably a little slow, but I had precious cargo with me. I had put mirrors on the headrests of the backseat so that I could see their little faces in the rearview mirror. As we went over a speed bump leaving the hospital, Charlotte's little head wobbled. Panicked, I reached back with my right hand and rested it on her head to stabilize it.

"Drew, what are you doing?"

"Her head was wobbling around. I'm holding it steady. Maybe you should sit back there so you can hold Henry's head."

She laughed at me. "Well, your head moves too."

"It's not the same. Didn't you listen to the nurse about how delicate their heads are right now? What if her head rolls too hard and snaps her neck?"

"Um, I don't think that could actually happen while she is tucked in her car seat and we're driving..." She leaned over and looked at the speedometer, rolling her eyes. "Seven miles an hour. I'm pretty sure they're safe back there."

"Laugh all you want, but I saw the video. I could kill them by barely shaking them. If we got hit by a car, there would be nothing protecting their little heads."

"Except the car seats."

He sighed heavily. "You're not taking this seriously."

"No, Drew. You're taking this way too seriously. Trust me. They'll be fine."

"How can you be so sure? I mean, no offense, but you're a first time mother."

She shrugged, thankfully not insulted by my remarks. "Call it mother's intuition."

"And you somehow gained this intuition in the span of a couple of days?"

"Don't worry, Drew. Your father's intuition will kick in soon enough." She blushed and started fumbling over her words. "Not that...I'm not... You're not...their father. I just mean that, you know, you'll get used to all this and...instincts will kick in."

I grinned at her obvious attempts to correct her previous statement. "So, even though I'm not their father, I'll still develop fatherly instincts? I guess that means I'll be helping out with the babies quite a bit," I said, sighing dramatically.

Her face blushed red and her eyes went wide. "No, I never implied that you would have to take care of the babies. I just meant that as you were around them, you would feel more in tune with their needs."

"So, I don't have to take care of them, but I need to spend time with them? Hmm..." I moved my head back and forth as if trying to decide if I could do that.

"Oh forget it. I wasn't implying anything."

I laughed at her frustration with me and drove us home. The normal twenty minute drive was closer to forty minutes because I was driving so slowly. Sarah kept craning her neck to look at the speedometer and then huffing, but I didn't care. This was my first time with the twins in the truck, and if I wanted to drive slowly, I would.

∽

TAKING care of twins was hell. There were three adults to take care of two little human beings and we were being run ragged. The babies went down for the night around six-thirty, but still woke up every two and a half hours to eat. Sarah had stopped tandem nursing because they screamed for about twenty minutes after waking. Something I learned very quickly about babies is that they poop a lot. Every time they woke up at night, they pooped. They had to be changed before they nursed because they would fall asleep nursing and you didn't want to wake them up after they went back to sleep.

So, both of them would wake up crying and need to be changed, but they would scream the longer it took for them to get their food. Cara and I took turns helping Sarah get the babies changed when they woke, and we found that if we got to the first one that started crying and calmed that one down, the other one wouldn't wake up.

Then, when the first was fed, we woke the second with a clean diaper and fed that one.

By the third day, the babies were eating every two hours, which actually meant two hours from the time they started. I didn't know how Sarah was doing it. She had to be exhausted, and her boobs had to be killing her from having babies constantly sucking on her tits. Sarah said that her milk was coming in and that's why they were nursing more frequently. Cara and I actually fell asleep on the floor of the babies' room because we were too tired to move from there.

Two nights ago, Charlotte started waking at ten o'clock screaming her little head off. Sarah would wrap her in a swaddling blanket really tight and then put Charlotte's stomach over her shoulder. She guessed that she was gassy and couldn't go to sleep. How could you be gassy when you shit that much?

Then, Henry started crying too, but nothing soothed him except me walking him up and down the stairs over and over again. He finally calmed down after about five minutes the first time, but I had to keep it up for a half hour before I could put him down. Now, whenever he started fussing, I took him over to the stairs for a little walk. My legs were killing me by the end, but I'd rather be tired than hear him scream for one more fucking minute.

At the end of the week I was very tempted to call Ryan and tell him I was coming back to work. I didn't know how much more of this I could take. Cara and Sarah were tired, but still stared at the babies like they hadn't just had their asses kicked by a newborn. Sarah must have sensed my need to get back to work because after a week at home she had a "talk" with me.

"I think it's time for you to get back to work."

I did my best to hide my excitement. "Really? Why's that?"

She rolled her eyes at me. "Don't play dumb with me, Drew. I know that you're itching to get out of here. You're great with the babies, but you don't have the patience to stay home with them. Call Ryan and tell him you're ready to go back."

I quickly grabbed my phone off the counter and started to dial, but when I looked up and saw her laughing at me, I shrugged. "Only if you think you're ready. Really, I don't mind hanging around another week."

Her lip quivered and she threw her head down on the table. "Oh, thank God. I can't do this anymore," she cried. Her tears about broke my heart, and I was torn between wanting to get back to work and staying with her so I didn't have to hear her cry. "You may have to take a third week off."

I panicked. I couldn't do a third week. It was too much. I would go insane.

"No take backs. You already told me I could go back!"

Her head popped up, her eyes twinkling with mirth. "We're fine. Go back to your manly work."

This time I dialed and told Ryan that I was coming back Monday. There was no way I could stay here all day for even one more day. It was torture.

~

"We're almost done with construction on Sarah's house."

Ryan had called me into his office at the end of the day to update me on the progress. It had been a little over a month since the babies were born and Thanksgiving was next week. I wanted to have a nice Thanksgiving for Sarah, but I didn't really know how to cook a large meal, and I didn't think that she would be up to it.

"That's great. I'm sure she'll be glad to get back to her own place."

I tried to sound happy, but I wasn't. I had grown used to having a house full of people. When I got home, there was someone to greet me. It had become my nightly ritual to rock with the babies after dinner. On especially long days, I dozed with them in my arms. I never thought I would be that happy again, that I would feel so much love for another human. These babies had worked their way into my frozen heart and melted it little by little.

"Yeah, I would say they should be done before Thanksgiving, and then she just needs to make some decisions on the finishing touches. I think she should be able to move in at the latest by the second week in December."

I swallowed hard, trying to pretend that I was happy, but my heart was breaking inside. It was like I was losing Iris all over again, only this time, it was this perfect little family I had created, including Cara.

"That's good. I'll be sure to let her know."

Ryan's cringe told me the fake smile I tried to plaster on my face was an epic fail.

"Dude, if you don't want her to move out, you're gonna have to say something. If you put that smile on your face, she's gonna know that something's wrong."

I sighed and ran my hand along the back of my neck. God, I wanted to tell her so badly that I wanted her to stay. I wanted to get down on my knees and plead with her, but if she wasn't ready, it wouldn't do me any good. Besides, she was overrun with emotions right now. She was in no position to make a decision like that.

"She's not ready. She wants time alone with the babies. She's all excited about having her house back. She tells me how great it's going to be and has me sit and look at paint colors with her. I smile along and pretend I'm totally okay with it. If she doesn't want to stay with me, I'm not gonna make her feel bad."

"You don't have to be a dick about it. Just tell her that you'd like her to stay. What's the worst that could happen? She says no? Big deal. You move on and try again later."

"It's not that simple. Sarah's stubborn. If I push too hard, she's going to put more space between us so I don't get *attached*, and I'm already attached to all of them. Even Cara, believe it or not. She does all the laundry and cooks the meals, and she's a really good cook."

"Yeah, well, all those years she lived with Sean, that's all she really had to do. Are you sure that you're not just attached to the idea of everything?"

"What do you mean? How can I be attached to an idea when they've been living with me?"

"Well, they aren't really yours. You've got yourself a ready made family. You haven't really had to put in any work that a relationship normally requires."

I bristled at his remarks. I was putting in the work. I had spent months building a friendship with Sarah that I hadn't even really wanted in the first place. When that loathing turned into interest and then friendship, I really tried to get to know her. It wasn't my fault that she was a closed book. Still, I wanted her and would be with her right now if she wasn't so damn stubborn.

"You don't know shit."

He held up both hands in surrender. "Look, I'm not trying to offend you, I'm just offering another perspective. How do you know she doesn't see it that way? A woman on her own with kids? It makes for an easy mark to be walked all over and pushed around."

"I would never do that to her."

"I know you wouldn't, but she's a single mother and she needs to be sure that you actually want the whole package. I mean, she's a good looking woman, right? I would be lying if I said that it didn't make me want what she has."

"You want her?"

"No." He rolled his eyes in frustration. "It's everything she has and what it represents—what's missing from my life. It's not that I want her, I want that whole package. The wife and a few kids, you know? It's the next step in life."

I nodded in acknowledgement. I knew exactly what he meant because I wanted the same thing, only I didn't need to see Sarah with kids to know it was what I wanted. It's what I had always wanted. I'd had that chance with Iris too little too late. I thought about what Ryan said the whole way home and tried to steel myself for Sarah's reaction when I updated her on the progress on her house.

When I walked in my house, Sarah and Cara were relaxing on the couches with what looked like Bloody Marys. I raised an eyebrow in question, wondering if it was okay for Sarah to be drinking while breastfeeding.

"It's virgin, but I really wish it wasn't."

"Mine's not, but since I'm not breastfeeding, I can drink all I want."

"Bitch. Don't rub it in."

I had noticed that Sarah and Cara really came out of their shells around each other. I had never seen either of them act like this with the other girls. I grinned as best I could as I sat down across from them. As I opened my mouth, my chest ached furiously. I hated doing this.

"I talked to Ryan today. He said that your house should be done before Thanksgiving, and they can finish the inside and have you moved in by early December."

"That's such great news. I'm sure you're ready to get rid of screaming babies that keep you up at all hours of the night."

I couldn't really tell if she was genuinely happy or if she was testing out the waters.

"I don't mind you being here. In fact, I think I'll be quite lonely when you leave."

"Does that include me too?" Cara asked.

"Yes, even you. Who will cook and clean for me when you're gone?"

"Aww, I guess you'll just have to hire a maid," she teased.

"Don't be silly. He can still come eat dinner with us."

"Yeah, what's one more mouth?"

I frowned at their teasing. They may not realize it, but this was impossible for me. They would go on and live their lives together, and I would be here all alone, invited over from time to time for a meal. All the while, I would be missing out on the everyday things that made my life so full right now. "Gee, don't sound too excited about having me over."

The girls chuckled at my pouting, but I just couldn't bring myself to be unhappy for them when they looked so excited. They seemed to be truly happy about being able to move home. It wouldn't make things any easier on Sarah if I gave her a hard time.

"Well, as long as you bake me a cake every now and then, I suppose it won't be that bad."

"We can do a Sunday dinner or something and have a big meal!" Sarah said excitedly. A little too excitedly if you asked me. The idea that I would only get to see them every once in a while really grated on me.

"Yeah. Sounds great." I grumbled and then stood, stomping upstairs to sulk. I stopped just outside the babies' room, walking slowly inside to stare at the angels sleeping in their pack 'n plays. They were so sweet when they slept, and despite how much their crying grated on my nerves, I also loved every second of it. And now it was all about to be ripped away.

Gritting my teeth, I walked out of the room and headed to my bedroom, sitting down on my bed. I dropped my head in my hands and tried to come to grips with the fact that my life was about to be uprooted once again.

∼

THANKSGIVING CAME WAY TOO FAST, and before I knew it, December was here. Cara and Sarah had been slowly moving things back over to the other house for a few days now, and every time I came home there was less evidence that I had housemates. Today though, today was the day they officially left my home for good. Sarah had been running around all morning packing up the last of the baby items. I had taken down the pack n' plays after they woke up from their naps and moved them over to the nursery in Sarah's house.

Cara came downstairs with the babies on each hip while Sarah lugged some bags downstairs. I quickly ran over to her and grabbed them, carrying them over to her house. When I got back, the babies were all bundled up to go outside. Even though the walk would take only a minute, they were bundled in fleece bear suits, as if they were going out into a winter storm. They looked so damn cute.

"Okay, I'm pretty sure I have everything," Sarah said with her hands on her hips. She looked like she hadn't even bothered to get herself ready this morning, only throwing on clothes to run around in. Her hair was tossed up messily on her head and her buttons on her shirt were mismatched. Still, she looked like the most beautiful woman I had ever seen. I frowned, wondering when I had started thinking of her as the most beautiful woman and not Iris. I shook that thought from my head. It wouldn't help to think about that right now.

"If you don't, you only live across the yard from me. I can bring it over."

Sarah came over and gave me a hug. "Thank you so much for everything, Drew. I really appreciate it."

One minute I was holding Sarah and breathing in her motherly smell, and the next, all four of them were out the door before I even got to hold the babies one last time. I watched the door click shut as the girls hustled across the lawn, keeping the babies tucked into them to avoid the cold breeze.

My chest ached as they walked inside and slammed the door behind them. That was it. They were gone, leaving me all alone and unable to see my family anymore. *My family.* That's what they were to me, all four of them, but now they were gone.

I turned and looked at the living room. There were no baby blankets there, but I could envision them in their swings as we played with them. I could see Sarah leaning over them, making silly faces as she cooed at them. I saw myself walking Henry around as he fussed at all hours of the night. I could smell Charlotte's sweet scent as I snuggled her against me. My smile faded as the memories disappeared.

I headed to the kitchen, opening the fridge looking for bottles of breastmilk. There were none to be found. Suddenly, it was imperative that I find something of theirs, something that I could hold onto. I ran from room to room, checking for anything that I could hold. The room that was used as the nursery was empty. There wasn't even a burp cloth left behind. Cara's room held no traces either. The bathroom was cleared of all girly products and baby paraphernalia. The last room I looked in was Sarah's. Glancing around the room, my heart sank when I realized every last trace of her was gone.

An envelope on her pillow gave me hope. I pulled it open and read the handwritten letter inside.

DREW,

I just wanted to say thank you for all you've done for me. I don't know how I would have gotten through these past few months without you. You have been my rock, and as much as I want to stay with you, I know that I need to continue to build my life on my own for a while. I hope that when I'm ready you will still be waiting, but I know that may not happen. I know the babies will miss rocking with you at night, so please feel free to stop by whenever you want. My door is always open for you.

LOVE,
    Sarah

IT WAS by no means a love letter, but it did give me hope there could be something between us in the future. I walked downstairs and sat in the living room. The silence was overwhelming and I wished more than anything I would hear a baby cry. My thoughts drifted to Iris, and it dawned on me that it wasn't Iris that I wanted to hear or feel. It was the family that was now sitting in the house across the lawn from me. In fact, I couldn't remember the last time that I had felt Iris around me. Her absence wasn't sad, though. It was as it should be. She was gone, and this time I had a sneaking suspicion that she wouldn't be coming back.

CHAPTER 21

SARAH

The new year brought all kinds of changes in my life. I had officially started back to work the week after Christmas to prepare for New Year's Eve. As much as I would have liked to start after New Year's, I couldn't blame Hank for wanting me there that week. There was much to do to prepare for the celebration, and I was glad that I had been there to get things organized.

Cole and Alex had decided on a destination wedding in Hawaii for right after New Year's, but since I'd just started back to work, I didn't go. Drew went and said the wedding was beautiful. Cara hadn't gone either and offered to watch Ethan so that Harper wouldn't have to take him along. Her next child was due later in April.

Drew had taken me shopping for a new car right before Christmas. There was no way I would take the twins out in the death trap I called my car. I ended up getting a Toyota Camry and was completely satisfied, though Drew was convinced that only an SUV would do. He debated with the salesman for close to an hour about the safety of an SUV versus a car. Finally, I'd had enough and told the car salesman that Drew did not actually have any say in what car

I would be getting. That drew his attention from, well, Drew awfully fast.

Cara had been staying home alone with the twins for a few weeks now, and even though she seemed thoroughly exhausted at the end of the day, most days she still put food on the table. On days that she was too tired, I made dinner when I got home. The twins were three months old now and were finally gaining a little personality. I took lots of pictures and made sure to send them to Drew.

He stopped by after the twins had gone to bed tonight. He'd been working late nights, and frequently arrived after they were already asleep. I smiled at him, but it was hard knowing that he was missing out on so much.

"Drew," I smiled sadly.

"They're asleep, aren't they?"

I nodded, watching as he sighed, running his hands through his hair. "I miss out on so much now."

"You can still see them."

"I know, but they're not awake," he growled in frustration. "I miss them."

"I know," I said, gently laying my hand on his arm. "I know this is hard—"

"No, you fucking don't, Sarah," he snarled. "They were with me, living with me as part of my life. Now they're over here and I never see them. I never see *you!*"

"Drew..."

I didn't know what to say. I knew he missed them and even me, but I didn't know how to make that better. I hated to see him struggle like this. I hated the pained look on his face, knowing that he was missing them. But was he really missing the babies and me or just the idea of us? I didn't want to put my children out there, only for Drew to walk away when he realized it was all too much.

Sighing, Drew shoved past me and walked to the babies' room. I watched from the doorway as he leaned over Henry's bed, running the back of his knuckles over his cute, little cheeks.

"Hey, little man. You're getting so big."

Henry wiggled slightly, yawning just before his eyes popped open. He let out a small cry, and I almost walked in to take over, but Drew reached in and gently picked him up, holding him against his chest. His eyes slipped closed as he swayed back and forth, rubbing Henry's back.

"That's it, little man. You're okay."

Warmth wrapped around me as I watched my neighbor, the man I had been quickly falling for, take care of my son as if he was his own. The way he held him, rubbed his back like he was the most precious thing in the world, had my heart twisting. I was so torn, angry that Todd wasn't here to experience this, but so happy that Drew was. I knew Todd wasn't coming back. I knew he would want me to be happy, and that he would even approve of Drew. But it felt so wrong, like choosing to move on without him was hurtful to his memory.

But the more I watched Drew, the more my heart grew with love for the man in front of me. He pressed a kiss to Henry's cheek and gently laid him back down. Then he moved over to Charlotte's bed and smiled down at her.

"Hey, sweetheart. You're so beautiful, you know that? You're going to be a heartbreaker someday."

His grin told me all I needed to know. None of this was fake. He desperately loved my kids. He loved all of us. He wanted all of us. How could I ever think that he was just creating a family out of us. He was already part of us, whether I realized it or not.

When he turned to me, I swore I saw tears in his eyes. It broke my heart. He walked over to me and linked his hand with mine. I stared at our joined fingers, wondering what it would be like to have him in my bed again, his body wrapped around mine. What would it be like to have him hold me every night and kiss me the way he had once before?

"Drew..."

His hand came up and cupped my cheek, his thumb brushing

against my skin. I opened my mouth to tell him to stay, that I needed him as much as he needed us, but the words just wouldn't come yet. I swallowed hard as he moved in and pressed a sweet kiss to my cheek, then rested his forehead against mine.

"I'll be waiting, Sarah...when you're ready."

He wrapped his arms around me and pulled me in for a hug. I felt his lips against my head and his hot breath brushing against me. I held him tight to me, not wanting to let him go, but still needing just a little more time to come to terms with the fact that I really wanted this man.

He stepped back and gave me a pained smile, then headed for the door. I followed him, almost crying out for him, but the further away he walked, the more I knew, it just wasn't time yet.

∼

I ANTICIPATED his knock before it came. He was always here bright and early in the morning on the weekends. I swung the door open with a smile on my face, despite the poor sleep I'd gotten.

"You look awful," he said with concern as he stepped forward and brushed his hand over my cheek. "Didn't you sleep?"

"I tried, but..." I squinted just before a sneeze shook my whole body. Pulling my robe tighter around me, I fought the chills creeping over me. I felt awful, and no amount of lying around was helping. I couldn't leave it all to Cara.

Drew pressed his hand to my forehead and frowned. "You're burning up. You should be in bed."

I smiled ironically at him. "With twins? I can't leave it all to Cara."

"Yes, you can," Cara said as she walked into the room. "I've got this. Go to bed."

"She's right," he said, swooping me up into his arms. I just barely had time to wrap my arms around his neck before he hauled me down the hall to my bedroom.

"Drew—"

"No, you need to take care of yourself." He laid me down in bed and pulled the covers up over me. "You need sleep. I'll make some soup and bring it to you, and Cara and I will take care of the twins."

"But—"

He pressed his fingers to my lips, smirking slightly. "Don't argue with me. You won't win."

He pressed a kiss to my forehead and walked out of the room, closing the door behind him. My face warmed as I thought of him taking care of me. The ice inside me was cracking apart one chunk at a time, and I was finally able to start really letting him in.

I snuggled under the covers, thinking it would be hard to fall back asleep knowing my kids were out there, but after just a few minutes, I was dozing off, my eyes slipping shut as I fell into a deep slumber. I slept for what felt like hours, and when I woke, Drew was walking in with a tray of soup and water, a small smile on his face.

"Hey," I yawned, sitting up in bed. "What time is it?"

"Four."

"In the afternoon?" I asked stupidly.

"Well, yeah."

"I can't believe I slept that long," I said as I took the tray from him. Stirring the soup, I took my first sip and sighed. "This is delicious."

"Well, I can't take credit for it. Cara made it," he laughed.

"That's okay. It's still perfect."

Drew came to sit on the bed beside me, completely ignoring the fact that I was sick or that he was climbing into bed with me. "Drew, you're going to get sick."

"Like I give a shit."

I ate as much as I could, and then he took the tray, setting it on the floor. I thought he would get up and leave, but instead, he pulled me into his side and snuggled me into him. It felt so nice, so comforting that I sank into him willingly.

"I hate going home," he said quietly. "It's so empty in my house. I miss all of you so much."

I pressed my hand to his chest and nuzzled against him. "I miss you too."

His lips pressed against my head, melting my heart.

"It's been a year," I said quietly. I knew I couldn't say too much, but I figured this much was okay. "He's been gone for a year, and it feels so wrong to lay here with you. But I love every second of it. Is that wrong?"

His hand skimmed up and down my arm. "I think I'm the wrong man to ask about that. I mourned my dead wife for way too long. I don't think there's a right or wrong time. I think it's just about being ready."

I smiled against his chest. "He would have loved you."

Drew turned slightly to look down at me. "That's a little awkward."

I laughed, shaking my head. "I mean, he would love the way you are with the kids and me." Tears filled my eyes and for the first time, I admitted that it was time to let Todd go. "He would want me to be with someone who takes care of me, who loves my kids like his own. I can practically hear him telling me to just let him go and take a chance."

"I think Iris would say the same thing," he said quietly. "She's been gone for a while now."

I sat up and looked at him. "You don't feel her anymore?"

He shook his head. "Not for some time. She must have known that I was ready to move on. She doesn't come to me anymore."

"Drew—"

"It's okay," he said around a lump in his throat. "The thing is, when I think about what I want out of life, it's not her anymore." He turned and stared at me. "She's my past and I will always love her, but you're the one I want in my future. I want those kids so bad it hurts. I even want Cara. You've become the biggest part of my life. I look forward to seeing you at the end of the day, kissing those kids at night. And I think that's what she wanted for me."

"I want you in my life too. And not just as my neighbor. I miss you being in the same house with me. I know that I said I needed time, but I think I'm ready now, for whatever you can give me."

He pressed a searing kiss to my lips and kissed me hard. "I can give you all of me."

CHAPTER 22

DREW

Despite my talk with Sarah, I didn't just assume that we were a couple. I wanted that more than anything, but we'd had such a tumultuous relationship, going from angry neighbors, to friends, to what I hoped would be lovers. She fell asleep in my arms that day, wiped out from being sick, and I held her, soaking up every minute I got with her. But telling each other we were ready to move on didn't give me the right to stay here overnight.

As she slept, I snuck out of her room, hating that I had to leave. I checked in with Cara, helping her get the babies down for bed before heading home. I stood out on my back porch at sunset, waiting just to see if Iris appeared, but she didn't. Instead of being disappointed, I felt a weight ease in my chest. It was finally time to move on.

I went to bed that night feeling lighter than I had in years. I went into work the next day with a pep in my step that hadn't been there in so long, I'd forgotten what it was like to be happy.

"What's got you all happy today?" Ryan asked when he showed up on the job site.

"Things are progressing with Sarah."

He snorted. "It's about time."

"What's that supposed to mean?"

"I mean it's obvious that you're in love with her, but you dance around it instead of coming out and telling her."

"She wasn't ready," I admitted.

"But she is now?"

"I think so," I grinned.

"Did you ever find out what happened with the other guy?"

"Not exactly. I know he's dead, but she's never said if he was her husband or not. She wore a ring though."

"Well, it must have been her husband," he frowned.

I shrugged, not wanting to guess. "Whatever he was, she loved him. I know how devastating it is to lose the person you love."

He frowned, and I realized I had never told him. And as I started telling him about Iris, the familiar pang of sadness didn't appear. My chest wasn't tight, and I didn't feel like punching anyone. I just felt...light.

"So, that's why you've been such a grumpy bastard since you came to town?"

I smiled. "Well, not anymore. Sarah's given me something I thought I would never have."

"Yeah? What's that?"

"A family, someone to love unconditionally, kids that fill the house with noise...the whole package."

He gripped my shoulder, smiling at me. "I'm happy for you."

"Yeah, there's just one problem."

"What's that?"

"Well, I haven't actually figured out how to make this thing official."

He frowned at me. "Well, you asked her out on a date, right?"

My jaw dropped. I hadn't even thought about that. "Well..."

He laughed. "You might want to start there."

The whole way home, I felt like slapping myself. I was so stupid. After everything she'd been through, of course she would want to be taken out on a date. I didn't even remember what that was like. It had been so long. All I thought about was being with her, but she probably wanted the whole thing, dating and kissing...all the things that made a woman feel special. I'd have to plan something for this weekend.

On Saturday, I got dressed and headed over to her house, prepared to spend the day with the kids, but when Sarah opened the door, she was dressed up in a cute pair of jeans that hugged her curves and a warm sweater that made me want to snuggle into her. With ankle boots, some light makeup, and her hair done up, she looked like a new woman. I couldn't take my eyes off her. But then I had another thought...maybe she already had plans and I wouldn't get to spend the day with her.

"Are you going out?" I asked around the lump in my throat. "I thought we were spending the day together."

"Um, well, Cara said she could watch the kids and..." She cleared her throat as anger swirled inside me. She was going out and leaving me behind. I was too late. "I thought you and I could go out together."

Anger forgotten, confusion took over and I stared at her a moment, wondering what she was telling me. Did she want groceries? Did she need me to help her run errands? The fact was, it didn't really matter. I got to spend time with her away from everyone else. And even though I loved spending time with the kids, I wanted this time with her, no matter what we were doing.

I nodded, pretending that this was totally fine. "Are you ready to go now?"

"Yeah. Can you drive?"

"Sure. See you later, Cara." I gave her a nod, and she winked at me, which I thought was strange.

We walked to the truck, and I held the door for her like always. God, I wished this was a date.

"So, what would you like to do today?"

"I want to do something that has nothing to do with kids. I want to feel like a free adult for one day."

I grinned at her. "I've got you covered."

I pulled out of the driveway and headed down the road, pulling into a winery an hour later. It was brunch time and the sign outside said they hosted a brunch wine tasting every Saturday, and then an afternoon wine tasting and an evening wine tasting.

"How did you know about this?" she asked curiously, getting out of the truck and walking around to meet me in the middle. I grabbed her hand, not knowing if she was okay with it or not.

"Harper was saying how she had wanted to come here, but she couldn't because she was pregnant."

"How is she doing? She's about to have the baby, right?"

"Yeah. I think in another two weeks or so," I said thoughtfully.

"I stopped by to see Cece the other day. Their son, Archer, is so cute. He's almost three and a half months old. Time really flies by. I can't believe the twins are almost five months old. They seem huge to me."

"They're growing like weeds. You need to find out what Cara's feeding them when you're gone and tell her to stop."

We headed for the winery and I glanced down at our clasped hands, grinning slightly. This felt right. Everything about this was perfect. We spent the morning and part of the afternoon eating food and tasting wine. I watched her as she people watched. She looked so peaceful out here, more than I'd ever seen before. It was like the weight of the world was finally gone from her shoulders, and I hoped I had helped her achieve that.

Despite her protests, I bought her a few bottles of wine for when she stopped breastfeeding. She finished her wine and sighed.

"I probably shouldn't have drank so much, but I couldn't help myself."

"I doubt the babies will be affected after you drink one time."

"Still..." She stood and brushed the grass from her pants. "I'm going to call Cara and check up on the kids before we head back."

"Okay."

I listened as she practically grilled Cara on the phone about the twins, making sure they were eating and weren't too busy for her. I smiled as I heard the worry in her voice. She was a great mom, and when she finally hung up, she didn't actually look that relieved.

"Everything okay at home?"

"Yep. She said we could stay out longer if we wanted. Do you want to go somewhere else? Maybe grab some dinner?"

I really wanted this to be a date, but the way she talked, we were just friends hanging out. I knew she didn't mean it to hurt, but that didn't stop the pang that made my chest ache. So, I brushed it off, hoping I didn't come across as the sad fucker I was.

I grinned at her playfully, trying to disguise my true feelings. "Are you asking me out on a date, Sarah?"

"Yes, I am."

The tension in the air reached a fever pitch as the seriousness washed over me. She was ready. She was giving me the green light. I stepped forward and wrapped my hand around the back of her neck, pulling her closer to my lips. My breath hitched just before I brushed my lips against hers. She tasted sweet like the wine, and when she opened for me, I swiped my tongue inside her mouth, tasting her for the first time in months. She was fucking perfect.

Intense. That was the only way to describe what I was feeling, what Sarah did to me. She kissed me like I was the air she breathed, and she couldn't get enough. When I finally pulled away, she stumbled slightly, a dizzying smile filling her face. She was fucking perfect, and now she was mine. I would never let her go.

I smiled at her, chuckling slightly as I pulled her into me. "God, I've waited forever for that."

She buried her face into my chest, her fists clenching in my shirt. "This feels so right," she murmured.

"Sweetheart, there's never been anything more right."

I took her hand in mine, and together, we explored the countryside. With both of us fairly new to the area, there was plenty to see. We came across a small town of about five hundred people and stopped at the bar in town. I used the word town very loosely because there were about five houses in "town" and the rest were scattered in the countryside.

The burgers and onion rings were the best I'd ever tasted. We talked about the twins and laughed at things they were doing. It didn't feel weird to talk about the kids on our date. In fact, it felt like the most natural thing in the world. I felt like so much of their lives happened without me, so I soaked in everything she told me.

Pulling into the driveway was the worst feeling in the world. I knew I had to let her go, but I wasn't ready yet. I wanted to stay with her forever. But this was our first date. I couldn't push it with her. I walked her to the door, my fingers linked with hers. It was weird, remembering my first date with Iris, and now going on my first date with Sarah. They were so different, but so similar. I had those same amazing feelings rushing through me. I wanted to kiss her. I wanted to take her inside. God, I wanted to never let the night end.

I couldn't take her inside and make love to her the way I wanted, but I could damn well make sure she never forgot today. I backed her up against the door and inserted my leg between hers. Her breath caught as I pressed my body up against hers and took her mouth the way I had wanted all day. My hand wrapped around the back of her head, holding her to me as I kissed her deep and long, leaving her quivering in my arms. When I broke the kiss, she looked shaken in the best possible way. I slowly backed away, not sure if I could hold onto my control for much longer. And now that I knew she was ready, I wouldn't back off.

"I'll call you later, sweetheart."

I grinned as she nodded, fumbling with the doorknob before pushing inside. Smiling, I turned back home with my hands in my pockets, and for the first time in a long time, I felt light and carefree.

CHAPTER 23

SARAH

I walked in the door, still shellshocked from the most amazing date I'd ever had. Even with Todd, it had never felt that natural to be with a man. Maybe that was wrong, but Drew had become my best friend. With Todd, it was so different. We were always apart for long periods of time. Every time we got close, he was deployed. Drew was steady and always there. I got to know him better for it, and saw the man deep inside that was so caring.

But it wasn't fair to compare. They were different men. Todd loved me so much, he made the ultimate sacrifice. So, it wasn't about who was the better man. It was just the facts that one was no longer here, but there was another man here that wanted me, and I could tell that he already loved me. It was clear in the way he looked at me.

"How was it? Did he kiss you?"

Cara was right up in my face the moment I walked in the door. I was still in too much of a daze to think coherently.

"Good. It was good. How are the kids?"

"Good? That's it?" she screeched. "The kids are sleeping, so you better start talking."

We walked into the living room and I plopped down in the

nearest chair before my legs would collapse from the shaking that had overtaken them.

"It was so much better than good. It was...it just felt right, you know? It was easy and natural."

"And did he kiss you?"

My face grew warm with the blush that overtook my face.

"He did! I knew it! So tell me, how was it? Is he a good kisser?"

"He's amazing." I started fanning my face as I thought about the scorcher he placed on me before he left.

"I knew it! I knew it! I knew it!"

She was jumping up and down and yelling, acting like a total loon. I started laughing at how happy she was that I had been kissed. Never in my wildest dreams would I have imagined Cara being so excited over me kissing someone. When I first met her, she was bitchy and reserved around people, but over the past months that we'd lived together, she had come out of her shell around me. I knew what had happened to her, but I didn't bring it up. I figured that if she wanted to talk about it, she would.

"So when are you going to see him again?"

"I would imagine every day, just like I have for the past few months. I doubt that will change."

"Oh my gosh. I can't believe it's finally happening. I knew ever since I moved into Drew's house that he wanted you, but I didn't know if it would ever happen, the way you two were acting."

"What do you mean, the way we were acting?"

"He was all mopy because he wanted you, but didn't want to push you. You were all, *woe is me*, and I still don't know the reasons why. I'm sure it was a good reason, but you had someone right in front of you that wanted you and you couldn't see it."

"I could see it. I just wasn't ready until recently."

"Well, thank God you're ready because I wasn't sure how much longer I could see those looks of longing coming from him. It seriously depressed me."

I shook my head in disbelief. I had no idea that she saw so much.

Apparently, the only people Drew and I were fooling were ourselves. I went down the hall after a while and kissed the babies goodnight. As I looked at them, I could see Todd in every little feature on their tiny faces.

"I promise," I whispered, "I'll find some way to let you know about your dad, even if you never know who he really is."

Todd would always be their father, but Drew was the man in their lives, and that wasn't changing any time soon. Smiling, I went to bed dreaming about my neighbor and the future I could now see with him.

∽

DREW TOOK me out every chance he got over the past few months. I felt closer to him than I had anyone else in my life. There were times that I even felt closer to him than Todd. He'd been in the military for so long and there were long stretches that I didn't see him or hear from him and when he was home, he was distant. I understood, though. His job was hard and it was an adjustment. Then, when he left the military, there was another period where my life was thrown into chaos. He had only been home a few years before he was killed, and most of that was spent acclimating to being home and acclimating to his new job. Once he was fully on board at the security company, his hours were long and not always in sync with my schedule. It was a wonder we even managed to create the twins.

Finally, I felt like I had found someone that I could truly rely on. It wasn't that I was happier with Drew than with Todd, but I felt like I finally had someone to share my everyday life with. Drew took me out to restaurants and line dancing. Every day brought us closer together and made me more sure than ever that I was ready to move on. Drew and I had a hard time keeping our hands off one another lately and I knew he wouldn't want to hold out much longer. I had already decided that I was ready to take the next step in our relationship. The question was, where would it happen? I didn't want to leave the twins alone overnight with Cara, but I couldn't take this next step with Drew with two kids and another woman in the house.

Tonight we were going out to dinner, but I didn't know where. He told me to meet him at his house because he was running a little late. I grabbed my stuff and headed for the living room where Cara was hanging out with the twins.

"Cara, I was wondering if you could maybe handle the babies for the night?"

Her jaw dropped as she stared at me. "Are you serious?"

"I'm sorry. It was stupid to ask. Never mind."

"No, no, no. That's not what I meant. I'm just surprised it took you so long to ask. I thought this would never happen between you two."

I blushed furiously and fiddled with my purse. "Well, you know. It's been a few months. It's not like we just started dating."

"Don't even try to explain this to me. I've been waiting for you two to get your shit together for way too long. Go and have fun. The babies are sleeping through the night, so it's not like I'll need you here to help manage them in the middle of the night."

"Alright, but if you need me, please call me."

"Yeah, that's not gonna happen. Shoo." She waved her hand dismissively at me and went back to playing with the babies.

I headed over to Drew's house and was shocked when he opened the door and I smelled food wafting from his kitchen.

"I thought we were going out to dinner?"

"I changed my mind. I wanted to stay in tonight and cook for you. I hope that's alright."

"Yeah. That sounds good to me."

I set my purse down and made my way to the kitchen, watching him stir something on the stove before walking back over to me and pulling me into his arms. His lips left a burning trail down my neck and across my shoulder. I wrapped my arms around him, pulling him closer. My sex throbbed with need as I gave in to the tingling sensations he left on my body. His hands trailed lower until they firmly gripped my ass, pulling me against his erection. I couldn't wait any longer. I needed him.

I pulled back and walked over to the stove, shutting off the burners. When I turned back around, he looked confused as ever. I grabbed his hand and pulled him behind me up the stairs. He caught on rather quickly to my intentions because as soon as we reached the top of the stairs, he spun me around and threw me over his shoulder. I squealed as the air was pushed from my lungs.

When he reached the bedroom, he slowly lowered me to my feet, pulling my dress up over my head as I slipped to the ground. I stood before him in a nude, lacy bra and matching panties, slightly self-conscious of the twin pouch I now sported. I didn't think it would ever go away, but Drew didn't seem to notice or care. His gaze set my skin on fire as it trailed over my body. I couldn't help but stare at the rather large bulge that had emerged in his pants. I bit my lower lip as I thought of touching him. It was just over six months ago that I first saw his cock engorged in his pants in my kitchen.

I barely heard his low growl as he stalked toward me. Where I expected him to pull me into his arms, he stopped short and leaned forward as if he were going to kiss me. He didn't though. He lifted his hand and brushed it lightly across my face, trailing it down my neck and whispering it across my breasts. My nipples peaked in anticipation of his touch, needing to feel more from him. When his hand settled lightly on my hip, he squeezed gently before leaning forward and pressing a light kiss to my lips.

"I've been waiting forever for you."

At first I misconstrued what he said and assumed that he was saying he had been waiting for me to be ready to have sex, but when I looked in his eyes, I saw the sincerity there. He saw the uncertainty on my face as sure as I thought about his words.

"Do you doubt me?"

"I don't understand. You loved her so much. You mourned her for seven years. How can you feel that about me? I'm no one special."

I was so sure he wouldn't have an answer for me, but he just shook his head and laughed lightly. "Sarah, you really don't get it, do you? You're amazing. You're a smart, beautiful woman, and I am madly in love with you. Yes, I loved Iris very much, but like you said, I mourned her for seven years. It would have to be a pretty incredible woman to pull me back from the edge, don't you think? Only someone really special could have given me reason to hope again, to want to move on and love again. You've given me something I never thought I could have or ever want. You, Sarah, are a miracle to me."

He didn't give me time to respond as he kissed me hard and deep, lifting me and carrying me over to the bed, gently laying me down. His lips burned over my skin, trailing down my body as he slowly slid my panties. I gripped the sheets, as he spread my legs. Tears slipped from my eyes as his lips closed over me. I'd been desperate for him for so long now, and now that it was happening, I was bursting with emotion.

"Oh God, Drew," I cried out.

His hands were strong and gentle at the same time, every touch reminding me how wonderful it was to be touched by a man that loved me. I could hardly think as he trailed his hands up over my breasts and kissed my neck, sucking at my skin and lighting me on fire. Every touch was filled with a passion I hadn't ever known. He was the only man that had ever loved me like I was the air he breathed.

And when he slid his pants off and hovered over me, there was only a moment of hesitation before he slowly slid inside me. I wrapped my arms around his neck, pulling him in closer as he slowly thrust in and out of me. I was so lost in him, so wrapped up in the feel of him that nothing else mattered. All of my fears over the last year and a half were gone, because I now had a man that loved me and would do anything for me. He was my light in my darkest moments.

He made love to me and reminded me what it felt like to be loved. He kissed away my tears when my emotions became too strong. He held me as our sweaty bodies rocked together, and when he pushed me to orgasm, he held my quivering body, barely holding back as my body squeezed his. He stared into my eyes as he came inside me, leaning forward to slowly kiss me.

"I love you, Drew."

"I love you, too, Sarah."

He wrapped his body around mine, holding me into the early morning hours as neither of us spoke.

CHAPTER 24

DREW

Sarah and I had been dating for six months and sleeping together for three. Most nights I spent at her house since I didn't want to sleep without her. At first, both of us were a little wary of having sex with Cara in the house. It seemed a little strange, but her room was at the back of the house and we tried to stay quiet. Tried being the key word. The first night that we were really loud, Cara was dragging ass in the morning. She gave us the stink eye before smiling at us.

"I'll just be sure to turn on some white noise from now on."

From that night on, we were definitely more careful about being quiet. If we were loud enough to wake up Cara, would we wake up the babies? I really wanted to ask Sarah to just move back home with me and let Cara stay in her house, but I wanted to do this the right way. Sarah deserved to be courted and have a ring on her finger before I asked her to move in with me again.

There was one thing that had to be done before I asked her to marry me. I went out on my back porch as the sun was setting and waited for Iris. I wasn't sure if she would be there. She hadn't been in a long time, but I needed her tonight.

"Iris, if you're there, please come to me. I need you."

A faint warmth covered my body and I closed my eyes, feeling her for what I assumed would be the last time. I removed the chain from around my neck and held our rings in my closed hand.

"I know you wanted me to move on and I finally am. She's wonderful and I'm sure you'd love her. Your parents seem to think that you brought us together. I love her and I'm going to ask her to marry me. I...I wish that we could have had more time together, but I don't regret what happened either. If you hadn't died, I never would have met Sarah. That sounds really bad, doesn't it?"

I paused as I gathered my thoughts. It was strange that I thought I was fucking up what I wanted to say to my dead wife. Iris would laugh and tell me I was being ridiculous. That I shouldn't worry over what I was saying to a ghost. I smiled as I imagined her head thrown back, mouth wide, and eyes squeezed closed with laughter.

"I feel so conflicted because a huge part of me still mourns our baby and the life we would have had together, but I've learned to move on and love again. I know it's time for me to let you go and that means taking off my ring."

Emotion gripped me and my throat closed up as I prepared to say my final goodbyes. Tears filled my eyes as the warmth wrapped tighter around me, squeezing me and filling me with love.

"I will always love you, Iris. I hope you're happy in heaven with my little baby girl." Tears spilled down my cheeks and my words barely escaped as my throat tightened. "No matter what, you will always be a part of me, and I will always cherish my time with you and the man I am because of you. I'll see you again someday, sweet Iris."

The sun shone brighter for a few moments before dimming once again and setting a few minutes later. I stayed on my porch in the dark as I allowed my emotions to settle once more. I had said goodbye, and tomorrow I would start a new life. One that would revolve around the woman that had come to mean everything to me.

THE NEXT MORNING I called Harper and asked her to go shopping with me. She had a baby boy almost six months ago that she named Jacob. As much as she loved him, I knew she needed some time away, which made this trip perfect for her. When I picked her up, I didn't tell her where we were going. I just drove. So imagine her shock when we pulled up in front of a jeweler.

"You're shitting me! Drew, does this mean what I think it means?"

"Are you thinking that I want to buy you earrings?"

She reared back in surprise. "No, I was not thinking that."

"Good. Then it probably means what you think it means."

With that, I stepped out of the truck and walked into the shop with Harper finally snapping out of her wonderment and running to catch up. She pulled me around the store and showed me all the rings she thought would be perfect for Sarah. We narrowed it down to two rings. I wanted something unique that would show Sarah how special she was to me. The first ring was platinum with a garnet stone surrounded by tiny diamonds. It wasn't too big, which I knew she would like, but it was gorgeous. The second was platinum with an opal surrounded by diamonds. The cool thing about the opal was the fiery red that it took on in certain lights.

"What do you think of the red?" I asked Harper.

"Well, it's beautiful, but I don't know that I see Sarah as a red kinda gal. It seems too flashy for her."

"Yeah, but doesn't the opal seem a little too grandmotherly?"

"Grandmotherly? No. It's beautiful and simple. It's probably more along the lines of something Sarah would like. You know why?" I shook my head. "Because it's not as flashy. Sarah is a classy woman and doesn't strike me as the kind of woman to want to flash around a bright red ring."

"How about I give you some information about the rings that might help you make a decision?" the sales lady said.

"Sure."

Harper nodded vigorously while I was ready to roll my eyes and just pick the first ring that looked pretty at this point. I wanted it to be perfect, but I had expected to walk in and just know which one I wanted.

"Well, this one, 'the red one' as you call it, is actually a garnet and it symbolizes a new beginning. The 'grandmotherly' ring is called a Fiery Opal and it represents the fulfillment of desires."

She kept talking, telling me more about the pricing of the ring and the measurements of the diamonds and clarity of both rings, but all I could think about was how perfect that ring was. It expressed exactly what Sarah was to me. I knew at that moment which ring was right for me.

~

The babies' birthdays were tomorrow and we had quite the party planned. All our friends were coming out for a party at my house. Sarah had originally wanted to do it at her house, but there was no way we could fit that many people in her house. Since we started dating, Sarah and I had spent most of our time at her house so that we could be around the babies and not have to haul their stuff to my house. However, about a month ago, I went out and bought the essentials for my own house so they could spend some time here and give Cara breaks. Now, we were prepared for not only our babies, but the onslaught of babies to come. Cece and Logan's son, Archer, was almost ten months old. Jack and Harper's son, Jacob, was almost six months old and their older son, Ethan was twenty months old.

Everyone had said they would be at the party, so I was planning on a huge feast. With that many men in the house, I had to have lots of food. Not to mention, Alex, Cole's wife, was now pregnant with their first child. She was about four months along and from what Cole said, was eating them out of house and home.

"Hey, Drew. We're here."

I walked into the living room and helped Sarah and Cara with all the baby equipment they brought along.

"Did you bring the kids or just the baby paraphernalia?"

"Haha. They're right over there." She pointed to the corner of the living room where the twins were already pulling out toys from the toy box I had Cole build for them. Henry was walking already, but Charlotte was only pulling up. It was enough that she could at least grab toys, but then Henry would take the toy and toddle away. I grabbed up each of my babies and gave them each big hugs and kisses. I never could get enough of these two.

Charlotte was very reserved and played by herself most of the time. Everyone assumed that she was going to be this sweet, quiet child that never caused trouble, but they never saw the devil in her. When she didn't get her way, she scowled and babbled on, yelling at whoever pissed her off. Henry was wild and crazy. He toddled through the house, barely paying attention to what was in front of his feet. He tripped over everything, but got right up, laughing and reaching for more hugs.

Turning back to the girls, I just shook my head. "You know, there was a reason I went out and got all that stuff for the twins. It was so you didn't have to bring your whole house over."

"I know, but you know I like to be prepared."

"Yes, because if something happened, it would have been an awfully long walk back to your house." I deadpanned.

"Don't be a shit."

I wrapped her in my arms and laid a big ol' smacking kiss on those beautiful lips. Cara groaned from behind us.

"Get a room already. Aren't you two sick of each other yet?"

"I thought you were happy that we were together finally?" I teased her.

"Yeah, well I didn't think the honeymoon phase would last quite this long."

Sara and Cara set about putting everything away, while I continued preparing the food. Sarah walked into the kitchen fifteen minutes later looking frazzled.

"What's up, sweet pea?"

"Did you pick up the cake?"

"Yep." I walked over to the fridge and pulled out a cake that had a picture of Thing 1 and Thing 2 on it, along with writing wishing Henry and Charlotte a happy birthday. "As promised."

"Good. Good. I just want everything to be perfect today."

"I understand, but, babe, all of our friends are really chill. No one is going to care if everything goes according to plan. The guys are only coming for the food."

"Hey!"

"What? It's true. Going to a one year old's party isn't what most guys think of as fun. They'll have fun, but not because of the little kids. Which is why I stocked up on beer."

I pointed into the fridge, which was stocked with an array of beer for the men to choose from. Sarah rolled her eyes at me, but conceded that we were prepared. An hour later, everyone was here and we were ready to get this party started, or as much as you could with little kids. The day went off without a hitch. The kids played together and napped when they got cranky. The guys stayed in the kitchen while the women sat in the living room. Everyone was having a great time.

There was still one thing that needed to happen to make this day perfect. I asked all the guys to join me in the living room where all the women and kids were currently. Sarah was standing by the twins, trying to help them get the toys they wanted. I pulled her into me and gave her a big kiss. All the guys were staring, not knowing why they were asked to follow me. The women were still chattering away.

"Excuse me." Everyone but Harper stopped talking. She was still going on and on to Cece about the diaper explosion of 2016. Jack reached over and covered her mouth with his hand.

"Pretty girl, shut up." She wrenched his hand from her mouth and turned on him with a scowl.

"Don't you ever put your hand on my mouth and tell me to shut up. I'll rip your balls off."

Jack just shook his head. "Babe, that threat is getting a little old, don't you think? Time to come up with something new."

"Well, I could just take sex off the table."

She raised an eyebrow as he visibly paled. He looked at me and shook his head. "Sorry, Drew. Nothing's worth that."

"I want to thank all of you for coming today. As you may have realized, it's the twins' birthdays!"

"No shit? Is that what we're doing here?" Vira asked.

There was some laughter around the room and I waited for it to die down before I continued. I was a little nervous doing this in front of all our friends, and I prayed that she didn't turn me down. That would be a little embarrassing. Turning to Sarah, I took her hand in mine.

"Sarah, I don't know if you realize it, but a year ago today, you gave me the best gift ever. You gave me a family. They might not technically be mine, but I promise that I will always love them as mine. There's just one thing I need to make my family complete." I pulled out the ring and got down on one knee. "This grandmotherly looking ring is called a Fire Opal. It represents fulfillment of desires. That's what you are to me. You are everything I could have ever wanted. I hope that you'll wear this ring and fulfill my greatest desire and be mine forever. Will you marry me?"

Her eyes were shimmering and for a second, I feared she would say no, but then she threw herself at me, causing me to fall backward on my ass and started kissing me. I ran my hands up her back up to the nape of her neck, pressing her closer to me. Passion took over and pretty soon, I had rolled over and was kissing her hard, pressing my body into hers.

When the clearing of a throat finally broke through my lust filled haze, I pulled back from Sarah. Her lips were red and swollen from my kisses, but I didn't care.

"That was like watching soft porn." Vira's voice floated through to me and I smiled at Sarah's reddening face.

"Watch much of that, do you?" I was pretty sure that was Sean.

"Baby, you already know what I like. Don't pretend you didn't teach me a thing or two."

Sarah pressed her face into my chest as she laughed. I pulled her up into a sitting position and finally slipped the ring on her finger.

"I'm guessing you were saying yes, otherwise that was one hell of a rejection."

"Yes."

I kissed her again, but this time kept my tongue to myself.

"I think that might be our cue to exit. I'll grab the twins and take them home. You two..." Cara waved her hands at us in a continue gesture, then ran off to grab everything to take home.

In less than five minutes, everyone had vacated the house, and the guys had helped Cara take everything back over to Sarah's house. I had already worked it out with Cara for Sarah to stay at my place tonight, so we didn't have to worry about the twins in the morning. Cara had packed an overnight bag for Sarah, along with some lingerie that I planned to put to very good use tonight.

I dragged Sarah upstairs and pushed her down on the bed to make love to her. I wanted to own every bit of her body tonight, but before I got the chance, Sarah pushed me off her and stood at the foot of the bed. She kicked off her shoes, then slowly undid the buttons of her shirt. When I saw the creamy skin of her breasts spilling out of her bra, my cock hardened painfully. It took everything in me to stay where I was. She didn't take off her shirt, leaving it partially buttoned and only giving me a glimpse of what I wanted to see. Then she started to undo her pants, but again, only undid them and teased me with a glimpse of her panties.

She stepped between my legs and pushed her breasts in my face, allowing me to lick the swells. Her fingers ran through my short hair, her nails scraping against my scalp. I couldn't hold back anymore. I ripped her shirt in two and tore it from her body. Twisting her around, I pushed her back on the bed and pulled her pants down her legs. She spread her legs, allowing me to settle between them.

Pulling the cups of her bra down, I ran my tongue across each peak, sucking the little buds into my mouth. Little drops of breast-milk filled my mouth. When I released her nipple and massaged her breast, Sarah thrust her breast upward. Milk shot from her breast, squirting me in the face. I quickly closed my eyes to avoid getting milk in them. Sarah started laughing, covering her face to hide her embarrassment.

"Does that ever happen to the babies?"

"Never," she said laughing. "But they don't massage my breasts and get me riled up like you do."

I wiped the milk from my face and decided to steer clear of her breasts for now. I kissed her again, rocking my hips into her, my cock straining against my pants. With every pulse, I needed her more.

"Sarah, I need you now."

Her heavy breathing in my ear let me know she needed me too. Her fingers worked at my clothes, tearing and pulling to get me undressed. When I was finally naked, I settled back between her thighs and thrust to the hilt inside her.

"Oh, God. That's like heaven."

I continued to rock my body against her, picking up speed as she moaned her approval. Soon, I was pounding into her, unable to hold back. She drove me crazy with her little noises.

"Drew, more! I need more," she shouted.

A few more thrusts and we were both tipping over the edge. Her pussy clenched around my cock, and a few seconds later, I was pouring my cum inside her. I collapsed on the bed next to her, resting my head in the palm of my hand. My other hand traced the curves of her body, feeling her pulse slowly return to normal.

Sarah lifted her hand and examined the ring on her finger.

"Do you like it?"

"I love it. It's so beautiful. How did you come up with this ring? I mean, did you specifically look for a ring with that meaning?"

"No. I went shopping with Harper and I had it narrowed down to two rings. The sales lady was telling us more about the rings to help me make a decision. The other ring meant 'a new beginning', but I thought this ring better described how I felt about you."

"So what was the comment about it being a grandmotherly ring?"

"Harper said she thought this ring would be better because it was more understated. The other was red with diamonds around it, but Harper said it was too flashy. I told her I thought this ring looked grandmotherly."

"Well, I don't think it looks grandmotherly. I love it."

∼

When I woke the next morning, Sarah was tucked into me, still sleeping. My arm was numb from her sleeping on my shoulder all night, so I slowly extricated myself from her and got up to go to the bathroom. When I came back to bed, Sarah was awake and staring at her ring, watching the light change the colors of the opal.

"It's so beautiful."

She turned to me and I looked at her, completely stunned.

"What? What is it?"

"Your eyes. They're blue."

She paled a little and quickly got up from bed, heading into the bathroom. I looked down and saw her contacts laying on the bed. She must have rubbed her eyes at night, causing the contacts to come out. I gathered them up and brought them to the bathroom.

"Sarah, I have the contacts here."

She pulled the door open slightly and reached out for them. After five minutes, she came back out, gathering her clothes from around the room.

"Sarah, what's going on?"

"Nothing. I just need to get home and put in some new contacts. These are torn."

"Why do you wear color contacts?"

"I just don't like blue eyes."

"Really? My eyes are blue."

"I meant on me. I don't like them on me," she said almost anxiously. She was rushing around the room like a madwoman, and I was still trying to figure out what the big deal was.

She was almost dressed, ready to bolt out the door. It was then that I started putting more of the pieces together. She had blue eyes and there were times that I saw blonde at the tips of her roots. She always colored her hair pretty soon after her roots started showing, but now it made more sense. She was hiding who she was. The question was, who was she hiding from?

"Sarah, just stay here and talk to me."

"I need to get home to the babies. I'll call you later. Maybe you can stop by for dinner tonight."

"Why are you acting like we're just dating again? You're my fiancé now. You can talk to me. I'm not going anywhere."

"Everything is fine, Drew. I promise. I'll let you know what we're having for dinner later."

She kissed me quickly and then practically ran out the door. What the hell was going on? There were two people that knew, but they weren't talking and I doubted my engagement to her would change that. Something about her seemed familiar now that I saw her with blue eyes, but I just couldn't put my finger on it. Something about having blue eyes changed her appearance. Memories of Sean asking me to look out for her came to mind. He had said that she could be in trouble. My conversation with Sebastian had been very similar. There were things that she couldn't tell me. She obviously changed her appearance to hide from someone, but how did you even begin to look for a face that looked familiar?

I decided if my friends wouldn't help me, I would have to find a way to help myself. After a few searches on the internet, I found facial recognition software that I could download on my computer. I searched my phone and found a picture that I took of the two of us. Surprisingly, it didn't take long for the software to work. Within a few hours, I had all the information I could possibly want on Sarah Matthews, widow of Todd Matthews. Todd had been killed by a

Mafia hitman after Sarah and Todd witnessed the murder of the former Chief of Police for New York City.

Christ. Now I remembered the story. It had been in the news a lot right before Sarah moved here. As much as Sarah was being protected from the media, pictures of her had been scattered all over the news because it was such a high profile case. There had even been several articles in the local paper about it. No wonder Sarah kept to herself so much. If she was recognized, she would move to keep her family safe.

My stomach bottomed out as I read the police reports and testimony she had given against Giuseppe Cordano. Then I saw the date of her testimony against Marco Abruzzo. It had been not long after she moved here. That's when she left to go home to Texas for her father's funeral. She was surrounded by her "brothers". Shit. This was really bad. Sources were reporting that she had a five million dollar price on her head.

Not thinking twice about it, I grabbed my keys and headed out the door. Glancing over at her house, I saw everyone was inside. That was something at least. Not that I should be worried about someone taking a shot at her right now, but she was my family, and now it was time for me to get the whole truth.

Jumping in my truck, I headed out to find Sean. I dialed him, but when he didn't answer, I called Sebastian. Those were the two people that could give me the answers I needed.

"Yo. What's up?"

"I'm on my way to see you. Are you at the office or home?"

"Office. What's going on?"

"I'll see you in twenty."

I hung up before he could say any more. I made it to Reed Security in fifteen minutes and stormed into his office. When I saw it was only him in the office, I shut the door and got in his face.

"You tell me that she's safe. Tell me that no one's coming for her."

"Drew, you know I can't talk to you about—"

"I know! I saw her without her contacts this morning, and she's always dying her hair brown, but she has blonde hair. I ran her through facial recognition software. I know who she is! So you tell me right now if someone is after her!"

Sebastian took a step back and moved back around his desk. "Sit down so we can talk about this."

I didn't feel like sitting, but I also knew that pacing around his office wouldn't help me get my answers. I sat down and took a deep breath to prepare me for whatever he was going to say.

"She's safe, for now. There's a hit out on her, but she's being protected by WitSec. They can't know that anyone knows who she is. They'll pull her out of here so fast, you won't have a chance to say goodbye."

"What if we're married?"

"I don't know. The rules of WitSec are not widely known. That's how people stay safe. This is such a clusterfuck. Three people now know who she is. That's not safe for her."

"I would never say or do anything to put her in danger." I spat at him.

"I know that. Calm down. Sean and I would never say anything either, but it's more dangerous for anyone to know. I've been keeping an eye on the situation from here. No one here knows about her or even suspects that there's anything different about her. As far as people around here are concerned, she's just a friend of mine."

"Okay, so where do we go from here?"

"You go on with your life as if nothing has changed. You and Sarah should have an honest discussion about what happens if someone does find out about her. You should have a plan in place, map out some areas you might go, but don't keep any records of anything. No paper trails. I can handle vehicles for you if you need to leave in a hurry. I'll keep watching on my end, and I'll give you a heads up if I hear anything and so will Sean. As soon as I call you, I'll have vehicles ready for you, and I can put together some IDs for you. They won't pass all inspections, but they'll work until you settle somewhere else. You should also have some bags packed for all of you to keep in your closet. Not too much stuff, but enough to get by. Let me get some stuff together for you all over the next few days. Then let's meet up again."

I nodded, taking in all he was telling me. He must have thought I was unsure about all this, but really, it was just a lot to take in. "What would you do for the love of a good woman, Drew?"

I looked him dead in the eyes. "Don't ever doubt me. I won't ever let anything happen to her or the kids, and I would do anything for them. If we need to run, I'll be ready."

"I have no doubt in my mind. I'll call you in a few days."

"Thanks, Sebastian. I appreciate you looking out for her."

CHAPTER 25

SARAH

I paced around the house trying to figure out what I was going to do. Did I leave? Did I take the chance that Drew wouldn't want all the baggage that came with my life? I saw the look on his face when he saw me without contacts. There was a spark of recognition, and it wouldn't be too much longer before he put it all together. If he put it together and so did two other people, it wouldn't be long before others recognized me.

I had to leave. That was the only option. The kids and I would never be safe in this town. I would get on the road by tonight and take the twins somewhere we would never be found. I could cut my hair and give myself a different look. I ran to my closet and pulled out my suitcase, throwing items from my dresser inside.

"Sarah, what's going on? It sounds like you're tearing the house apart." Cara stood in the doorway and watched me acting like a lunatic. "What are you doing? Why are you packing all your stuff?"

"I need to leave. The kids and I are leaving."

"What? What are you talking about? You can't just leave. You have a life here, and Drew. Is this because of him? Did he do something?"

"No. It's not because of him. I just need to go. You can stay in the house as long as you want. It's paid for, so you'll just have to handle utilities and cable. I'm sure Drew can help you get it sorted."

I walked into the bathroom and grabbed my toiletries, not bothering to check if I had it all. I just needed to leave. "Cara, can you please get the babies ready? I need to leave as soon as possible."

"Sure. I'll go get them ready."

She walked out of the room and I heard her go into the twins' room. Okay. One less thing to worry about. With her getting the babies ready, all I had to worry about was packing our stuff. I should probably pack some food for the road also. Less stopping would leave less likelihood that someone would recognize me. I should probably change my contacts, too. Maybe go with green eyes. I could dye my hair red also. My skin was pale enough that I could pass as Scottish.

Grabbing my fireproof box under my bed, I opened it and grabbed cash for my wallet and put the box in a separate bag. Shit. I should call the Marshals. They could have me relocated by tonight if I told them that people recognized me. I opened the box back up and grabbed the card Agent Sanders gave me. I was just about to dial when the front door slammed.

"Sarah! Sarah!" Drew's voice echoed through the house with urgency. He appeared in my doorway a few seconds later with Cara hot on his heels.

"Sarah, what the hell is this? You aren't going anywhere."

"Cara, what did you do?"

"I'm sorry, Sarah, but he had to know you were leaving. He loves you and I wasn't going to let you run off without him."

"Cara, can you leave us alone so I can talk to Drew for a few minutes?"

"No. She's part of this family as much as me and she stays. We have things to discuss that affect her too."

"Drew, that's not a good idea. I can't."

"I know, sweetheart."

I shook my head. It was impossible. There was no way he knew. "No, you don't."

"Yes, I do. I know," he said pleadingly. "Let's go to the living room and talk this out. If you still need to leave after that, I'll go with you."

I thought about it, but I couldn't let Drew go with me. He would be giving up his whole life to go on the run and I couldn't allow that to happen. Still, the only way he would leave would be if I talked to him.

"Fine. Let's go talk."

We walked into the living room and I saw the twins were still in the same clothes and playing on the ground. Cara had never started to get them ready.

"Cara, there's stuff we're going to talk about that can never be shared with anyone. If you know, then you come with us if we leave. If that's not something you're prepared for, then you need to leave the house. You can still watch the kids, but we may disappear one day with no notice. I need you to decide right now if you're in or out." Drew was taking charge of the whole situation and part of me was extremely relieved that I wasn't alone anymore.

"Is this dangerous? Will I be in danger?"

"Right now, no, but I can't guarantee anything."

"If I go with you, if you need to leave, will I have a chance to say goodbye to anyone, or is this like we're running from bad guys and we leave or die?"

When Drew didn't say anything, Cara nodded. "Okay, well considering you two and the kids are the closest thing to family right now, I'm in."

My head swiveled quickly to hers. "What about Sean? He's your brother!"

"He already knows. He would understand that you couldn't say goodbye, though I'm not sure he would want you involved in this," Drew said warily.

"I love my brother very much, but right now, I just can't see leaving all of you behind. You guys have been so good to me, and I just don't think I could handle losing you. If you go, I go."

"Alright. Here's the deal. Sarah's real name is Sarah Matthews. She was married to Todd Matthews, who was murdered when he and Sarah came upon an Italian mob boss trying to extort the Chief of Police. The chief was murdered when he wouldn't give in, and Sarah and Todd witnessed it. A hitman came after them and Todd died helping Sarah escape. She testified against the mob boss and the hitman. She now has a price on her head. She's in WitSec and if they knew that now four people know who she is, she would be moved and we would never see her again."

A nervous laugh left Cara's mouth. "Wow. Is that all?"

"So you see, Cara, if we left, you would have to come with us so that we could protect you. If anyone linked you to Sarah, they would torture you to get any information they could from you."

I expected her to get up and run from the house, but instead she sat there calmly and asked questions.

"Okay, so what do we do from here?"

"Sebastian is getting together IDs for us. I'll add you to the list. He said he would have vehicles ready for us if we ever needed to run. For now, he's monitoring the situation, but he feels that we're safe. Sean is the only other person that knows. We need to pick a location to go to in case anyone comes for us. We should all be prepared that we may not get to leave together. The most important thing is keeping the twins safe. Whoever is with them should leave right away if there is immediate danger. Call Sebastian and get out of town. No waiting around."

"Shouldn't I contact WitSec if I'm found?"

"It would take them too long to get here. Sebastian can get us out of town the fastest. If the threat isn't imminent, we could call WitSec, but I don't know the rules. Would Cara and I be able to come along?"

"I'm pretty sure if I was married, you would be able to come, but I have no clue about Cara."

"Then I think for now, it's best if we stick with this plan. Sebastian will call us in a few days and we can all sit down and work out the details. I think we should ask Sean to be there also. Since he already knows, it's best if he knows you're involved.

"I can't do this. I can't ask you both to give up your lives to come with me."

"First of all, you're going to be my wife and those are my kids. There is no way that I won't be with you no matter what. Second, you aren't asking anything. I'm telling you that I will gladly give up everything and anything to be with you and make sure you're safe."

"I may not be related, but you two are my family."

"Then it's settled. Let's figure out where we'll go if we have to run."

∽

FOR THE NEXT FEW DAYS, we looked at maps of the United States to find the perfect location. After much debate over weather, job prospects, population size, and anything else that might sway us, we found a location. With that set, all we needed was to meet with Sebastian to put the final pieces in place. Drew asked Sean to be at the meeting, and we decided to meet at Drew's house so that no one at Reed Security grew suspicious.

When Sean walked in, he saw Cara sitting on the couch next to Sebastian.

"What is this? Are you two..." He waved his finger between the two of them and shuddered. "I do not need to know. We didn't need to have a meeting over who you're fucking, Cara."

"We aren't fucking, Sean." She rolled her eyes at him and after much scrutinizing, Sean seemed to accept it and took a seat. Sebastian stood and went to his bag, pulling out a large envelope.

"These are the new IDs for all of you. It won't pass an intense background check, but if you were to apply for a job, it should work for you. Just don't land yourself in jail. I also included a burner phone that has one number. It's my work phone and I always have it on. If you need something, you call me and I'll take care of it. There are two vehicles parked in the basement of Reed Security. They won't lead back to you in any way, and won't be traced to Reed Security either. The keys are in the envelope, but I would prefer you contact me first so I can make sure you get away clean. Have you chosen a location?"

"Whoa, hold on one fucking minute. What the hell is going on and why is my sister here?"

"If they leave, I'm going with them." Cara didn't look at Sean as she spoke softly.

"What? Cara, you can't be serious."

Cara stood and walked over to him. "Sean, I know you love me very much and you've given so much to help me, but this is my family too. They've helped me so much and I want to stay with them."

He looked a little hurt by that statement, but didn't say anything. Drew stood and walked over to them. "Sean, we aren't going anywhere. This is all just a precaution. We may not be able to say anything if we leave, but Sebastian would know."

"Well, I hope for your sake that you don't have to go anywhere, but I understand that you have to be prepared. Just tell me one thing. How did my sister get involved in all this?"

"She's been a part of our lives for a year now, day in and day out. I gave her an out, but she didn't want it. Frankly, she'd probably be safer with us. If they found out that she was living with Sarah, she would be a target. I don't think I have to tell you what they would do to her."

"Fuck. I didn't even think about that." Sean ran his hand over his head and settled it on the back of his neck. "I've been listening for anything from New York, but so far, they aren't having any luck in their search. There's every possibility this could go nowhere."

"I just wanted to live a quiet life. I'm so sorry that I've done this to all of you." My eyes filled with tears as this small group of people sat around and planned for the possibility of upending our lives and leaving this place I had come to call home.

Drew knelt in front of me and grabbed my hands. "Sweetheart, none of this is your fault, and I wouldn't change a thing about it. Well, maybe the murders, but even though your husband had to die, it brought me you and I'm selfish enough to be grateful for that."

I gave Drew a small smile. I wasn't happy that Todd was dead either, but he was right. Todd's death brought me to Drew and I couldn't feel sorry about that. "What do we do now?"

"You two need to get married now. You already planned on it, but now we need to move that timeframe up. That way, if you have to run, WitSec will move you together."

"I can do that. I'm ready to do this now."

"Hold on there, cowboy. I still want to go pick out a dress and have a few flowers."

"Why don't we do it here at sunset? It would be beautiful."

"But...wouldn't that be a reminder of...Iris?" I didn't want to be morbid, but that seemed weird to me that he would want to get married to me at the time of day that he used to cherish so much.

"I think it's time to make new memories at sunset."

And just like that, my heart melted. There was no denying how much Drew loved me. The fact that he was giving me something that had been so special to him meant everything to me.

"We would have to do it soon. It's pretty chilly at night."

"We can do it next weekend. I don't know about you, but the only family I have is our friends. It won't take that long to inform all of them. You can go shopping this week and find something to wear."

"Can we get a marriage license that fast?"

"The state of Pennsylvania requires a three day waiting period. If you applied this week, you should have it for next weekend," Sean said.

"Well, I guess we have a plan then. We're getting married next weekend."

THAT NIGHT, lying in bed with Drew, I got the distinct impression that he was trying to work up the courage to ask me something. Irritated with his attempts, I turned in his arms.

"Just ask. Whatever it is, just ask."

"Now that I know about your past, will you tell me about Todd?"

I sighed and looked at the ceiling. I wasn't sure I wanted to rehash this after I had finally moved on, but he had told me about Iris. It was only fair.

"I met him when I was just out of college. He was in the military and he was usually deployed six months at a time. I fell in love with him so fast, but I held back because I was afraid he would get killed over there. Eventually, he wore me down and I moved in with him. We got married and I finished school and got a job managing an art gallery. He was always a little different when he came home, but it was the adjustment period. He always had trouble with that. We decided to wait until he got out of the military to start a family. He was so worried about leaving a family behind." I huffed out a laugh. "Who would have thought he would survive war only to be killed by a crime boss at home?"

"I read in the testimony that he had some trouble when he came home."

"Yeah. He was having a nightmare and I stupidly walked over to him and tried to wake him up. He was still in the throes of his nightmare and attacked me. When he woke up, he was devastated. A neighbor heard and called the police. They took him in and he was ready to let them throw the book at him, but I wouldn't allow it. He was suffering from PTSD. There was no reason he should have been in jail to begin with. Anyway, after that, he got counseling and he got better. He went to work at a security firm he heard about from his buddies. He was so happy there, but it was like he was in the military all over again. He worked long hours and sometimes opposite schedules as me. We rarely saw each other. His job was important to him, and I could appreciate that, but I was ready to start a family. He was so happy that night when I told him. He wanted to take me out to celebrate."

Tears started sliding down my cheeks as I recalled that night. "We had a great night and then he was gone. I can still see his face. He wasn't paying attention because he wanted to be sure I got away. He was a really good fighter, but I distracted him."

Drew pulled me into his arms, kissing my temple. "Baby, you can't blame yourself. I'm sure that as soon as you stepped into that situation, he knew it would end badly. He wanted to give you every chance to get away, and he did. It wasn't your fault."

"It might not have been my fault, but the look on his face will haunt me forever. I can't make those images go away. That's not how he should be remembered, but I'm not even allowed to talk about him. My kids will never know who he was because it could put them in danger."

"You may not be able to talk about who he was, but you can tell them about the man he was. That's what's most important. They need to know that he was a strong man who loved you and them very much."

"I wish he could have met them."

"I know you do."

He kissed my forehead and suddenly I needed to know something. "Drew, when you were telling me about your wife, you said that she had made a decision on whether or not to keep the baby, but you never told me what she chose."

"I didn't, did I? She kept the baby."

"Were you upset with her that she didn't give herself a chance?"

"No. I wanted to be, but at our last doctor's appointment, the doctor said that the cancer had spread so fast to her brain that chemo probably wouldn't have helped. He said that most likely the cancer cells were already there. She would have been devastated if she'd given up the baby, and when the doctor told us that, I was glad that she had kept it. It made her feel better that she hadn't killed her child, and I was grateful that she had that peace of mind when she passed."

"Did the baby live until the end with her?"

"The baby died about a week before she did, but she was so out of it that she never knew. She never had to mourn the baby."

"How did they deliver the baby?"

"They didn't. She was so far gone, the doctors didn't think she would last much longer. It would have been too hard on her body. Our baby is still with her."

"Did you name the baby?"

"It was a girl. We had already talked about names and had decided on Hope. Iris always had hope that the child would survive. There wasn't ever really a chance for her. The cancer hit Iris hard right away, and she was so weak that the baby wasn't developing at the proper rate. She was really small and that's why they kept her in the womb so long. They hoped that as time went on, she would gain some weight and they could induce labor around twenty-five weeks, but she just quit growing. Iris was too weak and the baby wasn't getting what she needed to survive. We both knew that our child wouldn't make it, but I'm glad that Iris wasn't coherent when the baby died."

"That's so sad. I'm sure that they're in heaven watching you."

"I know they are. They brought us together."

CHAPTER 26

SARAH

Drew and I were married on a very cold day in October. There had been a snowstorm two days before our wedding and it made for a beautiful landscape. We decided to go ahead with the outdoor wedding. I wore a deep blue dress that would have shown off my eyes if I wasn't wearing contacts. It had a boat neck and three quarter length sleeves with a lace overlay and a mermaid fit. It was absolutely beautiful. I probably should have worn a coat outside, but I wanted to enjoy the moment, short as it was. I did, however, wear fur lined snow boots.

Drew wore a classic tux that made him look completely dashing, but he also wore a black cowboy hat, true to his southern nature. The scruff on his jaw made him look absolutely delectable. We opted for the twins to be bundled up in fleece snowsuits that had hoods with little ears. They were so adorable. Some of our friends bitched about the cold weather, but when the ceremony started, everyone was quiet. The sun was setting just as we said our vows and I felt warmth wrap around me. I knew Iris was there and that Drew felt her too because his eyes teared up.

After we kissed and started walking back toward the house, I heard his voice. *Be happy, baby. I'll always love you.*

Looking up at Drew, I knew I had made a good choice. No one would ever understand me like him or love me as fiercely. We shared something that no one could ever take from us.

∽

Four years after we were married, I got a call from Agent Sanders in WitSec.

"Agent Sanders, it's been a while. Is everything okay?"

"We're just calling to check up on you."

"I thought you said we wouldn't be talking again unless something happened. Did something happen?"

"Well, yes. As of two weeks ago, the Cordano crime family has been wiped out."

"Excuse me?" My heart beat wildly in my chest. What did this mean for us?

"There was a war between two families and the Cordano's were not the ones left standing. All of the major players have been killed, including Giuseppe Cordano and Marco Abruzzo, who were killed in jail. The rest of them are gone in the wind."

My heart thundered in my chest. "What does this mean?"

"It means that you can rest easy. We'll keep you in WitSec as a precaution, but it looks like you're in the clear. The bounty on your head has been withdrawn, and it appears no one is interested in you anymore."

"Oh my gosh. You aren't serious."

"I'm completely serious."

"Does this mean I can tell my friends who I am? Can I tell my kids about their father?"

"Well, don't go crazy. Your kids can know, but you'd still be taking a chance with anyone else. We believe the threat is gone, but it wouldn't be a bad idea to continue to fly under the radar."

"I can't believe this. I never thought I would hear this from you."

"Enjoy your life, Sarah."

I hung up the phone and stared at the ground for a minute. There was so much joy rushing through me that I didn't know quite how to handle it. Drew walked into the room moments later and caught me staring at the ground as I rubbed my swollen belly.

"Sarah, is everything okay? Who was on the phone?"

"Agent Sanders. We just got our lives back."

ALSO BY GIULIA LAGOMARSINO

Thank you for reading Drew and Sarah's story, but it's not over! Catch more of your favorite characters in upcoming books! And don't miss the next in series *Sebastian!*

Join my newsletter to get the most up-to-date information, along with new content in the Reed Security series.

https://giulialagomarsinoauthor.com/connect/

Join my Facebook reader group to find out more about my obsession with Dwayne Johnson!

https://www.facebook.com/groups/GiuliaLagomarsinobooks

Reading Order:

https://giulialagomarsinoauthor.com/reading-order/

To find the individual series, follow the links below:

For *The Love Of A Good Woman* series

Reed Security series

The Cortell Brothers

A Good Run Of Bad Luck

The Shifting Sands Beneath Us- Standalone

Owens Protective Services

Printed in Great Britain
by Amazon